# DJINN

*and*

# LA MAISON DE
# RENDEZ-VOUS

# ALAIN ROBBE-GRILLET

# DJINN

Translated from the French by
Yvone Lenard and Walter Wells

## *and*

# LA MAISON DE RENDEZ-VOUS

Translated from the French
by Richard Howard

GROVE PRESS/*New York*

Published by Grove Press, Inc.
920 Broadway
New York, N.Y. 10010

Library of Congress Cataloging-in-Publication Data

Robbe-Grillet, Alain, 1922–
    La maison de rendez-vous; & Djinn.

    1. Robbe-Grillet, Alain, 1922–     —Translations, English. I. Robbe-Grillet, Alain, 1922–    . Djinn. English. 1987. II. Title. III. Title: Maison de rendez-vous. IV. Title: Djinn.
PQ2635.0117A24 1987     843'.914     87-7387
ISBN 0-802-13017-8

Manufactured in the United States of America

First Edition 1987

10 9 8 7 6 5 4 3 2

# CONTENTS

# DJINN

# PROLOGUE

There is nothing—I mean no incontrovertible evidence—that might allow anyone to place Simon Lecoeur's story among tales of pure fiction. In the contrary, one can observe that numerous and important elements of that unstable, incomplete text, fissured as it seems, coincide with facts (commonly known facts) with a strange recurrence that is therefore disconcerting. And, while other elements of the narrative stray deliberately away from those facts,

7

they always do so in so suspicious a manner that one is forced to see there a systematic intent on the part of the narrator, as though some secret motive had dictated those changes and those inventions.

Such motive, of course, escapes us, at least for the time being. Were we to discover it, it would shed light on the whole affair. It is permissible, in any case, to think so.

About the author himself, little is known. His true identity is itself open to question. Nobody knew any of his relatives, distant or close. After his disappearance, a French passport was found at his home, in the name of Boris Koershimen, an electronics engineer, born in Kiev. But the police in charge of the investigation claim that document to be a crude fake, probably manufactured abroad. Yet, the photograph it bears, according to all witnesses, seems indeed to be that of the young man.

As for the officially listed last name, it hardly sounds Ukrainian. Besides, it is under a different spelling and a different first name that he had been employed at the American School of the rue de Passy,* where, for the last few months, he had been teaching contemporary literary French: "Robin Körsimos, known as Simon Lecoeur." The name would seem to indicate, this time, rather a Hungarian, or a Finn, perhaps yet even a Greek; but this last guess would be given the lie by the looks of that tall and

* The Franco-American School in Paris (E.F.A.P.) 56, rue de Passy 75016 Paris

slender young man, with light blond hair and pale green eyes. Finally, one must note that his colleagues at school, as well as his students (girls for the most part) called him only "Yann," which they spelled Ján when they wrote him brief memos; none of them could ever say why.

The text that concerns us—ninety-nine pages, typed double spaced—had been prominently placed on his desk (in the modest furnished room he rented at 21, rue d'Amsterdam), next to an ancient typewriter, which, according to experts, was indeed the one on which it had been typed. Yet, the date on that typescript was several weeks, probably even several months, old; and there again, the proximity of the typewriter to the papers could have been the product of some staging, a falsification invented by that elusive character in order to cover his tracks.

Reading that narrative, your first impression is that you are dealing with material for a textbook, meant for the teaching of language, such as there must be hundreds. The regular progression of the grammatical difficulties of the language appears clearly, in the course of eight chapters of increasing length, which would roughly correspond to the eight* weeks of an American university quarter.

Nevertheless, the story told in these pages remains quite far removed from the resolutely innocuous texts generally found in works of that type. As a matter of fact, the ratio of probability of the reported

* There are actually ten weeks in a quarter (Translator's note).

events is almost always too low, in relation to the laws of traditional realism. Thus, it is not ruled out to see a mere guise in this pretense of a pedagogical intent. Behind that guise, something else must be concealed. But what?

Here, in its entirety, is the text in question. At the top of the page appears this simple title: *The Rendez-vous.*

# CHAPTER ONE

I arrive exactly at the appointed hour: it is six-thirty. It is almost dark already. The hangar is not locked. I walk in, pushing the door, which no longer has a lock.

Inside, all is silent. Listening more attentively, the straining ear registers only a faint sound, clear and steady, fairly close by: water dripping from some loose faucet, into a tank, a basin, or just a puddle on the ground.

Under the dim light that filters through the large

windows with dirt encrusted, partly broken panes, I can barely make out the objects that surround me, piled on all sides in great disarray, no doubt cast off: ancient discarded machinery, metallic carcasses, and assorted old hardware, which dust and rust darken to a blackish and uniformly dull tint.

When my eyes become somewhat accustomed to the semidarkness, I finally notice the man, facing me. Standing, motionless, both hands in the pockets of his trench coat, he watches me without saying a word, without so much as the slightest greeting in my direction. The character is wearing dark glasses, and the thought crosses my mind: he is perhaps blind. . . .

Tall and slender, young by all appearances, he leans a casual shoulder against a pile of oddly shaped crates. His face is not quite visible, because of the glasses, between the turned-up collar of the trench coat and the brim of the hat pulled down over his forehead. The whole figure brings irresistibly to mind some old detective movie of the thirties.

Having now myself stopped five or six steps away from the man who remains as motionless as a bronze statue, I enunciate clearly (but in a low voice) the coded message of recognition: "Monsieur Jean, I presume? My name is Boris. I come about the ad."

And all I hear again is the steady dripping of water in the silence. Is that blind man a deaf mute as well?

After several minutes, the answer finally comes: "Do not pronounce it *Jean*, but Djinn. I am an American."

My surprise is so great that I can barely hide it. The voice is, indeed, that of a young woman: lilting and warm, with husky undertones that give it a hint of senuous intimacy; yet, she does not correct the title *Monsieur,* which she therefore seems to accept.

A half smile plays upon her lips. She asks: "It bothers you to work for a girl?"

There is a challenge in the tone of her words. But I promptly decide to play the game: "No, sir," I say, "on the contrary." In any case, I have no choice.

Djinn does not seem in a hurry to speak any more. She is watching me carefully and without kindness. She is, perhaps, forming an unfavorable judgment of my abilities. I dread the verdict, which falls at the end of her examination: "You are a rather good-looking guy," she says, "but you are too tall for a Frenchman."

I feel like laughing. This young foreigner hasn't been in France long, I guess, and she has come with ready-made ideas. "I am French," I say by way of justification. "That is not the question," she answers after a silence.

She speaks French with a slight accent, which carries a lot of charm. Her lilting voice and her androgynous looks evoke, for me, the actress Jane Frank. I love Jane Frank. I go to see every single one of her movies. Unfortunately, as "Monsieur" Djinn says, that is not the question.

We remain that way, watching each other, for a few minutes more. But it is getting darker and darker. To hide my embarrassment, I ask: "So, what is the question?"

Relaxing for the first time, or so it seems, Djinn smiles the delightful smile of Jane. "You are going to have to pass unnoticed in the crowd," she says.

I am very much tempted to return her smile, accompanied by a compliment on her looks. I don't dare: she is the boss. I fall back on apologies: "I am not a giant." As a matter of fact, I am barely six one, and she herself is not short.

She wants me to move forward. I take five steps toward her. At closer range, her face has a strange pallor, a waxen immobility. I am almost afraid to move closer. I stare at her mouth. . . .

"Closer," she says. This time, there is no doubt: her lips do not move when she speaks. I take one more step and I place my hand on her chest.

This is not a woman, nor a man. What I have in front of me is a plastic mannequin for display windows. The dim light explains my mistake. The lovely smile of Jane Frank must be credited to my imagination alone.

"Touch again, if you like," says the seductive voice of Monsieur Djinn ironically, underlining the ridiculousness of my situation. Where does that voice come from? The sounds do not issue from the mannequin itself, most likely, but from a loudspeaker hidden nearby.

So, I am being watched by someone invisible. This is most unpleasant. It makes me feel clumsy, threatened, guilty. The girl who is talking to me probably happens to be sitting several miles away; and she is watching me, as though I were some bug caught in a trap, on her television screen. I am sure she is making fun of me.

"At the end of the center aisle," says the voice, "there are some stairs. Walk up to the second floor. The steps do not go any farther." Happy to part company with my lifeless doll, I am relieved to carry out these instructions.

Arriving at the first floor, I see the stairs stop there. This is therefore a second floor American style. This confirms my opinion: Djinn does not reside in France.

I am now in some sort of a vast attic, which quite resembles the ground floor: same dirty panes, and same arrangement of aisles between piles of assorted junk. There is only a little more light.

I glance left and right, seeking a human presence in this mess of cardboard, wood and iron.

Suddenly, I have the disturbing feeling that a scene is being repeated, as in a mirror: facing me, five or six steps away, stands the same motionless figure, in a trench coat with turned-up collar, dark glasses and felt hat with a turned-down brim, that is to say a second mannequin, the exact reproduction of the first, in an identical posture.

I approach, this time without hesitation; and I reach forward. . . . Fortunately, I stop my gesture in time: the thing has just smiled, and this time, beyond

15

any doubt, unless I am crazy. This fake wax mannequin is a real woman.

She withdraws her hand from her pocket, and
very slowly, she raises her arm to push away mine,
which remains half raised, paralyzed by surprise.

"Don't touch, boy," she says, "danger zone!" The
voice is the same indeed, with the same sensuous
allure, and the same Boston accent; except that, from
now on, she speaks to me with patronizing im-
pertinence.

"Sorry, baby," I say, "I am an idiot." In the same
severe and final tone, she replies: "According to reg-
ulations, *you* must always speak to me courteously."

"Okay," I say, without abandoning my apparent
good humor. Yet, all this staginess is beginning to get
on my nerves. Djinn is probably acting that way on
purpose, because she adds, after a moment's reflection: "And don't say *okay*, that's very vulgar, especially in French."

I am anxious to terminate this unpleasant interview: I have nothing to hope for, after such a
welcome. Yet, at the same time, this insolent girl fas-
cinates me in some disconcerting way. "Thank you,"
I say, "I appreciate the language lessons."

As though she had guessed my thoughts, she adds
then: "Impossible for you to leave us. It is too late,
the exit is guarded. Meet Laura, she is armed."

I turn around, toward the stairs. Another girl,
wearing exactly the same costume, with dark glasses
and slouch brim hat is there, at the top of the stairs,

hands pushed deep into the pockets of her raincoat.

The position of her right arm and the bulge in her pocket give some likelihood to the threat: that young lady is aiming a heavy-gauge revolver at me, hidden by the fabric. . . . Or else, she is pretending to.

"Hello, Laura, how are you?" I say in my coolest thriller-diller style. "How are you," she affirms in an echo, Anglo-Saxon style. She must be without rank in the organization, since she speaks that politely.

An absurd thought crosses my mind: Laura is nothing but the inanimate mannequin from the ground floor, who, having climbed the steps behind me, faces me again.

To tell the truth, girls are no longer the way they used to be. They play gangsters, nowadays, just like boys. They organize rackets. They plan holdups and practice karate. They will rape defenseless adolescents. They wear pants. . . . Life has become impossible.

Djinn probably feels that explanations are in order, for she breaks, at this point, into a longer speech: "I hope that you'll forgive our methods. We absolutely have to work this way: keep on the lookout for possible enemies, and watch over the loyalty of our new friends: in short, we must operate with the greatest precautions, as you have just seen."

Then, after a pause, she goes on: "Our action is secret, by necessity. It carries major risks for us. You are going to help us. We will give you precise instructions. But we prefer (at least at first) not to reveal to you the exact purpose of your mission nor the general goal of our undertaking. That is for reasons of security, but also of efficiency."

I ask her what will happen should I refuse. But she leaves me no choice: "You need money, we pay. Therefore, you accept without an argument. It is useless to ask questions or to make comments. You do what we ask of you, and that's all there is to it."

I like my freedom. I like to feel responsible for my own actions. I like to understand what I am doing. . . . And, yet, I agree to this weird deal.

It is not the fear of that imaginary gun that motivates me, nor such a great need for money. . . . There are many other ways to earn a living, when you are young. Why, then? Curiosity? Bravado? Or a more obscure motivation?

In any case, if I am free, I have the right to do what I feel like doing, even against my own good sense.

"You've got something on your mind that you are not telling," says Djinn. "Yes," I say. "And what is it?" "It has nothing to do with the job."

Djinn then removes her dark glasses, allowing me to gaze upon her lovely pale eyes. And finally, she smiles at me, the enchanting smile I have been hoping for all along, and giving up the superior tone of her position, she whispers in her warm and sweet voice: "Now, you tell me what's on your mind."

"The struggle of the sexes," I say, "is the motor of history."

# CHAPTER TWO

Alone again, walking briskly along the streets, now brightly lit by streetlights and shop windows, I find that my mood has radically changed: a brand new exhilaration quickens my body, churns my thoughts, colors every little thing around me. It is no longer the mindless indifference of this morning, but a sort of happiness, and even enthusiasm, without precise cause. . . .

Without cause, indeed? Why not admit it? My

19

meeting with Djinn is the obvious cause of this sudden and remarkable transformation. At every moment, for any reason or for no reason at all, I think of her. Her image, her silhouette, her face, her gestures, the way she moves, above all her smile are much too present in my mind; my job certainly does not require that I pay that much attention to the person of my employer.

I look at the shops (rather unattractive in this part of town), the passersby, the dogs (usually I hate dogs), with benevolence. I want to sing, to run. I see smiles on every face. Ordinarily, people look dumb and sad. Today, they have been touched by some inexplicable grace.

My new job is certainly fun: it has the taste of adventure. But it has more than that: It has the taste of an adventure that is a love affair. . . . I have always been a romantic, and fond of make-believe, that's for certain. I should, therefore, be doubly careful in this matter. My runaway imagination might well cause errors in my judgments and even gross mistakes in my actions.

Suddenly, a forgotten detail surfaces in my memory: I am supposed to pass unnoticed. Djinn said so, and she insisted on it several times. Well, I happen to be doing exactly the contrary: no doubt everyone notices my joyful euphoria, and this thought calms me down considerably.

I walk into a café, and I order a black espresso. The French like only Italian coffee; "French" coffee is not strong enough. But worst of all, for them, is American coffee. . . . Why am I thinking of America? Because of Djinn, once more! This is beginning to get to me.

A paradox: in order not to be noticed, in France, one asks for an Italian espresso. Is there such a thing, as "the French," or "the Americans"? The French are like this. . . . The French eat this, and not that. . . . The French dress this way, they walk that way. . . . Where eating is concerned, yes, it might still be true, but less and less. A sign above the counter lists foods and prices; I read: hot dog, pizza, sandwiches, roll-mops, merguez. . . .

The waiter brings a small cup of very black liquid, which he places on the table in front of me, with two cubes of sugar wrapped together in white paper. Then, he walks away, picking up on his way a used glass left on another table.

I realize then that I am not the only customer in this bistro which was, however, empty when I came in. I have company, a young woman sitting nearby, a student apparently, wearing a red jacket and en-grossed in a heavy medical textbook.

While I observe her, she seems to sense my stare, and raises her eye in my direction. I think ironically: now, I've done it, I've really struck out, I've been noticed. She gazes at me silently, at length, as though not seeing me. Then she returns her attention to her book.

But, a few seconds later, she examines me again,

and this time she says in a neutral voice, with a sort of quiet assurance: "It's five past seven. You are going to be late." She hasn't even looked at her watch. I check mine automatically. It is indeed five past seven. And I do have an appointment at quarter past seven at the Gare du Nord.

So, this girl is a spy, staked out by Djinn on my path to check my professional dedication. "You work with us?" I say after a moment's reflection. Then, since she does not answer, I ask further: "How come you know so much about me? You know who I am, where I am going, what I have to do, and at what time. You're a friend of Djinn, then?"

She looks me over with cold interest, also no doubt with disapproval, because she finally states flatly: "You talk too much." And she turns her attention back to her work. Thirty seconds later, without raising an eye, she pronounces a few words, slowly, as though speaking to herself. She seems to be deciphering a difficult passage of her book: "The street you are looking for is the third on the right, straight down the avenue."

To tell the truth, this guardian angel is right: If I hang around here arguing, I'm going to be late. "I thank you," I say, showing my independence by an overly formal bow. I rise, I go to the counter, I pay for my coffee and I push the door.

Once outside, I glance backward toward the large, brightly lit room empty but for the girl in the red jacket. She is no longer reading. She has closed her heavy book on her table, and she follows me with her eyes, showing no embarrassment, with a hard and steady expression.

In spite of my desire to do just the contrary, to assert my freedom, I continue walking in the right direction, on the avenue, among the crowd of men and women returning home from work. They are no longer carefree and attractive. From now on, I am convinced they are all watching me. At the third intersection, I turn right into a dark and deserted, narrow street.

Devoid of any automobile traffic, even of parked cars, and lit here and there only by a few old-fashioned street lamps that cast a yellow flickering light, abandoned—so it seems—by its very inhabitants, this infrequented side street contrasts completely with the major thoroughfare I have just left. The houses are low (two stories at most) and poor, no lights in the windows. Anyway, it's mostly hangars and workshops here. The ground is uneven, cobbled in the old style, in very bad condition, with puddles of dirty water where the paving stones are missing.

I hesitate to venture farther into this long and narrow passage, which looks very much like a dead end: in spite of the darkness, I can make out a blind wall that appears to block the far end. Yet, a blue enamel plaque at the entrance bore the name of a real street; I mean one passable at both ends: "Rue Vercingétorix III." I wasn't aware of the existence of a third Vercingétorix, or even a second. . . .

Reflecting, I thought there might, indeed, be a passage at the far end, to the right or the left. But the total absence of automobile traffic is disquieting. Am I really on the right track? My thought was to take the next street, with which I am familiar. I am certain that it leads to the railway station almost as quickly. Only the intervention of the medical student has sent me on this so-called shortcut.

Time is short. My appointment at the railway station is, by now, less than five minutes away. This Godforsaken alley might mean a worthwhile saving of time. It is in any case, good for going fast: no vehicles or pedestrians impeding progress and no crossing either.

Having accepted the risk (somewhat at random, unfortunately), I must, in the absence of a sidewalk, place my feet carefully where the ground is even . . . taking the longest possible strides. I'm going so fast I have the feeling I'm flying, as in a dream.

I am ignorant, for the time being, of the exact meaning of my mission: it consists only in spotting a certain traveler (whose precise description I have memorized) arriving on the train from Amsterdam at 7:12 P.M. Next, I am discreetly to tail the character all the way to his hotel. That's it for now. I hope to learn the rest soon.

I haven't yet gone halfway down this endless street, when suddenly a child bursts across ten yards in front of me. He comes from one of the houses on the right, one a little taller than its neighbors, and he runs across the street as fast as his little legs will carry him.

On the run, he trips over an uneven paving stone and falls into a puddle of blackish mud without a cry. He lies still, sprawled with his arms thrown out in front of him.

A few quick strides and I am bending over the motionless little body. I turn him over carefully. He is a boy, about ten years old, dressed strangely: like a kid from the last century, with breeches, knee socks, and a full smock, rather short, cinched at the waist by a wide leather belt.

His eyes are wide open: but his pupils are fixed. His mouth isn't closed, his lips tremble slightly. His limbs are limp and inert, as well as his neck; his entire body is like a rag doll.

Luckily, he did not fall into the mud, but just on the edge of that hole full of dirty water. This water, looked at more closely, seems viscous, brown, almost red rather than black. A strange anxiety suddenly overwhelms me. Does the color of this unknown liquid scare me? Or what else?

I check my watch. It is 7:09. Impossible, now, to be at the railway station in time for the train from Amsterdam. My whole adventure, born just this morning, is already over, then. But I can't find it within me to abandon this injured child, even for the love of Djinn. . . . Oh well! Anyway, I've missed the train.

A door on my right is wide open. The boy undoubtedly comes from that house. Yet, there is no light that I can see inside, neither at the ground floor, nor the one above. I lift the boy's body in my arms. It is extremely thin, light as a bird.

Under the faint glow of the streetlight nearby, I get a better look at his face: he has no apparent injury, he is calm and handsome, but exceedingly pale. His skull must have hit a paving stone, and he is still unconscious from the impact. Yet, he has fallen forward, arms outstretched. His head did not, therefore, hit the ground.

I pass over the threshold of the house, the frail burden draped over my arms. I proceed with caution, down the long corridor that runs perpendicular to the street. All is dark and silent.

Having found no other way to go—no door or cross hall—I come upon a wooden staircase. I seem to glimpse a faint light from the floor above. I walk up slowly, for I'm afraid of stumbling or hitting some invisible obstacle with the legs or the head of the still-unconscious kid.

Two doors open onto the landing of the second floor. One is closed, the other slightly ajar. This is where the faint light comes from. I push the door with my knee and enter a room of very large dimensions, with two windows looking out onto the street.

There is no light in the room. There is only the glow of the streetlights that comes from outside through the curtainless windowpanes. It allows me to make out the shapes of the furniture: a bare wooden table, three or four unmatched chairs, their seats more or less caved in, an iron bedstead and a large number of trunks of various shapes and sizes.

The bedstead holds a mattress, but no sheets or blankets. I place the child, with all possible care, onto this crude couch. He is still unconscious, with no sign of life except for a very faint breathing. His pulse is almost imperceptible. But his large eyes, remaining open, shine in the gloomy light.

I glance around for an electric switch or something else that might provide light. But I see nothing of the kind. I notice, at this point, that there isn't a single light—chandelier, shaded lamp or bare bulb—in the entire room.

I step back out on the landing and I call out, in a low voice at first, then louder. No answer whatsoever reaches my ears. The whole house is plunged into total silence, as though abandoned. I don't know what else to do. I am abandoned myself, outside of time.

Then, a sudden thought takes me back to the windows of the room: Where was the kid going on his brief run? He was crossing the road from one side to the other, straightaway. He might, therefore, live on the other side.

But, on the other side of the street there are no houses: only a long brick wall with no apparent opening at all. A little farther on the left there is a fence in disrepair. I go back to the stairs and I call out again, still in vain. I listen to the pounding of my own heart. I have a very strong feeling, now, that time has stopped.

A faint creaking sound, in the room, calls me back to my patient. Two steps away from the bed I am jolted, instinctively recoiling. The boy is in exactly the same position as before, but now he has a large crucifix laid on his chest, a dark wooden cross with a silver Christ, that reaches from shoulder to waist.

I glance all around. There is no one but the child lying outstretched. So my first thought is that he himself is responsible for this macabre setting: he pretends to have fainted, but he moves when my back is turned. I examine his face very closely; his features are as frozen as those of a wax figure, and his complexion just as pallid. He looks like an effigy sculpted upon a tomb.

At that moment, looking up, I become aware of the presence of a second child, standing at the threshold of the room; a little girl of about seven or eight, motionless in the doorway. Her eyes are fixed upon me.

Where does she come from? How did she get here? No sound has signaled her approach. In the dim light, I clearly distinguish, nevertheless, her white, old-fashioned dress with fitted bodice and wide gathered skirt, full but rather stiff, falling all the way to her ankles.

"Hello," I say, "is your mama here?"

The girl keeps staring at me silently. The whole scene is so unreal, ghostly, frozen, that the sound of my own voice rings strangely off-key to me, unlikely, as it were, in this spellbound atmosphere under the weird bluish light. . . .

As there is nothing else to do but venture a few words, I force myself to speak this innocuous sentence:

"Your brother fell."

My syllables fall, too, awakening neither response nor echo, like useless objects deprived of sense. And silence closes in again. Have I really spoken? Cold, numbness, paralysis begin to spread through my limbs.

# CHAPTER THREE

How long did the spell last?

Suddenly making up her mind, the little girl walks decisively toward me without a word. I make an immense effort to pull out of my pervading numbness. I rub my hand over my forehead, over my eyelids, again and again. I finally manage to come back up to the surface. Little by little, I am regaining my senses.

To my great surprise, I am now seated on a straw

chair at the head of the bed. By my side, the boy is still asleep, lying on his back, his eyes open, the crucifix on his chest. I manage to stand without too much effort.

The little girl holds before her a brass candelabrum which shines like gold; it is fitted with three unlit candles. She walks without the slightest sound, gliding in the manner of an apparition, but that is because of her felt-sole slippers.

She places the candelabrum on the chair I have just left. Then she lights the three candles, one after another, with care, each time lighting a new match and blowing out the flame after use, to return the blackened stub to the box afterward with total concentration.

I ask: "Where is there a telephone? We are going to call a doctor for your brother."

The little girl watches me with a kind of condescension, as one does when addressed by a maniac or a half-wit.

"Jean is not my brother," she says. "And the doctor is of no use, since Jean is dead."

She speaks in the conciliatory tone of a grown-up, not at all like a child. Her voice is well modulated and sweet, but expresses no emotion. Her features very much resemble those of the unconscious boy, in a more feminine way of course.

"His name is Jean?" I say. The question is superfluous; but suddenly the memory of Djinn overwhelms me and I feel, once more, a violent despair. It

is now past seven-thirty. The affair is pretty well finished, I should say pretty badly finished. . . . The little
girl shrugs her shoulders:

"Obviously," she says. "What do you want to
call him?" Then, still with the same grave and reasonable air, she goes on: "Already, yesterday, he died."

"What are you talking about? When one dies, it's
forever."

"No, not Jean!" she states with such categorical
certainty that I myself feel shaken. I smile inwardly,
nevertheless, at the idea of the bizarre spectacle that
she and I are making, and of the absurd dialogue we
are exchanging. But I choose to play the game.

"He dies often?"

"These days, yes, rather often. Other times, he
will go several days without dying."

"And it lasts long?"

"An hour perhaps, or a minute, or a century. I do
not know. I do not have a watch."

"He comes out of death by himself? Or you must
help him?"

"Sometimes he comes back by himself. Generally,
it's when I wash his face; you know: the last rites."

I am beginning to grasp, now, the likely meaning
of this whole scene: the boy must have frequent
fainting spells, probably of nervous origin; cold water
on his brow serves to revive him. I cannot, however,
leave these children alone until the boy regains
consciousness.

The candle flame now casts a pink glow on his
face. Warmer highlights soften the shadows around

his mouth and his nose. His pupils, under this new glow, reflect dancing lights, breaking the fixed stare of his eyes.

The little girl in the white dress sits down carelessly on the bed, at the feet of the would-be corpse. I can't refrain from reaching out, to protect the boy from her jolting the metal box spring. I get, in return, a scornful glare.

"The dead do not feel anything. You should know that. They are not even here. They sleep in another world, with their dreams. . . ." Lower, more confidential tones muffle the timbre of her voice, which grows softer and more faraway to whisper: "Often, I sleep next to him, when he is dead; we leave together for heaven."

A feeling of void, an immeasurable anguish, once more, assaults my mind. Neither my good will nor my presence serve any purpose. I want to leave this haunted room; it weakens my body and my reason. If I can manage to get a satisfactory explanation, I will leave immediately. I repeat my first question:

"Where is your mama?"

"She is gone."

"When is she coming back?"

"She is not coming back," says the little girl.

I no longer dare to insist any further. I sense here some family drama, painful and secret. I say, to change the subject:

"And your papa?"

"He died."

"How many times?"

33

The stare of her eyes, widened by surprise, full of pity and reproach, soon make me feel guilty. After a remarkably long time, she finally condescends to explain:

"You are talking nonsense. When people die, it is final. Even children know that." Which is logic itself, by all evidence.

I am not getting anywhere. How can these kids live here alone, all by themselves, without father or mother? Perhaps they live elsewhere, with grand-parents or friends, who have taken them in as an act of charity. But, more or less left to themselves, they wander all day here and there. And this empty, run-down building, without electricity or telephone, is only their favorite playground. I ask:

"Where do you live, you and your brother?"

"Jean is not my brother," she says. "He is my husband."

"And you live with him in this house?"

"We live where we want to. And if you don't like our house, why did you come? We didn't ask any-thing of anyone."

After all, she is right. I have no idea myself what I am doing here. I sum up the situation in my head: a phony medical student redirects me into an alley I did not choose; I see a kid run just in front of me; he falls and faints dead away; I carry his body to the nearest shelter; there, a grown-up sounding and mys-tical little girl holds forth without rhyme or reason on the subject of the absent and the dead.

"If you want to see his portrait, it's hanging on the wall," she says by way of conclusion. How did she guess I was still thinking of her father?

On the wall she points to, between the two windows, a small ebony frame does hold the photograph of a man, about thirty, in the uniform of a petty officer. A commemorative sprig of boxwood has been slipped under the black wood of the frame.

"He was a sailor?"

"Obviously."

"He died at sea?"

I am sure she is going to say "Obviously" again, with that barely perceptible shrug of the shoulders. But, in fact, her answers always disappoint my expectations. And, this time, she only rectifies it, like a teacher correcting a pupil: "Lost at sea," which is the accurate expression when speaking of a shipwreck.

Yet, such distinctions are hardly what one would expect coming from a child that age. And I suddenly feel that she is mouthing a well-rehearsed lesson. Under the photograph, a careful hand has written these words: "For Marie and Jean, their loving Papa." I half turn to the little girl:

"You are called Marie?"

"Obviously. What else do you want to call me?"

While I examine the portrait, I can suddenly sense a trap. But already the little girl goes on:

"And you, you are called Simon. There is a letter for you, Si."

I have just noticed a white envelope protruding

slightly from under the sprig of boxwood. So I don't have time to mull over the surprising changes in Marie's behavior: now, she knows my first name and uses it as though she knew me well.

I carefully grasp the letter with two fingers, and I pull it out of its hiding place without damaging the leaves of the boxwood. Light and air will soon turn this kind of paper yellow. Yet, it is neither yellowed, nor old, as far as I can tell under this poor light. It can't have been here long.

The envelope bears the complete name of the addressee: "Monsieur Simon Lecoeur, alias Boris"—that is to say, not only my own name, but also the password of the organization for which I have been working barely a few hours.

More strangely yet, the writing resembles in every way (same ink, same pen, same hand) that on the dedication of the sailor's photograph. . . .

But, at this very moment, the little girl shouts at the top of her lungs, behind me: "All right, Jean, you may wake up. He has found the message."

I turn with a start, and I see the inanimate kid sit up suddenly on the edge of the mattress, legs dangling, next to his delighted sister. Both of them applaud in unison and shake with mirth as the metal box spring vibrates under their laughter for almost a minute. I feel like a complete idiot.

Then Marie, as abruptly as before, turns serious again. The boy soon does likewise; he obeys—I think—this little girl who is clearly younger than he, but sharper. She declares then for my benefit:

"Now, it is you who are our papa. I am Marie Lecoeur. And this is Jean Lecoeur."

She leaps to her feet to point to her accomplice, ceremoniously, while taking a bow in my direction. Next, she runs to the door that opens onto the landing; there, she apparently presses an electric switch (placed outside), for suddenly a brilliant light fills the entire room, as in a theater at intermission.

The many lamps, antique sconces shaped like birds, are as a matter of fact quite visible; but when unlit, they can well pass unnoticed. Marie, quick and light, has come back to the bed where she sat again close to her big brother. They whisper in each other's ear.

Then, they stare at me again. They now have a quiet and attentive look. They want to see what comes next. They are at the theater, and I am on the stage, performing an unknown play, written for me by a man I do not know . . . or perhaps a woman?

I open the unsealed envelope. In it, there is a sheet of paper, folded in four. I unfold it carefully. The handwriting is still the same, that of a left handed man, no doubt, or, more accurately, of a left handed woman. My heart leaps when I see the signature. . . .

Not only that, but I can suddenly understand better my instinctive suspicion, of a moment ago, at the sight of the letters slanting backward, under the black framed portrait: very few people, in France, write with their left hand, especially in that sailor's generation.

The letter is hardly a love letter, undoubtedly. But a few words mean a lot, especially when they come from someone whom one has just lost forever. In high spirits now, facing my youthful audience, I read the text aloud, like a comedian:

"The Amsterdam train was a false track, meant to mislead suspicions. The true mission begins here. Now that you have met, the children will lead you where you are supposed to go together. Good luck."

The letter is signed "Jean," that is to say Djinn, without any possible error. But I don't get the part about suspicions. Who's supposed to be suspicious? I refold the paper, and I slip it back into its envelope. Marie applauds briefly. Jean imitates her, with some delay, unenthusiastically.

"I'm hungry," he says. "I get tired being dead."

The two children then come toward me, and each grabs one of my hands, with authority. I let them, since these are the instructions. Thus we leave, the three of us, going first out of the room, then out of the house, like a family on an outing.

The staircase and the downstairs hall, like the upstairs landing, are now also brilliantly lit by powerful bulbs. (Who in the world has turned them on?) Since Marie, as we leave, doesn't turn off the lights or close the door, I ask her why. Her answer is no more surprising than the rest of the situation:

"It doesn't matter," she says, "since Jeanne and Joseph are here."

"Who are Jeanne and Joseph?"

"Well, Joseph is Joseph and Jeanne is Jeanne . . ."

I complete her sentence myself: ". . . obviously."

She pulls me by the hand toward the large avenue, walking with a quick step, or sometimes hopping, hopscotch fashion, on the uneven paving stones. Jean, on the contrary, lets himself be dragged along. After a few minutes, he repeats:

"I am very hungry."

"It is time for his dinner," says Marie. "He's got to be fed. Otherwise he is going to die again; and we haven't got the time anymore to play that game."

Saying these last words, she bursts into a short, shrill laugh that doesn't sound right. She is quite mad, like most children who are too grown-up for their age. I wonder how old she could be, in fact. She is short and petite, but she might be a lot older than eight.

"Marie, how old are you?"

"It's bad manners, you know, to question ladies on the subject of their age."

"Even at this age?"

"Obviously. There is no age to learn manners."

She delivered this pronouncement in a sententious tone, without the slightest smile of connivance. Is she or is she not conscious of the absurdity of her reasoning? She has turned to the left, onto the avenue, pulling us both, Jean and me, after her. Her step, as decisive as her character, does not encourage questions. But she suddenly stops short to ask one herself, staring up at me sternly:

"What about you? Do you know how to lie?"

"Sometimes, when it's necessary."

"I can lie very well, even when it's pointless. When one lies out of necessity, it has less value, obviously. I can go for a whole day without saying a single true thing. I even won a lying award, at school, last year."

"You are lying," I say. But my reply doesn't bother her for a second. She goes on, brooking no interruption, with quiet self-assurance:

"In our Logic class this year, we are doing lying exercises of the second degree. We are also studying first-degree lying with two unknowns. And sometimes, we lie in harmony. It's very exciting. In the advanced class, the girls do second-degree lying, with two unknowns, and lying of the third degree. That must be hard. I can't wait till next year."

Then, just as suddenly, she springs forward again. As for the boy, he doesn't open his mouth. I ask:

"Where are we going?"

"To the restaurant."

"We have time?"

"Obviously. What was written in the letter?"

"That you are going to take me where I'm supposed to go."

"Then, since I am taking you to the restaurant, you must therefore go to the restaurant."

That is indeed logic itself. Anyway, we arrive in front of a coffee shop. The little girl pushes the glass door with authority, and surprising vigor. We walk in behind her, Jean and I. I immediately recognize the café where I met the medical student in the red jacket. . . .

She is still there, sitting at the same place, in the center of the large empty room. She stands up when she sees us enter. I am convinced that she has been watching for my return. Passing close to us, she gives Marie a little sign and says in a low voice:

"Everything's okay?"

"Fine," says Marie, very loud and unconcerned. And she adds immediately: "Obviously."

The phony student leaves, not favoring me with a glance. We sit at one of the rectangular tables in the back of the room. For no apparent reason, the children choose the least-lighted one. They seem to avoid overly bright lights. In any case, it is up to Marie to decide.

"I want a pizza," says Jean.

"No," says his sister, "you know very well they stuff them with bacteria and viruses, on purpose."

Well, I say to myself, prophylaxy is gaining ground among the young generation. Or else, are these kids raised by an American family? As the waiter approaches, Marie orders *croque-monsieur* for everyone, two 7-Ups, "and a beer for Monsieur, who is a Russian." She makes an awful face at me, while the man walks away, still silent.

"Why did you say I was Russian? Anyway, Russians don't drink any more beer than the French, or the Germans . . ."

41

"You are a Russian, because your name is Boris. And you drink beer like everybody else, Boris Lecoeurovich!"

Then changing both her tone and her subject, she leans toward my ear to whisper in a confidential tone:

"Did you notice the face on that waiter? That's him in the photograph, in the sailor's uniform, in the mourning frame."

"He is really dead?"

"Obviously. Lost at sea. His ghost comes back to serve in the café where he used to work in days gone by. That's why he never says a word."

"Ah well," I say. "I see."

The man in the white jacket appears suddenly in front of us with the drinks. His resemblance to the sailor is not obvious. Marie tells him, acting very worldly:

"I do thank you. My mother will come around tomorrow to pay the bill."

# CHAPTER FOUR

While we were eating, I asked Marie how that waiter could be employed in a café before his death, since he was a sailor. But that did not cause her to lose her poise:

"That was obviously during his shore leaves. As soon as he hit shore, he would come to see his mistress, who worked here. And he would serve with her, out of love, glasses of white wine and cups of coffee. Love, it makes one do great things."

"What about his mistress? What became of her?"

"When she heard of her lover's tragic end, she committed suicide, by eating a mass-produced pizza."

Next, Marie wanted me to tell her how people live in Moscow, since she had just granted me Russian citizenship. I told her that she ought to know, since she was my daughter. She then made up another cock-and-bull story:

"Oh, but no. We did not live with you. Gypsies had kidnapped us, Jean and me, when we were just babies. We lived in caravans, crisscrossed Europe and Asia, begged, sang, danced in circuses. Our adoptive parents even forced us to steal money, or things from stores.

"When we disobeyed, they would punish us cruelly: Jean had to sleep on the flying trapeze, and I in the tiger's cage. Fortunately, the tiger was quite nice; but he had nightmares and he would roar all night long. This would wake me up with a start. When I got up in the morning, I had never had enough sleep.

"You, in the meantime, were searching the world for us. You would go every night to the circus—a new circus every night—and you would roam backstage to question all the little children you found. But I bet you were mostly looking at the pretty bareback riders. . . . So it is only today that we found each other again."

Marie was speaking fast, with a sort of anxious certainty. Suddenly, her excitement fell. She thought for a moment in a sudden dreamy mood, then she concluded sadly:

"And still, we're not certain that we have found each other. Perhaps it is not us, nor you, either. . . ."

Probably judging that she had spoken enough nonsense, Marie next declared that it was my turn to tell a story.

Since I ate faster than the children, I have finished my croque-monsieur some time ago. Marie, who chews every mouthful slowly and carefully in between her lengthy speeches, doesn't seem anywhere near having finished her meal. I want to know what kind of a story she wishes to hear. She says—that's definite—"a story of love and science fiction." So I begin:

"Here you go. A robot meets a young lady. . . ."

My listener allows me to go no further.

"You don't know how to tell stories," she says. "A real story has to be in the past."

"As you wish. A robot, then, met a . . ."

"No, no, not that way. A story has to be told like a story. Or else nobody knows it's a story."

She is probably right. I think it over for a moment, unaccustomed to that manner of speech, and I start again:

"Once upon a time, in the long, long ago, in the fair Kingdom of France, a robot who was very intelligent, even though strictly metallic, met at a royal ball a young and lovely lady of the nobility. They danced together. He whispered sweet nothings in her ear. She blushed. He apologized.

"By and by, they danced again. She thought he was a bit rigid, but charming with his stiff manners, which gave him a great deal of distinction. They were married the very next day. They received sumptuous wedding presents and departed on their honeymoon. . . . Is it okay this way?"

"It's no great shakes," says Marie, "but it will do. In any case, you're telling it like a real story."

"Then, I'll go on. The bride, whose name was Blanche, as compensation, because she had raven black hair, the bride, I said, was naïve, and she did not notice right away that her spouse was a product of cybernetics. Yet, she could see that he would always make the same gestures and that he would always say the same things. Well, she thought, here is a man who knows how to follow up on his ideas.

"But one fine morning, having risen earlier than was her custom, she saw him oiling the mechanism of his coxo-femoral articulations, in the bathroom, with the oil can from the sewing machine. Since she was well bred, she made no remark. From that day on, however, doubt invaded her heart.

"Small, unexplained details now came back to her mind: nocturnal creaking sounds, for example, which couldn't really come from the box spring, while her husband embraced her in the secrecy of their alcove; or else the curious ticktock that filled the air around him.

"Blanche had also discovered that his gray eyes, rather inexpressive, would sometimes light up and blink, to the left or to the right, like a car about to change direction. Other signs, as well, mechanical in nature, eventually increased her concern to the utmost.

"Finally, she became certain of even more disturbing peculiarities, and truly diabolical ones: her husband never forgot anything. His stupefying memory, concerning the slightest daily events, as well as the inexplicable rapidity of the mental calculations he effected at the end of each month, when they would check their household accounts together, gave Blanche a treacherous idea. She wanted to know more, and conceived then a Machiavellian plan. . . ."

The children, meanwhile, have both emptied their plates. As for me, I am burning with impatience, anxious as I am to leave this café, and to know at last where we are going next. I rush my conclusion accordingly.

"Unfortunately," I say, "the Seventeenth Crusade broke out right at that moment, and the robot was drafted into the colonial infantry, third armored regiment. He embarked at the port of Marseilles and went to fight the war, in the Near East, against the Palestinians.

"Since all the knights wore articulated stainless steel armor, the physical peculiarities of the robot passed henceforth unnoticed. And he never returned to Sweet France, for he died absurdly, one summer night, without attracting anyone's attention, under the ramparts of Jerusalem. The poisoned arrow of an Infidel had pierced his helmet and caused a short circuit inside his electronic brain."

Marie pouts:

"The ending is idiotic," she says. "You had a few good ideas, but you did not know how to exploit them intelligently. And, above all, you never succeeded, at any time, in giving life to your characters or in making them sympathetic. When the hero dies, at the end, the audience is not moved at all."

"When the hero expired, wast thou not moved?" I joke.

This time, I did win at least a pretty smile of amusement from my too demanding professor of narration. She answers in the same tone of parody:

"I had, nonetheless, a certain pleasure in listening to thee, my dear, when thou recounted the ball whereat they met and courted. When we had consumed our repast, Jean and I deplored it, for that curtailed thy story: We could divine thy sudden haste at that point. . . ." Then, changing her tone: "Later, I want to study to become a heroine in novels. It is a good job, and it allows one to live in the literary style. Don't you thinks that's prettier?"

"I'm still hungry," says her brother at that point. "Now, I want a pizza."

It must be a joke, for they both laugh. But I don't understand why. It must be part of their private folklore. There follows a very long silence which feels to me like a hole in time or like a blank space between two chapters. I conclude that something new will probably happen. I wait.

My young companions seem to wait, too. Marie takes up her knife and her fork, and she plays for a moment at balancing them, one against the other, by placing the ends together; then she arranges them in a cross in the center of the table. She puts such seriousness into these innocuous exercises, such calculated precision, that they acquire in my eyes the value of cabalistic signs.

I, unfortunately, do not know how to interpret these figures. And perhaps they have no real significance. Marie, like all children and poets, enjoys playing with sense and nonsense. Having completed her construction, she smiles to herself. Jean drinks up the rest of his glass. They are both silent. What are they waiting for like this? It is the boy who breaks the silence:

"No, he says, "have no fear. The pizza, that was just to get a rise out of you. Anyway, it's been several months that in this café they sell only *croque-monsieur* and sandwiches. You were wondering what we were waiting for here, right? The time to get going had not come, that's all. Now, we are going to leave."

Just like his sister, this boy expresses himself almost like an adult. He, furthermore, seems more respectful. He hasn't spoken that many words since I saw him for the first time more than an hour ago. But now, I have understood why he remained so obstinately silent.

His voice is, indeed, in the midst of changing; and he fears seeming ridiculous because of the cracks which happen, unexpectedly, in the middle of his sentences. That might also explain, perhaps, why his sister and he were laughing: the word *pizza* must contain sounds that are especially fearsome to his vocal chords.

Marie then supplies me, at last, with the next phase of our program: she herself has to go back home (what home?) to do her homework (homework in lying?), while her brother takes me to a secret meeting, where I am to receive precise instructions. But I must, for my part, remain ignorant of the locale of that appointment. I am therefore going to be disguised as a blind man, with totally opaque, black glasses.

The precautions and mysteries, maintained around its activities by this clandestine organization, are becoming more and more extravagant. But I am convinced that it is largely a game and, in any case, I have decided to pursue the experiment to its end. It is easy to guess why.

I pretend therefore to see nothing strange in the quasimiraculous appearance of the objects necessary to my disguise: the aforementioned goggles, as well as a white cane. Jean has quite naturally gone to pick them up in a corner of the café room, where they were waiting, very close to the spot where we were eating.

The two children had evidently chosen that table, inconvenient and poorly lit, because of its immediate proximity to their hiding place. But who put those props there? Jean, or Marie, or else the student in the red jacket?

That girl must have followed me since I left the workshop with the mannequins, where Djinn engaged me in her service. She could have brought the cane and the glasses already. She followed me to that café, which she entered a few seconds after me. She may have immediately placed these objects in this corner, before sitting at a table close to mine.

Yet, I am surprised to have noticed nothing of these comings and goings. When I discovered her presence, the student was already sitting and quietly reading her big anatomy textbook. But I was indulging, at that moment, in amorous reveries, vague and euphoric, which probably numbed my sense of the realities.

Another question perplexes me even further. It was I who decided to have a cup of coffee in this particular café, the phony student did nothing but follow me in. As it happens, I could, as well, have chosen another establishment on the avenue (or even drink no coffee). How, under these conditions, were the children forewarned, by their accomplice, of the spot where they were going to find the cane and the glasses?

On the other hand, Marie was talking to the waiter, upon our arrival, as though she knew him very well. And Jean knew which dishes were available, among those which are listed, more or less misleadingly, on the sign hanging above the bar. Finally, they claimed their mother was going to come soon, to pay the bill for our meal; whereas all they had to do was let me pay that modest sum myself. The waiter voiced no objection. He visibly trusts these children, who behave like regular customers.

Everything happens, therefore, as if I had walked, by chance, precisely into the café they use as their canteen and headquarters. That's rather unlikely. However, the other possible explanation seems stranger still: it wasn't "by chance"; I have, on the contrary, been led, unaware, to this bistro by the organization itself, in order to meet the student who awaited me there.

But, in that case, how have I been "led"? In what manner? By means of what mysterious method? The more I think about it all, the less clear things become, and the more I conclude the presence here of an enigma. . . .

If I could first solve the problem of the connection between the children and the medical student . . . Unfortunately, I solve nothing at all.

While I turned these thoughts over in my head, Jean and his sister adjusted the black goggles over my eyes. The rubber rims of the frames fitted perfectly to my forehead, my temples, my cheekbones. I immediately realized that I could see neither to the sides, nor down below, and neither could I distinguish anything through the lenses, which are really opaque.

And now, we are walking on the sidewalk along the avenue, side by side, the kid and I. We are holding each other by the hand. With my free hand, my right one, I point the white cane forward, its sharp point sweeping the space in front of me, searching for possible obstacles. After a few minutes, I am using this accessory with complete ease.

I reflect, while allowing myself to be guided like a blind man, upon this curious progressive deterioration of my freedom, since walking, at half past six in the evening, into the hangar with the mannequins, crowded with cast-off merchandise and junked machinery, where "Monsieur Jean" had asked me to report.

There, not only did I agree to obey the orders of a girl my age (or even younger than I), but furthermore, I did so under the insulting threat of a revolver (a hypothetical one at least), which destroyed any impression of voluntary choice. Moreover, I accepted without a word of protest, this total ignorance of my exact mission and of the goals sought by the organization. I wasn't bothered in the least by any of that: I did, on the contrary, feel happy and lighthearted.

Next, a rather ungracious student, in a café, forced me, with her air of a school inspector, or of a teacher, to take a path that did not seem the best to me. This led me to having to care for a supposedly injured boy, who was lying unconscious on the ground, but who in fact was making a fool of me.

When I found out, I did not complain of this unfairness. And I soon saw myself obeying, this time, a girl barely ten years old, a liar and a compulsive one at that. In the last place, I ended up by agreeing to relinquish as well the use of my eyes, after having in succession given up that of my free choice and that of my intelligence.

Things have reached the point where I now behave without understanding anything of what I am doing, or of what is happening to me, without even knowing where I am going, entrusted to the lead of this taciturn child who is perhaps an epileptic. And I seek in no way to infringe upon the orders received, by cheating a little with the black glasses. It is probably enough to push the frames slightly, as though I were scratching my eyebrow, so as to create a space between the rubber rim and my nose. . . .

But I undertake no such thing. I have willingly become an irresponsible agent. I did not fear to let myself be blindfolded. Soon, if it pleases Djinn, I shall myself become some sort of rudimentary robot. I can already picture myself, in a wheelchair, blind, mute, deaf . . . and what else yet?

I smiled to myself at that image.

"Why do you laugh?" asks Jean.

I answer that my present situation seems to me rather comical. The boy takes up, then, as a quote, a phrase I have already heard from the lips of his sister, while we were in the café:

"Love," he says, "it makes one do great things."

At first, I thought he was making fun of me, and I answered, with a certain annoyance, that I couldn't see the relationship. But, upon reflection, this remark of his seems to me above all inexplicable. How would he know of this hoped-for love (quasi-absurd and, in any case, secret) that I have barely acknowledged to myself?

"Oh, but yes," he goes on in that voice of his that

wavers constantly between low and sharp, "there is an obvious relationship: love is blind, that's well known. And, in any case, you mustn't laugh: being blind, that's sad."

I am going to ask him if he concludes therefore that love is sad (which seems the evident conclusion, in a perfect syllogism, of his two propositions concerning the status of the blind), when there occurs an event that puts an end to our conversation.

We had stopped, for a few moments, at the edge of a sidewalk (I had felt the stone edge with the iron tip of my cane) and I had thought that we were waiting for the traffic light that gives pedestrians the right to cross. (We do not have a musical signal for the blind, as is the case in many cities in Japan.) But I was mistaken. This place must have been a taxi stand, where Jean waited for the arrival of a free cab.

He helped me, as a matter of fact, to climb into a car, a fairly large one, it seems, judging by the width of the doors that I negotiate gropingly (I have relinquished my cane to my guide). I settle down on what seems to be the rear seat, spacious and comfortable.

While I was sitting down, Jean slammed the door, and he must have walked around the car, in order to climb in himself through the left door: I can hear it open, and someone getting in and sitting next to me. And that someone is the kid, all right, for his voice, with its inimitable cracks, says, in the direction of the driver:

"We are going here, please."

I can make out at the same time the slight rustling of paper. Instead of saying aloud where we wish to go, Jean has most likely handed the driver a piece of paper on which the address has been written (by whom?). Such subterfuge allows them to leave me ignorant of our destination. Since it is a child using it, this method can't surprise the driver.

And suppose it wasn't a taxi?

# CHAPTER FIVE

While the car rolled on, I thought again about the absurdity of my situation. But I did not succeed in making the decision to put an end to it. This obstinacy of mine surprised me. I blamed myself for it, all the while complacently enjoying it. The interest that I harbor for Djinn could not be its only cause. There also had to be, quite certainly, curiosity. And what else yet?

I felt pulled along in a chain of episodes and encounters, in which chance probably played no part at all. I was the only one who did not grasp its profound causality. These successive mysteries made me think of a sort of treasure hunt: one progresses from clue to clue, and discovers the solution only at the very end. And the treasure, it was Djinn!

I wondered, as well, about the kind of work the organization expected of me. Were they afraid to tell me openly about it? Was it so disreputable a job? What was the meaning of these endless preliminaries? And why did they leave me so little initiative in the matter?

This total absence of information, I hoped just the same that it was only temporary: perhaps I was first supposed to pass through this initial phase, where I would be put to the test. The treasure hunt thus became, in my romantic mind, like a journey of initiation.

As for my recent transformation into this classic character of a blind man led by a child, it was meant no doubt to arouse people's sympathy, and thereby put their suspicions to rest. But, as for passing unnoticed in the crowd, as I had been sternly instructed to, it seemed to me a very dubious way.

Beyond that, a precise subject of concern kept coming back to preoccupy me: where were we going now? Which streets, which boulevards were we following? Towards which suburbs were we thus driving? Towards what revelation? Or else, toward what new secret? Was the trip to get there going to be long?

This last point above all—the length of the car ride—nagged at me, without a specific reason. Perhaps Jean was authorized to tell me? Taking a chance, I asked him about it. But he answered that he had no idea himself, which seemed even stranger to me (inasmuch, at least, as I believed it).

The driver, who could hear all we were saying, then intervened to reassure me:

"Don't worry. We'll get there soon."

But instead, I perceived, in these two sentences, a vague threat I couldn't explain. In any case, it didn't mean much. I listened to the sounds of the street, around us, but they provided no indication of the sections of town we were driving through. Perhaps, however, the traffic here was less intense.

Next, Jean offered me a mint lozenge. I answered that I would take one. But it was rather out of courtesy. So, he touched my left arm, saying:

"Here, give me your hand."

I offered it to him, my palm extended. He placed in it a piece of half melted candy, sort of sticky, like all children carry in their pockets. I really didn't feel at all like it anymore, but I dared not confess it to the donor: once I had accepted the candy, it became impossible to return it.

So I put it into my mouth, quite against my will. I immediately thought it had a weird taste, flat and bitter at the same time. I felt very much like spitting it out again. I abstained, once more to spare the kid's feelings. For, unable to see him, I could never know whether he was not precisely watching me at that very moment.

I was discovering here a paradoxical consequence of blindness: a blind person can no longer do anything secretly! Those poor people who can't see constantly fear being seen. In order to escape this unpleasant feeling, in a rather illogical reflex, I closed my eyes behind my black glasses.

I slept, I am sure of it; or, at least, I dozed off. But I don't know for how long.

"Wake up," said the kid's voice, "we're getting off here."

And he was shaking me lightly, at the same time. I now suspect that mint lozenge, with its suspicious flavor, was drugged with sleeping medicine; for I am hardly in the habit of falling asleep this way in cars. My friend Jean has drugged me, that is most likely, just as he must have been ordered to. This way, I won't even know the length of the trip we have just taken.

The car has stopped. And my youthful guide has already paid the fare (if, however, it is really a cab, which seems to me to be less and less certain). I no longer sense any presence in the driver's seat. And I have the confused feeling that I am no longer in the same car.

I find it hard to regain my wits. The darkness in which I am still steeped makes waking even more difficult, and also leaves it more uncertain. I have a feeling that my sleep continues, while I dream that I am coming out of it. Furthermore, I no longer have the slightest idea of the time.

"Hurry. We are not early."

My guardian angel is growing anxious and lets me know straightaway, in his funny voice that goes off-key. I extract myself with difficulty from the car, and I stand as well as I can. I feel quite woozy, as though I had been drinking too much.

"Now," I say, "give me back my cane."

The kid places it in my right hand, and then he grabs the left one to pull me vigorously along.

"Don't go so fast. You're going to make me lose my balance."

"We're going to be late, if you drag your feet."

"Where are we going now?"

"Don't ask me. I'm not allowed to tell you. And besides, it doesn't have a name."

The place is, at any rate, quite silent. It seems to me that there is no longer anyone around us. I can hear neither voices nor footsteps. We are walking on gravel. Then the feeling of the ground changes. We step over a threshold and we enter a building.

There, we follow a rather complex course the kid seems to know by heart, for he never hesitates when changing direction. A wooden floor has replaced the stone of the entryway.

Possibly, there is someone else, now, who is walking beside us, or rather ahead of us, to show us the way. Indeed, if I stop for a second, my young guide, who holds me by the hand, stops also, and I seem then to detect, just ahead, a third footstep that continues for a few seconds more. But it is difficult to say for sure.

"Don't stop," says the kid.

And a few feet farther:

"Pay attention, we're coming to some stairs. Take the banister in your right hand. If your cane is in the way, give it to me."

No, instinctively, I prefer not to relinquish it. I can sense a danger of sorts closing in on us. So I grasp, with the same hand, the iron banister and the curved handle of the cane. I stand ready for any eventuality. If something too disquieting happens, I am getting ready to suddenly pull my black goggles off with my left hand (which the kid holds rather loosely in his own), and to brandish, with the right, my iron tipped cane to serve as a defensive weapon.

But no alarming event occurs. After having climbed one floor, up a very steep staircase, we soon arrive at a room where a meeting, it seems, is in progress. Jean has warned me before walking in, adding in a whisper:

"Don't make any noise. We are the last ones. Let's not get ourselves noticed."

He has softly opened the door, and I follow him, still led by the hand, like a small child. There is a crowd in the room: I can tell right away because of the very faint—but numerous—assorted sounds, breathing, suppressed coughing, the rumpling of fabric, slight impacts or furtive sliding sounds, soles imperceptibly scraping the floor, etc.

Yet, all these people remain motionless, I am convinced of it. But they have probably remained standing, and they move a little in place, that can't be helped. Since I haven't been shown a seat, I remain standing, too. Around us, no one says anything.

And suddenly, in this silence quickened by many attentive presences, the long-awaited surprise comes at last. Djinn is here, in the room, her lovely voice rises a few feet from me. And I feel, suddenly, rewarded for all my patience.

"I have gathered you here," she says, "in order to give you some explanations, henceforth necessary. . . ."

I imagine her at a podium, standing as well, and facing her audience. Is there a table in front of her, as in a classroom? And how is Djinn dressed? Is she still wearing her raincoat and her felt hat? Or else, has she taken them off for this meeting? What about her dark glasses, has she kept them on?

For the first time, I am dying to remove mine. But nobody has yet give me permission; and this is not after all the right moment, with all these people nearby who can see me. Not counting Djinn herself . . . I must therefore be satisfied with what is offered me: the delicious voice with its hint of an American accent.

". . . clandestine international organization . . . partitioning the tasks . . . great humanitarian enterprise . . ."

What great humanitarian enterprise? What is she talking about? Suddenly, I become aware of my frivolity: I'm not even listening to what she says! Charmed by her exotic intonations, quite busy imagining the face and the mouth from which they come (is she smiling? Or else is she putting on that phony gang-leader look?), I have forgotten the main thing: to pay attention to the information contained in her words; I am savoring them instead of registering their meaning. And all the time, I claimed to be so anxious to learn more about my future work!

But now, Djinn has stopped speaking. What has she just said, exactly? I try in vain to remember. I have the vague idea that they were only words of greeting, of welcome into the organization, and that the most important part remains yet to come. But why is she silent? And what are the other members of the audience doing in the meantime? Nobody moves around me, nor evidences any surprise.

I don't know if it's emotional, but a bothersome itching is annoying my right eye. Vigorous blinking does not succeed in getting rid of it. I try to find a way to scratch discreetly. My left hand has remained held in the kid's, and he is not letting go, and the right one is encumbered with the cane. Yet, unable to stand it any longer, I attempt with that right hand to rub at least the area around my eye.

Inconvenienced by the curved handle of the cane, I make a clumsy gesture, and the thick frame of the glasses slides upward, to my eyebrows. As a matter of fact, the goggles have barely moved, but the space created between my skin and the rubber rim is still enough to allow me to glimpse what is directly on my right. . . .

It leaves me stupefied. I had hardly guessed anything like this. . . . I slowly move my head, in order to sweep a wider angle through my narrowed field of vision. What I see, on all sides, only confirms my initial stupefaction: I have the feeling that I am in front of my own image, multiplied twenty or thirty-fold.

The entire room is, in fact, full of blind men, phony blind men as well, most likely: young men my own age, dressed in various ways (but, all in all, pretty much like me), with the same heavy black goggles over their eyes, the same white cane in the right hand, a kid just like mine holding them by the left hand.

They are all turned in the same direction, toward the stage. Each pair—a blind man and his guide—is separated from the others by an empty space, always about the same, as if one had taken care to arrange, on carefully marked squares, a series of identical statuettes.

And, suddenly, a stupid feeling of jealousy tightens my heart: It isn't me then that Djinn was speaking to! I did know she was addressing a large assembly. But it is quite something else to see, with my own eyes, that Djinn has already recruited two or three dozen guys, who are little different from me and treated in exactly the same way. I am nothing more, to her, than the least remarkable among them.

But just at that moment, Djinn resumes speaking. Most strangely, she picks up her speech right in the middle of a sentence, without repeating the words that came before so as to preserve the coherence of her remarks. And she says nothing to justify this interruption; her tone is exactly the same as if there had not been any.

". . . will allow you not to awaken suspicions . . ."

Having abandoned all prudence (and all obedience to the orders that I suddenly can't bear any longer), I manage to turn my head sufficiently, by twisting my neck and raising my chin, so as to place the center of the stage in my visual field. . . .

I don't understand right away what's going on. . . . But soon I must surrender to the evidence: there is a lecturer's table all right, but no one behind it! Djinn is not there at all, nor anywhere else in the room.

It is just a loudspeaker that is broadcasting her address, recorded I know not where nor when. The machine is placed on the table, perfectly visible, almost indecent. It had probably stopped, following some technical trouble: a technician is just now checking the wires, which he must have just plugged back in. . . .

All the charm of that fresh and sensuous voice

has disappeared suddenly. No doubt the rest of the recording is of the same excellent quality; the words continue their lilting song from beyond the Atlantic; the tape recorder faithfully reproduces its sonorities, the melody, down to the slightest inflection. . . .

But, now that the illusion of her physical presence has vanished, I have lost all feeling of contact with that music, so sweet to my ears a moment before. My discovery of the ruse has broken the magical spell of the speech, which has then become dull and cold: the magnetic tape now reels it off with the anonymous neutrality of an airport announcement. So much so that, now, I no longer have any trouble at all listening to its words nor discovering meaning in them.

The faceless voice is in the process of explaining to us our roles and our future functions. But she does not divulge them entirely, she gives us only their broad outlines. She elaborates more on the goals to be pursued than on the methods: it is because of a concern for efficiency that she prefers, she says again, to divulge to us, for the moment, only that which is strictly necessary.

I have not followed well, as I said, the beginning of her exposé. But it seems to me however that I have grasped the essentials: what I am now hearing allows me in any case to assume that I did, for I can find in it no major obscurities (except those intentionally worked in there by the speaker).

We have then, she informs us, been enlisted, the

others and I, in an international movement of struggle against machinism. The classified ad that led me (after a brief exchange of letters, with a post-office box) to meet Djinn in the abandoned workshop, had already led me to assume it as much. But I had not fully fathomed the consequences of the slogan being used: "For a life more free and rid of the imperialism of machines."

In fact, the organization's ideology is rather simple, simplistic even or so it seems: "The time has come to free ourselves from machines, for they, and nothing else, oppress us. Men believe that machines work for them. While men, on the contrary, henceforth work for machines. More and more, machines command us, and we obey them.

"Machinism, above all, is responsible for the division of work into tiny fragments devoid of all meaning. The automated tool demands the performance by each worker of a single gesture, he must repeat from morning to night, all his life long. Fragmentation is evident then in manual work. But it is also becoming the rule in any other branch of human activity.

"This, in all cases, the long-term product of our work (manufactured goods, service, or intellectual study) escapes us entirely. The worker never knows either the form of the whole, or its ultimate use, except in a theoretical and purely abstract way. No responsibility accrues to him, no pride can he reap from it. He is nothing but an infinitesimally small link in the immense chain of production, bringing only a modification of detail to a spare part, to an isolated cog, that have no significance in themselves.

"No one, in any domain, any longer produces anything complete. And man's conscience and awareness have been shattered. But mark my word: it is our alienation by the machine that has brought forth capitalism and Soviet bureaucracy, and not the contrary. It is the atomization of the entire universe that has begotten the atomic bomb.

"Yet, at the beginning of this century, the ruling class, the only one to be spared, still kept decision-making power. Henceforth, the machine that thinks—that is to say, the computer—has taken these away as well. We are no longer anything more than slaves, working toward our own destruction, in the service—and for the greater glory—of the Almighty God of the Mechanical."

On the subject of the means for raising the consciousness of the masses, Djinn is more discreet and less explicit. She speaks of "peaceful terrorism" and "dramatic" actions staged by us in the midst of the crowd, in the subway, in city squares, in offices and in factories. . . .

And yet, something disturbs me about these fine words: it is the fate meant for us, we, the agents of the program's execution: our role is in total contradiction to the goals that it proposes. Up to now at least, this program has hardly been applied to us. We, on the contrary, have been manipulated, without any regard for our free will. And now still, it has been admitted that only partial knowledge of the whole is permitted us. They want to raise our consciousness, but they start out by preventing us from seeing. Finally, to top it all off, it's a machine that talks to us, persuading us, directing us. . . .

Once again, I am filled with mistrust. I sense some unknown, obscure danger floating over this trumped-up meeting. This roomful of phony blind men is a trap, in which I have allowed myself to be caught. Through the narrow slit, which I have carefully maintained under the right edge of my cumbersome glasses, I glance at my closest neighbor, a tall blond guy who wears a white leather windbreaker, rather chic, open over a bright blue pullover. . . .

He has also (as I suspected a moment ago), managed to slip by a fraction of an inch the tight-fitting contraption that blinded him, so as to glimpse the surroundings on his left; in such a way that our sidelong glances have crossed, I am certain of it. A slight tightening of his mouth gives me, besides, a sign of connivance. I return it, in the form of the same grimace, which can pass for a smile in his direction.

The kid who accompanies him, and who holds his left hand, has noticed nothing of our carryings-on, it seems to me. Little Jean hasn't either, certainly, for he, he is clearly located outside this limited exchange. Meanwhile, the harangue goes on, calling out to us in no uncertain terms:

"The machine is watching you: fear it no longer!

The machine gives you orders: obey it no longer! The machine demands all your time: surrender it no longer! The machine thinks itself superior to men: prefer it over them no longer!"

At this point, I see that the character in the white zippered jacket, who has like me kept his blind man's cane in his right hand, slips it discreetly behind his back, toward his left, so as to bring its sharp tip closer to me. With that iron tip, he noiselessly draws complicated signs on the ground.

Indeed, this colleague of mine, as rebellious as I, is trying to communicate something to me. But I can't seem to understand what he wants to tell me. He repeats several times for me the same series of short, straight lines and intertwining curves. I persist vainly in my attempts to decipher them; my very limited view of the floor, distorted furthermore by the excessive angle, doesn't help, that's for sure.

"We have discovered," the recorded voice goes on, "a simple solution to save our brothers. Make them aware of it. Put it in their head without telling them, almost without their knowing it. And turn them themselves into new propagandists . . ."

At this point, I sense a sudden agitation behind me. Hurried footsteps, very near, break the silence. I feel a violent shock, at the base of my skull, and a very sharp pain. . . .

# CHAPTER SIX

Simon Lecoeur awoke, feeling hung over, as though he had drunk too much, in the midst of piled-up crates and junked machinery. He regained consciousness little by little, with the vague feeling that he was coming out of a long nightmare. Soon, he recognized the scene around him. It was the abandoned workshop where he had met Djinn. And, almost immediately, there returned to his mind the starting point of his mission.

"I must," he thought, "go to the Gare du Nord.

In fact, I must hurry, for it is most important that I be on time for the arrival of the train from Amsterdam. If I do not creditably carry out this first assignment, I very much fear that I won't be trusted later on, and that I won't be allowed to go any further. . . ."

But Simon Lecoeur felt, in some confused way, that all this business of railroad station, a train, a traveler he was supposed not to miss, was out of date, done with: this future already belonged to the past. Something was scrambling space and time. And Simon did not seem able to define in it all his own situation. What had happened to him? And when? And where?

On the one hand, he was finding himself lying on the floor, unable to grasp the reason for it, in the dust and assorted debris that littered the workshop, among the discarded materials and machinery. On the other hand, it was broad daylight. The sun, already high, of a fine spring morning, brightly illumined from outside the dusty panes of the skylight; while, on the contrary, night had been falling when Djinn materialized, in these same forlorn premises, with her raincoat and her fedora. . . .

Simon suddenly remembered a recent scene, seeing it again with extreme precision: a boy of about ten, probably dead, considering his total immobility, his excessive rigidity and his waxen complexion, who was lying on an iron bedstead with a bare mattress, a large crucifix placed on his chest, under the flickering light of the three candles in a brass candelabrum. . . .

Another image followed this one, just as sharp and swift: that same boy, still clad in the fashion of the last century, was leading a blind man, holding his left hand. The invalid tightly held, in his other hand, the curved handle of a white cane, which he used to reconnoiter the ground in front of his steps. Heavy black goggles half hid his face. He wore a fine white leather windbreaker with a zipper, wide open over a bright blue sweater. . . .

A sudden thought crossed Simon Lecoeur's mind. He felt his chest with his hand. His fingers did not find the ebony crucifix (although he himself was lying supine in the exact position of the kid at the wake), but he acknowledged the presence of the lambskin windbreaker and the cashmere pullover. He recalled having chosen them, in fact, for tonight's appointment, although this blue and white outfit, at once elegant and casual, did not seem to him perfectly suited to job hunting. . . .

"But of course," he said to himself, "this cannot be tonight's meeting. Tonight hasn't come yet, and the appointment has already taken place. Therefore, it must have been last night. . . . As for those two scenes in which the same kid figures, the second one had to take place before the first, since, in the first, the child is lying on his deathbed. . . . But where do these images come from?

Simon did not know whether he should grant them the status of recollections, as though they were events of his real life; or else whether they were not, instead, images such as are shaped in dreams and file through our head at the moment of awakening and usually in reverse chronological order.

In any case, there was a gap in his timetable. Indeed, it seemed hard to conceive that Simon might have slept more than twelve hours in that uncomfortable place . . . unless sleeping pills, or harder drugs, were the cause. . . .

A new image, come from he knew not where, arose unexpectedly in his disordered memory: a long straight alleyway, badly paved, feebly lit by old-fashioned streetlights, between ramshackle fencing, blind walls, and half-ruined cottages. . . . And again, the same kid, springing forth from one of the houses, taking five or six running steps, and sprawling head-long into a puddle of reddish water. . . .

Simon Lecoeur stood up painfully. Every joint hurt, he was uncomfortable, his head heavy. "I must have a cup of coffee," he thought, "and take an aspirin." He recalled having seen, on his way down the broad avenue nearby, a number of coffee shops and restaurants. Simon made a few swipes, with the flat of his hands, at the white fabric of his trousers, now rumpled, shapeless and stained with black dust; but he did not manage, evidently, to restore its normal look.

Turning around to leave, he saw that someone else was lying on the floor, a few yards from him, in an identical position. The body was not wholly visible: a large size crate was hiding from view the upper torso and the head. Simon approached cautiously. He was startled to discover the face: it was Djinn's without the least possible doubt.

The girl was lying across the passageway, still wearing her buttoned-up raincoat, her sunglasses, and her slouch felt hat, which had strangely remained in place when she had dropped, mortally wounded in the back by some knife blade or bullet of a gun. She showed no visible wound, but a puddle of blood, already coagulated, had formed under her chest and had spread onto the darkish concrete floor all around her left shoulder.

Minutes ran out slowly before Simon decided to make a move. He was standing there, motionless, uncomprehending, and inspired with no idea of what he should do. At length, he bent down, overcoming his revulsion, and wanting to touch the hand of the cadaver. . . .

Not only was the hand stiffened and cold, but it seemed to him much too hard, too rigid, to pass as one made of flesh and human joints. In order to dissipate his last doubts, and although an inexplicable revulsion still held him back, he forced himself to feel as well the limbs, the chest, the skin of the cheeks and the lips. . . .

The obvious artificiality of the whole thing quite convinced Simon of his mistake, which duplicated, after all, given the interval of a few hours, the one he had made upon his arrival: he was once more in the presence of a papier-mâché mannequin. Yet, the dark red puddle was not plastic: Simon verified, with his fingertips, its slightly damp and viscous quality. One could not swear, nonetheless, that it was real blood.

All this seemed absurd to Simon Lecoeur; yet, he feared, in some obscure way, that there might be a precise meaning to these simulations, although that meaning eluded him. . . . The murdered mannequin was lying at the exact place where Djinn had stood at the time of the brief interview of the previous day; although Simon remembered very well having seen it, at that time, on the ground floor. . . . Unless he was now confusing the two consecutive scenes, the one with Djinn and the one with the mannequin.

He decided to get out as fast as possible, for fear other enigmas might come to complicate the problem further. As it was, he had already enough of them for several hours of reflection. But, at any rate, the more he thought it over, the less he could find the guiding thread.

He went downstairs. On the ground floor, the facsimile of Djinn was still in its place, casually leaning against the same crates, both hands in the pockets of her trench coat, an imperceptible smile frozen on her waxen lips. The figure upstairs was, therefore, a second mannequin, in all respects identical. The thin mocking smile, on her lips, no longer at all resembled Jane Frank's. Simon had only the unpleasant feeling that someone was making fun of him. He shrugged, and walked to the half-glass door opening onto the courtyard.

. . . Even before he had passed the door, the phony mannequin straightened up a little, and her smile widened. The right hand came out of the trench-coat pocket, moved up to her face, and slowly removed the dark glasses. . . . The seductive pale green eyes reappeared. . . .

It was Simon himself, who, while on his way, imagined this ultimate mystification. But he didn't bother to turn around, to destroy completely its feeble likelihood, so certain did he remain that he had, this time seen only a waxwork American girl. He crossed the yard, passed through the outside gate; then, at the very end of the alley, he turned, as expected, onto the wide avenue teeming with passersby. Simon felt intensely relieved, as though he were at last returning to the real world, after an interminable absence.

It might have been close to noon, to judge from the position of the sun. Since Simon had not rewound his watch in time, the previous night, it had of course stopped; he had just noticed it. In full possession of himself now, he walked with a brisk step. But he could see no café or bistro, although, in his memory, they were plentiful all along the avenue; cafés, probably, started in fact a little farther on. He walked into the first one he saw.

Simon immediately recognized the place: this was where he had already drunk a black coffee, upon leaving, for the first time, the abandonned workshop. But many patrons had taken up places there today, and Simon had trouble finding a free table. Eventually, he spotted one, in a dark corner, and sat there, facing the room.

The taciturn waiter of the day before, in his white jacket and black trousers, was not on duty today, unless he had gone to the kitchen for some hot dish. A middle-aged woman, wearing a gray smock, was replacing him. She came over to the new arrival to take his order. Simon told her he wanted only a cup of black coffee, very strong, with a glass of tap water.

When she returned, carrying on a tray a small white cup, a carafe and a large glass, he asked her, looking as indifferent as he could, whether the waiter wasn't there today. She didn't answer right away, as though she was thinking the question over; then she said, with something like concern in her voice:

"Which waiter are you talking about?"

"The man in the white jacket, who works here, usually."

"I am always the one who works here," she said. "There is no one else, even during busy hours."

"But yesterday, however, I saw . . ."

"Yesterday, you could not see anything: that was the day we close."

And she walked away, pressured by her work. Her tone of voice was not really unpleasant, but full of weariness, sadness even. Simon observed his surroundings. Was he confusing this establishment with another one similarly arranged?

Putting aside the presence of numerous patrons, workmen and office workers of both sexes, the resemblance was, in any case, disconcerting. The same glazed partition separated the room from the sidewalk, the tables were the same, and lined up in identical fashion. The bottles, behind the bar, were lined up in the same way, and the same signs were posted above the upper row of bottles. One of them offered the same fast foods: sandwiches, *croque-monsieur,* pizza.

"Although they no longer serve pizza here, and haven't for some time," thought Simon Lecoeur. Next, he wondered that such a certainty had come to him, with such sudden conviction. He drank his coffee in a single gulp. Since the posted signs listed the price of pizzas, he could no doubt order some. Why had Simon suddenly believed differently? He evidently possessed no special information that might allow such a thought.

But, while he was examining the other signs posted behind the bar, his attention was drawn to a fairly small photo portrait, framed in black, which had also been hung there, off to the side a little, next to the ordinance forbidding the sale of alcoholic beverages to minors. Seized with a curiosity that he himself couldn't explain every well, Simon Lecoeur stood up, feigning a trip to the men's room, and took a few steps out of his way, in order to pass in front of the photo. There, he stopped, as though by chance, to examine it more closely.

It showed a man about thirty, with strange pale eyes, in the uniform of a naval officer, or more exactly of a noncommissioned officer. The face reminded Simon of something. . . . Suddenly he understood why: it was the waiter who had served him the day before.

A sprig of boxwood, slipped under the black wood frame, protruded substantially on the right side. Withered by the years, the dusty stems had lost half their leaves. Under the photograph, in the yellowed margin, someone obviously lefthanded had penned this dedication: "For Marie and Jean, their loving Papa."

"Is it the uniform you find puzzling?" said the waitress.

Simon had not heard her coming. The woman in the gray smock was wiping glasses, behind the counter. She went on:

"That's my father you're looking at. He was a Russian."

Simon, who hadn't noticed it, acknowledged that the uniform, indeed, did not belong to the French navy. But, since the man wasn't wearing his cap, the difference wasn't obvious. In order to say something, he asked, rather stupidly, whether the sailor had died at sea:

"Lost at sea," the lady corrected him.

"And your name is Marie?"

"Of course!" she said with a shrug.

He walked down to the basement level, where the ill-smelling toilets were located. The walls, painted a cream color, were being used by the regulars to inscribe their political opinions, their business appointments and their sexual fantasies. Simon thought that, perhaps, one of these messages was meant for him; for instance, that phone number, insistently repeated, written in red crayon, in every direction: 765-43-21. The figures were, in any case, easy to remember.

Walking back to his seat, his eyes stopped on the recessed angle formed by the imitation wood paneling, just behind the chair he occupied. A white cane, like those used by the blind, was leaning in the corner. That wall, very poorly lit, had not captured his attention when he first arrived. The cane must have been there already. Simon Lecoeur sat down again. As the sad waitress passed by, he beckoned to her:

"I'll have a pizza, please."

"We haven't been serving them for months," answered the gray woman. "The health authorities have forbidden us to sell them."

Simon drained his glass of water and paid for the coffee. He was heading for the door, when he remembered something. "Well," he said to himself, "here I go, forgetting my cane." No other table was close enough to the thing, so that it could not belong to another patron. Simon retraced his steps rapidly, picked up the white cane without hesitation and crossed the crowded room, looking serene, holding it under his left arm. He left, without arousing any suspicion.

In front of the café door, a street vendor was displaying on the sidewalk fake tortoiseshell combs and other assorted cheap merchandise. Although they seemed greatly overpriced to him, Simon Lecoeur bought sunglasses, with very large and very dark lenses. He liked the frames, because of their close fit. The bright spring sun hurt his eyes and he didn't want its slanting rays to penetrate through wide side openings. He immediately put on the glasses; they fit him perfectly.

Without knowing why—simply as a game, perhaps—Simon closed his eyes, sheltered behind the dark lenses, and started to walk, feeling the pavement in front of his feet, with the iron tip of his cane. This gave him a sort of restful feeling.

As long as he remembered the disposition of his surroundings, he was able to progress without too much difficulty, although he was forced to slow down more and more. After about twenty steps, he no longer had any idea of the obstacles around him. He felt completely lost and stopped, but did not open his eyes. His status as a blind man protected him from being jostled.

"Sir, would you like me to help you cross?"

It was a young boy who addressed him thusly. Simon could easily guess his approximate age, because his voice was obviously just beginning to change. The sound originated from a clearly definable level, indicating further the height of the child, with a precision that surprised the phony invalid.

"Yes, thank you," answered Simon, "I would like that."

The boy grabbed his left hand, gently and firmly.

"Wait awhile," he said, "the light is green and cars go fast, on the avenue."

Simon concluded that he must have stopped just at the edge of the sidewalk. He had therefore strayed considerably, in a few yards, from his original direction. Yet, the experiment still attracted him, fascinated him, even; he wanted to carry it out until some insurmountable difficulty put an end to it.

He easily located, with the iron tip, the edge of the stone margin and the difference in level, that he would have to negotiate in order to reach the surface of the street. His own idiotic obstinacy surprised him: "I must have one hell of an Oedipus complex," he thought smiling, while the kid pulled him forward, cars having finally given way to pedestrians. But soon his smile vanished, replaced by this inward thought:

"I mustn't laugh: it is sad to be blind. . . ."

The hazy image of a little girl in a gathered white dress, cinched at the waist with a wide ribbon, after wavering momentarily in an indefinable recollection, finally settles behind the screen of, his closed eyelids. . . .

She stands motionless in the frame of a doorway. It is so dark around her that practically nothing is visible. In the dim light, only the white gauze dress, the blond hair, the pale features emerge. The child carries, in front of her, in both hands, a large three-branched candelabrum, polished and shiny: but its three candles are out.

I wonder, once more, where these images might

come from. This candelabrum has already appeared in my memory. It has been placed on a chair, lit that time, at the head of a young boy lying on his death-bed. . . .

But we have now reached the other side of the street, and I fear that my guide might abandon me. Since I am not yet comfortable in my part as a blind man, I wish that we might continue to walk together, for a few extra minutes. In order to gain time, I question him.

"What's your name?"

"My name is Jean, sir."

"You live around here?"

"No, sir, I live in the fourteenth district."

We are, however, at the other end of Paris. Although there might be a number of reasons to explain the presence here of that child, I am surprised that he wanders around, this way, so far from his home. About to question him on this subject, I suddenly fear that he might find my indiscretion strange, that it might alarm him, and that it could even cause him to flee. . . .

"Rue Vercingétorix," specifies the kid, in that voice of his that breaks from sharp to low, and in the middle of a word as well.

The name of the leader of the Gauls surprises me: I think there is, to be sure, a rue Vercingétorix that opens onto this avenue, and I don't think there is another one elsewhere, not in Paris in any case. It is impossible that the same name would be used for two different streets in the same city, unless there are also two Vercingétorixes in French history. I convey my doubts to my companion.

"No," he answers, without an hesitation, "there is only one Vercingétorix and only one street by that name in Paris. It is in the fourteenth arrondissement."

I must then be confusing it with another street name? . . . It happens rather often this way, that we believe in things that are quite false: it is enough that some fragment of a memory, come from elsewhere, enters into some coherent pattern open to it, or else that we unconsciously fuse two disparate halves, or still that we reverse the order of the elements in some causal system, to fashion in our minds chimerical objects, having for us all the appearances of reality. . . .

But I put off until later the solution to my problem of topography, for fear the kid might eventually tire of my questions. He has let go of my hand, and I doubt that he wants to go on serving as my guide for much longer. His parents are perhaps expecting him for the midday meal.

As he hasn't said anything else for a fairly long time (long enough for me to be aware of it), I even fear for a moment that he has already gone, and that I may, henceforth, have to go on alone, without his providential support. I must look rather forlorn, for I hear his voice, reassuring to me in spite of its strange sonorities.

"It doesn't seem that you're accustomed to walking alone," he says. "Do you want us to stay together a little longer? Where are you going?"

I am at a loss to answer. But I must keep my improvised guide from noticing my embarrassment. In order not to let him find out that I do not myself know where I am going, I answer with assurance, without thinking:

"To the Gare du Nord."

"In that case, we shouldn't have crossed over. That's on the other side of the avenue."

He is right, of course. I give him, again quickly, the only explanation that comes to mind:

"I thought this sidewalk would be less crowded."

"As a matter of fact, it *is* less crowded," says the kid. "But in any case, you were supposed to make a right turn immediately. You're taking the train?"

"No, I am going to meet a friend."

"Where is he coming from?"

"He is coming from Amsterdam."

"At what time?"

I have once again ventured upon dangerous ground. Let's hope there is really such a train in the early afternoon. Fortunately, it is quite unlikely that this child would know the train schedules.

"I don't remember the exact time," I say. "But I am sure that I am quite early."

"The express from Amsterdam pulls into the station at 12:34," says the kid. "We can be there on time if we take the shortcut. Come on. Let's hurry."

# CHAPTER SEVEN

"We'll take the alley," says the kid. "It will be faster. But you'll have to be careful where you put your feet: the paving stones are quite uneven. On the other hand, there won't be any more cars or pedestrians."

"Good," I say, "I'll be careful."

"I'll guide you as well as I can between the holes and the bumps. When we come to some particular obstacle, I'll squeeze your hand harder. . . . Well, here we are: we have to turn right."

I'd better open my eyes, of course. It would be safer, and at any rate, more convenient. But I have decided to walk like a blind man for as long as possible. This has to be what is known as a losing bet. It looks, after all, as though I'd be behaving like a scatterbrain or a child, a behavior that is hardly customary for me. . . .

At the same time, this darkness to which I am condemning myself, and which I doubtlessly enjoy, seems to me to fit perfectly the mental uncertainty in which I have been struggling since waking up. My self-imposed blindness would be some sort of metaphor for it, or its objective correlative, or a redundancy. . . .

The kid pulls me vigorously by the left arm. He advances with long steps, light and sure, and I can barely keep pace with their rhythm. I should let go, take more chances, but I don't dare: I feel the ground in front of me with the tip of my cane, as though I feared to find myself suddenly in front of some chasm, which would be, after all, quite unlikely. . . .

"If you don't walk any faster," says the kid, "you won't get there on time for the train, you'll miss your friend, and then we'll have to look for him all over the station."

The time I get there hardly matters to me, and for good reason. Yet, I follow my guide with confidence and earnestness. I have the funny feeling that he is leading me towards something important, of which I know nothing, and which might well have nothing to do with the Gare du Nord and the Amsterdam train.

Propelled, most likely, by this obscure idea, I venture more and more boldly on this surprise-laden ground to which my feet are getting accustomed little by little. Soon, I feel quite comfortable here. I almost feel as if I were swimming in a new element. . . .

I didn't think that my legs would function so easily and by themselves, without control, so to speak. They would like to go even faster still, pulled along by a force in which the kid has no part. I would run, now, if he asked me to. . . .

But it is he who suddenly stumbles. I don't even have time to hold him back, his hand slips out of mine, and I can hear him falling heavily, just in front of me. I could almost, carried along by my impetus, fall too on top of him, and we would roll together in the dark, one on top of the other, like characters out of Samuel Beckett. I burst out laughing at that image, while struggling to regain my balance.

As for my guide, he does not laugh at his misadventure. He doesn't speak a word. I don't hear him move. Could he be injured through some unlikely bad luck? Could his fall have caused some trauma to his skull, his head having hit a raised cobblestone?

I call him by his first name, and I ask him if he's been hurt: but he answers nothing. A great silence has suddenly descended, and it goes on, which is beginning to concern me seriously. I feel the stone with the iron tip of my cane, taking infinite precautions. . . .

The body of the kid lies across our path. He

seems motionless. I kneel down and I bend over him. I let go of my cane in order to feel his clothes with both hands. I get no reaction, but, under my fingers, I feel a sticky liquid, the nature of which I cannot determine.

This time, I am seized by fear for good. I open my eyes. I remove my dark glasses. . . . I remain dazed, at first, by the bright light to which I am no longer accustomed. Then, the surroundings come into focus, become clearer, take on a consistency, as would a Polaroid photograph, where the picture would appear little by little on the glazed white paper. . . . But it is like the setting in a dream, repetitive and full of anguish, with convolutions from which I could not manage to free myself. . . .

The long, deserted street, stretching in front of me, reminds me indeed of something, the origin of which however I could not determine: I only have the feeling of a place where I would already have come, recently, once at least, several times perhaps. . . .

It is a straight alley, fairly narrow, empty, solitary, you can't see the end of it. It looks like it has been abandoned by everyone, quarantined, forgotten by time. Each side is lined with low structures, uncertain, more or less dilapidated: crumbling houses with yawning apertures, ruined workshops, blind walls and ramshackle fences. . . .

On the crude old-fashioned pavement—which has probably not been repaired for a hundred years—

a kid about twelve, clad in a gray smock, billowing and cinched at the waist, such as little boys used to wear last century, lies prone, stretched to his full length, seemingly deprived of consciousness. . . .

All of this then would have taken place already, previously, once at least. This situation, however exceptional, that I confront here, would only be the reproduction of a previous adventure, exactly identical, one whose events I myself would have lived, and in which I play the same part. . . . But when? And where?

Progressively, the memory dims. . . . The more I attempt to close in on it, the more it escapes me. . . . A last glimmer, still. . . . Then nothing more. It will all have been but a brief illusion. I am well acquainted, anyway, with these sharp and fleeting impressions, which I, as well as many others, experience frequently, and which are sometimes called: memory of the future.

It might instead be, in fact, an instantaneous memory: we believe that what is happening to us has already happened before, as though the present time were splitting in two, breaking in its own midst into two parts: an immediate reality, plus a ghost of that reality. . . . But the ghost soon wavers. . . . One would like to grasp it. . . . It passes again and again behind our eyes, diaphanous butterfly or dancing will-o'-the-wisp that toys with us. . . . Ten seconds later, it has all fled forever.

As to the fate of the injured boy, there is, in any

case, one reassuring fact: the viscous liquid that stained my fingers, when I felt the ground close to the gray linen smock, is not blood, although its color could make you think of it, as well as the way it feels.

It is nothing but an ordinary puddle of reddish mud, colored by rusty dust, that has probably remained in the hollow of the pavement since the last rain. The child, luckily for his clothes, which are threadbare, but very clean, has fallen just on the edge. He was trying perhaps to guide me away from that obstacle towards which I was rushing, when he himself lost his balance. I hope the consequence of his fall will not be too serious.

But I ought to do something about it, it is an emergency. Even if nothing is broken, the fact that he has fainted could make me fear some serious injury. And yet, I do not see, as I turn over the frail body with maternal care, any injury to either the forehead or the jaw.

The whole face is intact. The eyes are closed. It looks as though the kid is asleep. His pulse and his breathing seem normal, though very weak. In any case, I have to take action: nobody will come to my help in this deserted place.

If the surrounding houses were lived in, I'd go there to seek assistance. I'd carry the child there, kind women would offer him a bed, and we would call the paramedics, or some neighborhood physician who would be willing to come over.

But are there any tenants in these crumbling

buildings open to the weather? That would surprise me greatly. There ought to be living there, at this point, no one except some vagabonds who would laugh at me were I to ask them for a bed or a telephone. Perhaps even, were I to disturb them in the midst of some suspicious pursuit, they would manage an even worse reception for me.

Just then, I spot, directly on my right, a small two-story building, where the windows have remained in place in their frames and still retain all their panes. The door is ajar. . . . It is there, then, that I shall attempt my first visit. As soon as I have placed the injured boy under some shelter, I will already feel better.

But it seems to me, inexplicably, that I already know the rest: pushing the half open door with my foot, I shall penetrate into that unknown house, with the unconscious child that I shall be holding carefully in my arms. Inside, all will be obscure and deserted. I shall perceive, however, a dim bluish light, which will be coming from the second floor. I shall slowly climb a wooden staircase, steep and narrow, with steps that will creak in the silence. . . .

I know it. I remember it. . . . I remember that entire house, with hallucinating precision, and all those events that would therefore already have taken place, through whose succession I would already have lived, and in which I would have taken an active part. . . . But when was that?

At the very top of the stairs, there was a half-open door. A young woman, tall and slender, with pale blond hair, was standing in the doorway, as though she had been waiting for someone's arrival. She was wearing a white dress, of some light fabric, gauzy, translucent, whose folds, floating at the whim of an unlikely breeze, caught the reflections of that blue light that fell I knew not from where.

An undefinable smile, very gentle, youthful and faraway, played upon her pale lips. Her large green eyes, widened still in the semidarkness, shone with a strange brilliance "like those of a girl who would have come from another world," thought Simon Lecoeur, as soon as he saw her.

And he remained there, motionless on the threshold of the room, holding in his arms ("like an armful of roses offered in tribute," he thought) the unconscious little boy. Struck with enchantment himself, he gazed upon the otherworldly apparition, fearful at each instant that she might disappear in a wisp of smoke, especially when a stronger gust of air (to which yet no other object in the room seemed exposed), blew her veils around her like "ash-colored flames."

After a time, probably very lengthy (but impossible to measure with any certainty), during which Simon did not manage to compose, in his mind, any phrase that might have been appropriate to this extraordinary situation, he finally, for lack of anything better, spoke these ridiculously simple words:

"A child has been hurt."

"Yes, I know," said the young woman, but after such a delay that Simon's words seemed to have traveled, before reaching her, immense distances. Then, after another silence, she added: "Hello. My name is Djinn."

Her voice was soft and faraway, alluring yet elusive, like her eyes.

"You are an elf?" asked Simon.

"A spirit, an elf, a girl, as you like."

"My name is Simon Lecoeur," said Simon.

"Yes, I know," said the strange girl.

She had a slight foreign accent, British perhaps, unless these were the melodious tones of sirens and fairies. Her smile had become imperceptibly more pronounced with these words: it seemed she was speaking from elsewhere, from very far away in time, that she was standing in a sort of future world, in the midst of which everything would already have been accomplished.

She opened the door wide, so that Simon could walk in without difficulty. And she gestured to him gracefully with a movement of her bare arm (which had just emerged out of a very ample and flaring sleeve) toward an old-fashioned brass bed. Its head, resting against the back wall under an ebony crucifix, was framed by two gilt bronze candelabra that sparkled, bearing numerous tapers. Djinn started to light these, one after the other.

"It looks like a deathbed," said Simon.

"Won't all beds be deathbeds, sooner or later?"

answered the young woman in a barely audible whisper. Her voice took on a little more substance to declare, with sudden maternal care: "As soon as you have laid him upon these white sheets, Jean will fall into a dreamless sleep."

"So you even know that his name is Jean?"

"What else would he be called? What strange name would you want him to bear? All little boys are called Jean. All little girls are called Marie. You would know that, if you were from here."

Simon wondered what she meant by the words *from here*. Did she mean this strange house? Or this whole abandoned street? Simon very gently laid the still-inanimate child on the funeral bed. Djinn folded his hands across his chest, as is done for those whose soul is departing.

The child let her without offering the slightest resistance, nor showing any other reaction. His eyes had remained wide open, but his pupils were fixed. The flame of the candles lit them with dancing lights, which imparted to them a feverish, supernatural, disconcerting life.

Djinn, now, stood motionless again, next to the bed she surveyed serenely. To see her there, in her filmy white dress, almost immaterial, she looked like an archangel watching over the repose of a restless heart.

Simon had to shake himself back to reality, in the oppressive silence that had fallen upon the room, to ask the young woman some new questions:

"Can you tell me, then, what ails him?"

"He is afflicted," she answered, "with acute dysfunction of the memory, which provokes partial losses of consciousness, and which might end up killing him completely. He should rest, or else his overwrought brain will tire too soon, and his nervous cells will die of exhaustion, before his body reaches adulthood."

"What kind of dysfunction, exactly?"

"He remembers, with extraordinary precision, events that have not yet taken place: what will happen to him tomorrow, or even what he will do next year. And you are, here, nothing but a character out of his afflicted memory. When he wakes up, you will immediately disappear from this room, where, as a matter of fact, you have not yet set foot. . . ."

"So, I will come here at a later date?"

"Yes. Beyond any doubt."

"When?"

"I don't know the exact date. You will walk into this house, for the first time, about the middle of next week. . . ."

"And what about you, Djinn? What would become of you if he woke up?"

"I, too, will disappear from here upon his awakening. We would both disappear at the same time."

"But where would we go? Would we stay together?"

"Oh, no. That would be contrary to the rules of chronology. Try to understand: you will go where you ought to be at that time, in your present reality. . . ."

"What do you mean by *present?*"

"It is your future self that is here by error. Your present day self is several miles away from here, I think, where you are attending some ecological meeting, that opposes electronic machinism, or something of the sort."

"What about you?"

"I, unfortunately, am already dead, and have been for almost three years, so I will not go anywhere. It is only Jean's malfunctioning brain that has brought us together in this house, by chance: I belong to his past, while you, Simon, you belong to his future existence. You understand, now?"

But Simon could not manage to grasp—except as a total abstraction—what all this could mean in the here and now. In order to test whether he was—yes or no—nothing but someone else's dream, it occurred to him to pinch his ear hard. He felt a normal pain, quite real. But what did that prove?

He had to struggle against the vertigo to which these confusions of time and space subjected his reason. This diaphanous and dreamlike woman was perhaps quite insane. . . . He raised his eyes toward her. Djinn was watching him with a smile.

"You pinch your ear," she said, "in order to know whether you are not in the midst of a dream. But you are not dreaming: you are being dreamed, that is quite different. As for me, although I am dead, I can still feel pain and pleasure in my body: these are my past joys and sufferings, recalled by that overly receptive child, and imbued by him with new life, barely dulled by time."

Simon was the prey of contradictory emotions. On the one hand, this strange girl fascinated him, and, without admitting it to himself, he feared to see her disappear; even if she came from the realm of shadows, he wanted to stay close to her. But at the same time, he was angry to hear all that nonsense: he had the feeling that he was being told, to mock him, tales without rhyme or reason.

He tried to reason calmly. This scene (which he was, at that very moment, living) could have belonged to his future existence—or to that of the child—only if the characters present in the room were, indeed, to be gathered there a little later—the following week, for instance. However, that became an impossibility, under normal conditions, if the girl had died three years before.

Owing to the same anachronisms, the scene now taking place here could not have happened in Djinn's past existence, since he had never met her before, while she was alive. . . .

A doubt, suddenly, shook that overly reassuring conviction. . . . In a flash, a recollection crossed Simon's mind, of a past meeting with a blond girl, with pale green eyes and a slight American accent. . . . Soon this impression vanished, suddenly, just as it had come. But it left the young man perturbed.

Had he confused her, for a fleeting moment, with some image of the actress Jane Frank that would have strongly impressed him, in a movie? That explanation was not convincing. A fear seized him, more strongly than ever, that the child would regain consciousness, and that Djinn would vanish before his eyes, forever.

At that moment, Simon became aware of a significant peculiarity in the decor, to which, very strangely, he had not yet paid any attention: the curtains of the room were drawn. Made of some heavy, dark-red fabric, probably quite old (worn threadbare along the folds), they completely masked the window-panes that must have opened onto the street. Why were they kept drawn that way, in broad daylight?

But Simon reflected then on that idea of broad "daylight." What time could it be? Stirred by a sudden anxiety, he ran to the windows, which emitted no light at all, neither through the fabric or along the sides. He hastily raised a fold of the curtain.

Outside, it was pitch black. For how long had it been? The alley was steeped in total darkness, under a starless and moonless sky. Not the slightest light—electric or otherwise—in the windows of the houses, themselves almost invisible. A single old-fashioned streetlight, fairly distant, way off to the right, gave off a faint bluish light in a radius barely a few feet wide.

Simon let the curtain fall back. Would night have fallen that fast? Or else was time flowing "here" according to other laws? Simon looked at his wristwatch. He wasn't even surprised to see that it had stopped. The hands showed exactly twelve o'clock. That was noon as well as midnight.

On the wall, between the two windows, hung a photographic portrait under glass, framed in black wood, with a sprig of boxwood protruding from the back. Simon looked at it more closely. But the light that came from the candelabra was not enough for him to make out the features of the person, a man in some military uniform, it seemed.

A sudden desire to see the face better seized Simon, for whom the image was suddenly taking on an inexplicable significance. He returned quickly to the bed, grabbed one of the candlesticks, and returned to the portrait, which he lighted as best he could with the flickering light of the candles. . . .

He could almost have bet on it: it was his own photograph. No mistake was possible. The face was perfectly recognizable, although older perhaps by two or three years, or barely more than that, which brought to it an expression of seriousness and maturity.

This left Simon petrified. Holding at arm's length the heavy bronze candelabrum, he could not take his eyes off his double, who smiled imperceptibly at him, a smile both fraternal and mocking.

He wore, in that unknown photo, the uniform of the navy and the braid of a chief petty officer. But the costume was not exactly like that worn in the French forces, not at that time, in any case. Simon, furthermore, had never been either a sailor or a soldier. The print was of a sepia tint a little washed out. The paper seemed yellowed by time, marked by small gray and brownish stains.

In the lower margin, two short, handwritten lines slanted across the blank space. Simon immediately recognized his own handwriting, slanted backwards like that of left-handed people. He read in a low voice: "For Marie and Jean, their loving Papa."

Simon Lecoeur turned around. Without his hearing her, Djinn had moved closer to him; and she was gazing upon him with an almost tender, playful pout:

"You see," she said, "that's a photo of you taken a few years from now."

"Then it also belongs to Jean's abnormal memory, and to the future?"

"Of course, as does everything else here."

"Except you?"

"Yes, that's right. Because Jean mixes up times and tenses. That's what confuses things and makes them hard to understand."

"You were saying just now that I would come here a few days hence. Why? What will I come here for?"

"You will bring back an injured little boy in your arms, obviously, a little boy who must, besides, be your son."

"Jean is my son?"

"He 'will be' your son, as proved by the dedication on this photograph. And you will also have a little daughter, who will be called Marie."

"Can't you see that's impossible! I cannot, next

week, have an eight-year-old child who is not born today, and whom you would have known, yourself, more than two years ago!''

"You really reason like a Frenchman, positivist and Cartesian. . . . In any case, I said that you would come here in a few days, 'for the first time,' but you will come back many times after that. You will probably even live in this house with your wife and your children. Why, otherwise, would your photo hang on this wall?''

"You are not French?''

"I was not French. I was American.''

"What was your occupation?''

"I was a movie actress.''

"And what killed you?''

"A machine accident. caused by a crazed computer. That is the reason why I militate now, against mechanization and data processing.''

"But what do you mean, 'now'? I thought you were dead!''

"So what? You too, are dead! Didn't you notice the portrait in black wood, and the holy boxwood that watches over your soul?''

"And what did I die from? What would I die from? I mean, what will I die from?'' shouted Simon with growing exasperation.

"Lost at sea,'' replied Djinn calmly.

This was too much. Simon made a last, desperate effort to extricate himself from a situation which could be nothing else but a nightmare. He thought he should first relax his overwrought nerves: he had to scream, he had to hit his head against the walls, break something. . . .

In a rage, he dropped the flickering candelabrum to the floor, and he walked with deliberate step toward that overly desirable woman who was mocking him. He grabbed her. Far from resisting him, she wound her arms around him like a blond octopus, with a sensuousness Simon had hardly expected.

Her flesh was too warm and too sweet to belong to a ghost. . . . She was pulling him toward the bed, from which the little boy had fled, wakened no doubt by the commotion. Upon the floor, the spilled candles continued to burn, threatening to set fire to the curtains. . . .

This is the last clear view of the room that Simon had, before he surrendered to ecstasy.

# CHAPTER EIGHT

When I arrived in France, last year, I met, by chance, a guy my age named Simon Lecoeur, who was known as Boris, I never knew why.

I liked him right away. He was rather good-looking, tall for a Frenchman, and above all he had a wild imagination that made him, at every moment, turn daily life and its simplest events into strange, romantic adventures, like those found in science fiction stories.

But I also thought, almost from the start, that I'd no doubt need a lot of patience, at times, if I were willingly to accept his extravagant fabrications; I should even write: his follies. "I'll have to like him enormously," I told myself that first day; "otherwise, very soon, we won't be able to stand each other."

We met in a way that was both weird and ordinary, because of an ad read in a daily newspaper. We were both looking for work: some little part-time job that would allow us to buy, without too much effort, if not the necessities, at least little luxuries. He said he was a student, as am I.

A short ad, then, written in telegraphic style, with somewhat unclear abbreviations, was seeking a y.m. or a y.w. to take care of two children, a boy and a girl. It was probably a matter of looking after them at night, picking them up at school, taking them to the zoo, and other things of that sort. We both showed up at the interview. But nobody else came.

The person placing the ad must, in the meantime, have given up the plan, or else, found through another means, what he needed. The fact is that, Simon and I, finding ourselves face to face, each of us believed, at first, that the other was his eventual employer.

When we discovered that this wasn't the case, and that the person placing the ad had actually stood us up, I was personally rather disappointed. But he, without losing his cool poise for an instant, took pleasure in prolonging his misconception, even starting to speak to me as though I was henceforth to become his boss.

"It wouldn't bother you," I asked him then, "to work for a girl?" He answered that, on the contrary, he liked that very much.

He said "liked," and not "would like," which meant that he was going to play the game. So, I pretended, in turn, to be myself what he was making me out to be, because it seemed amusing to me, especially because I found him droll and charming.

I even added that these children, that he would watch for me, from now on, were a handful: they belonged to a terrorist organization that blew up nuclear power plants . . . It's a stupid idea that, I don't know why, had suddenly occurred to me.

Next, we walked to a café, on the boulevard nearby, where he bought me coffee and a *croque-monsieur*. I wanted to order a pizza, but he launched right away into new tales about that bistro, in which poisoned foods would supposedly have been served to enemy spies in order to get rid of them.

As the waiter wasn't very talkative, morose, with a rather sinister look, Simon claimed that he was a Soviet agent, for whom the two kids were in fact working.

We were both in a very happy mood. We whispered in each other's ear, so the waiter couldn't hear us, like conspirators or lovers. We were amused by everything. Everything seemed to be happening in a singular atmosphere, privileged, almost supernatural.

The coffee was terrible. But my companion explained, quite seriously, that if I kept drinking my coffee too strong, it would cause me to become blind, on account of the pale green color of my eyes. He took advantage of that, of course, to pay me a few conventional compliments on my "mysterious look" and even on "the unearthly brilliance" of my eyes!

I had to go to the Gare du Nord, to meet my friend Caroline, who was due to arrive on the train from Amsterdam. That wasn't very far from the place where we were. Simon, who of course wished to accompany me, proposed that we walk there. Rather I should write: "Simon decided we would walk" for his incessant fantasizing, paradoxically, was joined by a rather strong authoritarianism.

So we set out, happily. Simon did his best to invent all kinds of stories, more or less fantastic, concerning the places we were walking through and the people we came across. But he made us take a strange, complicated path, of which he wasn't sure enough: alleyways more and more deserted, which were, he said, supposed to constitute a shortcut.

We ended up completely lost eventually. I was afraid of being late, and I was finding Simon a great deal less amusing. I was very glad, finally, to be able to jump into a cruising taxicab, whose unexpected presence in that deserted place seemed a godsend to me.

Before leaving my deplorable guide, who was refusing—for extravagant reasons—to climb into that car with me, I nevertheless made a date with him for the next day, under an absurd pretext (intentionally absurd): to resume the visit of that desolate quarter—devoid of any tourist appeal—at exactly the place where we were parting company, that is to say in the middle of a long, straight alleyway, lined with old fences and half tumbling walls, with a ruined pavilion as a landmark.

As I feared that I would not be able to find the place by myself, we decided to meet, for that excursion, in the same café where we had already stopped today. Their beer might be more palatable than their black coffee.

But the taxi driver was getting impatient; he claimed that his vehicle was holding up traffic, which was quite stupid, since there was no traffic at all. Yet, it was getting close to train time, so Simon and I said brief good-byes. At the last moment, he called out a phone number where I could reach him: seven sixty-five, forty-three, twenty-one.

Once settled into the cab, which was old and in even worse shape than the New York City cabs, I noticed that it was also that bright yellow color we are used to at home, but which is very unusual in France. Simon, however, was not surprised.

And still thinking about it some more, I began to wonder how that car had appeared precisely along our way: taxis are not accustomed to cruising such deserted places, practically uninhabited. That would be hard to understand. . . .

I became even more concerned when I realized the driver had placed his rearview mirror, atop the windshield, in such a way that he could easily observe me, instead of watching the street behind us. When I met his eyes, in the small rectangular mirror, he didn't even look away. He had strong, irregular, asymmetrical features. And I thought he looked sinister.

Disturbed by these dark, deep-set eyes, that remained fixed upon me in the mirror (was he then familiar with this maze of alleyways, that he could drive through them this way at a good speed almost without looking at the road?), I asked if the Gare du Nord were still far away. The man then twisted his mouth horribly, in what was perhaps a failed attempt at a smile, and said, in a slow voice:

"Don't you worry, we'll be there soon enough."

That innocuous reply, spoken in a mournful tone (someone prone to panic might even have found it threatening), only increased my concern. Then, I blamed myself for my excessive mistrust, and thought that Simon's wild imagination was probably contagious.

I had thought I was very close to the station, when we had parted, Simon and I. However, the cab drove on for a long time, through neighborhoods where nothing was familiar, and which looked to me more like distant suburbs.

Then, suddenly, at a turn in the street, we found ourselves in front of the well-known facade of the

Gare du Nord. At the edge of the sidewalk, at a place where cabs unload their passengers after a quick U-turn, there was Simon waiting for me.

He opened the door for me politely, and he must have paid the fare himself, because, after I saw him lean briefly into the driver's open window, the cab sped away, full speed, without waiting for anything else. However, that exchange of words (inaudible) had been extremely short, and I do not recall having seen, between the two men, the slightest gesture in any way related to some transaction.

I was, besides, absolutely flabbergasted by this unexpected reappearance of Simon. He smiled sweetly, looking happy, like a child who has played a good trick. I asked him how he had got there.

"Ah well," he said to me, "I took a shortcut."

"You walked?"

"Of course. And I've been waiting for you for ten minutes already."

"But that's impossible!"

"It may be impossible, but it's true. You took a very long time to drive that short distance. Now, you have missed your train, and your friend."

It was unfortunately true. I was almost ten minutes late, and I was going to have a hard time finding Caroline in the crowd. I was supposed to be waiting for her as she got off the train, just at the gate exit from the platform.

"If you want my opinion," Simon added moreover, "that driver took you the long way around on purpose, just to make it a bigger fare. Since you took so long to get here, I even thought for a moment that you'd never arrive: yellow cabs are always the ones used in kidnappings. It's a tradition in this country.

"You'll have to be more suspicious from now on: more than a dozen pretty girls, in just this way, disappear every day in Paris. They'll spend the remainder of their short lives in the luxurious brothels of Beirut, Macao, or Buenos Aires. Just last month they discovered . . ."

Then suddenly, as though he had in a flash remembered some urgent business, Simon broke off, in the midst of his fabrications and lies, and declared hurriedly:

"Excuse me, I must be gone. I have lingered here too long. Till tomorrow, then, as agreed."

He had spoken, to remind me of our meeting the next day, in a low and mysterious voice, like one who might have feared the indiscreet ears of possible spies. I answered: "See you tomorrow!" and I saw him watched him hurry away. He was soon lost in the crowd.

I then turned back toward the entrance of the station, and I saw Caroline coming out, walking toward me with her broadest smile. To my great surprise, she was holding by the hand a little blond girl, very pretty, maybe seven or eight years old.

Caroline, whose right hand was encumbered with a suitcase, let go of the little girl's hand to wave at me cheerfully with her left. And she called out to me, unconcerned about the travelers hurrying in all directions between her and me:

"So, that's the way you wait for me on the platform! You just stand there, talking with guys, without caring about when my train comes in!"

She ran up to me and kissed me with her usual exuberance. The little girl looked the other way, with the discreet air of a well-bred young lady who hasn't been introduced yet. I said:

"Yes, I know, I am a bit late. Forgive me. I'll explain to you . . ."

"There's nothing to explain: I saw you with that good-looking guy! Here, this is Marie. She's the daughter of my brother Joseph and of Jeanne. She was entrusted to me in Amsterdam, to bring her back to her parents."

The child then performed for my benefit, with earnestness, a complicated and ceremonious curtsey, such as young ladies were taught fifty or a hundred years ago. I said: "Hello, Marie!" and Caroline continued her explanations with animation:

"She was spending her vacation at an aunt's, you know: Jeanne's sister who married an officer in the Russian Navy. I already told you the story: a man named Boris, who asked for political asylum when his ship made port in The Hague."

Speaking in the reasonable tone of a grown-up, and in surprisingly sophisticated language for a child her age, little Marie added her own commentary:

"Uncle Boris is not really a political refugee. He's

a Soviet agent, disguised as a dissident, whose mission is to spread discontent and disorder among workers in the nuclear industry.

"And you found that out all by yourself?" I asked her with amusement.

"Yes, I did," she answered, unperturbed. "I did see that he had his spy number tattooed in blue on his left wrist. He tries to hide it under a leather wristband, which he wears supposedly to strengthen that joint. But that can't be true, since he does no physical work."

"Don't pay any attention to Marie," Caroline told me. "She's always inventing absurd stories of science fiction, espionage, or the occult. Children read far too much fantastic literature."

At that moment, I realized that a man was watching us, a few steps away from us. He stood a little way back, in an angle of the wall, and stared at our little group with abnormal interest. At first, I thought it was Marie who was attracting his rather unwholesome interest.

He might have been about forty, perhaps a little more, and he wore a gray, doublebreasted suit of classic cut (with matching jacket, vest and pants), but it was old, threadbare, shapeless with wear, and his shirt and tie were as beat up as though he had slept in his clothes during some very long train trip. He carried in his hand a small, black leather case, which made me think of a surgeon's kit, I don't exactly know why.

Those dark and piercing eyes, deeply set, that face with its heavy, asymmetrical, sharply etched, unpleasant features, that wide mouth twisted into a kind of smirk, all that reminded me brutally of something . . . a memory, however recent, that I could not manage to bring into focus.

Then, suddenly, I remembered: it was the driver of the yellow cab who had brought me to the station. I experienced such a sharp sense of discomfort, almost physical, that I felt myself blushing. I turned my head away from that unpleasant character. But a few seconds later, I glanced at him again.

He had neither moved, nor changed the direction of his stare. But it was rather Caroline, to tell the truth, whom he seemed to be watching. Did I forget to mention that Caroline is a very beautiful girl? Tall, a great body, slender, very blond, with a short haircut and a sweet, slightly androgynous face, one that brings to mind that of the actress Jane Frank, she always attracts the homage, more or less indiscreet, of men of all ages.

I must also confess something else: people claim that there is an extraordinary resemblance between us. We are generally mistaken for two sisters, often even for twins. And it has happened several times that friends of Caroline addressed me, thinking they were speaking to her, which one day triggered a strange adventure. . . .

But Caroline interrupted the course of my thoughts:

"What's the matter with you?" she asked, scrutinizing my face with concern. "Your expression has changed. You look like you've just seen something scary."

Marie, who had guessed the cause of my emotion, explained calmly, in a loud voice:

"The guy who's been following us since we got off the train is still here, with his little suitcase full of knives. He's a (sex) pervert, obviously, I could tell right away."

"Don't talk so loud," whispered Caroline, bending over the child while pretending to smooth the rumpled folds of her dress, "he's going to hear us."

"Of course he can hear us," answered Marie without lowering her voice. "That's what he's here for."

And, suddenly, she stuck out her tongue at the stranger, and at the same time smiled her most angelic smile at him. Caroline burst out laughing, with her customary unconcern, while scolding Marie as a matter of principle, without any conviction. Then she said to me:

"In fact, the child might be right. Besides, I think that character took the same train we were on. It seems to me that I saw him prowling in the corridor, and that I had already spotted him on the departure platform, in Amsterdam."

Raising my eyes once more toward the suspicious character with the black case, I then witnessed a scene that only served to increase my astonishment.

The man was no longer turned toward us; he was now looking at a blind man who walked toward him, feeling the ground with the iron tip of his cane.

He was a tall, blond young man, twenty or twenty-five, wearing an elegant windbreaker made of very fine leather, cream colored, and open over a bright blue pullover. Black goggles hid his eyes. He held in his right hand a white cane with a curved handle. A little boy of about twelve was leading him by the left hand.

For a few seconds, I imagined, against all likelihood, that it was Simon Lecoeur, who was returning disguised as a blind man. Of course, looking at him more carefully, I soon recognized my error: the few points of resemblance that one could find in the general appearance, the dress, or the hairstyle of the two men, were in fact minor.

When the young man with the white cane and his guide got close to the character with the baggy clothes and the physician's bag, they stopped. But none of them gave any sign whatever. There were no salutations, none of those words or gestures of welcome that might have been expected in such circumstances. They remained there without saying a word, face to face, motionless now.

Then, with deliberate precision, in the same even motion, precisely as if the same mechanism were activating three heads, they turned toward us. And they remained that way, petrified once again, motionless now like three statues: the young man with the fair face half-hidden behind his bulky glasses, framed between the little boy on his left and the short man in the shapeless gray suit on his right.

All three kept their eyes fixed on me, the blind man too, I could have sworn it, behind his enormous black lenses. The skinny face of the boy had an extreme, abnormal, ghostly pallor. The ugly features of the short man had frozen into a horrible grimace. The whole group suddenly seemed to me so terrifying that I wanted to scream, as one does to end a nightmare.

But, just as in nightmares, no sound came out of my mouth. Why wasn't Caroline saying anything? And what about Marie, who was standing between the two of us, why wasn't she breaking the spell, bold and casual as children will be? Why was she standing there frozen, rendered speechless too, held in thrall by what enchantment?

Anguish was growing in me so dangerously, relentless, that I feared I might faint. To struggle against this unbearable malaise, so unlike my nature, I tried to think of something else. But I could no longer find anything to hold on to, except one of the idiotic tirades Simon was delivering for my benefit an hour or two earlier:

I was not, he claimed, a real woman, but only a highly sophisticated electronic robot built by a certain Dr. Morgan. Dr. Morgan was now subjecting me to various experiments in order to test my performance. He was putting me through a series of tests, while having me watched by agents in his employ, placed everywhere along my way, some of whom, themselves, would be nothing but robots as well. . . .

The gestures of that phony blind man, who had just arrived as though by chance in front of me, did they not, precisely, seem to me mechanical and staccato? Those strange goggles, which seemed to be growing monstrously larger, were probably not covering real eyes, but a sophisticated recording system, perhaps even some device that emitted rays, which were working, unbeknownst to me, on my body and on my consciousness. And the surgeon-cabdriver was none other than Morgan himself.

The space between these people and me had emptied, I know not through what chance circumstance, or what supernatural action. The travelers milling around here in large numbers a moment earlier, had disappeared now. . . . With incomprehensible difficulty, I managed to turn my head away from those three pairs of eyes that hypnotized me. And I sought help in the direction of Marie and Caroline.

They too were staring at me with the same icy, inhuman eyes. They were not on my side, but on that of the others, against me. . . . I felt my legs giving way, and my reason tumbling, into the void, in a vertiginous fall.

When I woke up this morning, my head was empty, heavy, and my mouth felt pasty, as though I had allowed myself, the day before, to drink to excess, or else taken some powerful sleeping drug. Yet that was not the case.

What did I do, exactly, the night before? I could not manage to remember. . . . I was supposed to go and meet Caroline at the station, but something prevented me. . . . I no longer knew what it was.

A picture, however, came back to my memory, but I couldn't tie it to anything. It was a large room, furnished with odd pieces, in very bad repair, like those sprung chairs and those broken iron bedsteads that used to be relegated to the attics of old houses.

There were, in particular, a very large number of old trunks, of different sizes and shapes. I opened one. It was full of old-fashioned women's clothing, corsets, petticoats, pretty faded dresses of another day. I could not very well make out the elaborate ornaments or the embroidery, because the room was lit by only two candelabra in which candle stubs burned with a yellow and vacillating flame. . . .

Next, I thought of the ad that Caroline had read me, over the phone, when she called to tell me the arrival time of her train. Since I was looking for a part-time job, in order to supplement the amount of my scholarship, I had decided to go to the address given in that weird job ad, which my friend had found while reading an ecological weekly. But I had overslept so long, today, that the time to get ready had already come, if I wanted to be there at the appointed hour.

I arrived exactly at six-thirty. It was almost dark

already. The hangar wasn't locked. I walked in by pushing the door, which no longer had a lock.

Inside, all was silent. Under the faint light that came through the windows with dirt-encrusted panes, I could barely see the objects that surrounded me, piled everywhere in great disarray, probably cast off.

When my eyes became used to the semidarkness, I finally noticed the man facing me. Standing, motionless, both hands in the pockets of his raincoat, he watched me without speaking a word, without so much as the slightest greeting in my direction.

Resolutely, I stepped forward toward him. . . .

# EPILOGUE

Here stops Simon Lecoeur's story.
I do say "Simon Lecoeur's story" because no one—neither our people, nor those on the side of the police—thinks that Chapter Eight, supposedly written by a woman, was really written by anyone else: it is too clearly integrated into the whole, from the grammatical point of view as well as according to the logic of the plot locales and the narrative twists.

Simon—all testimony agrees on this point—came

as usual to teach his class, at the school on the rue de Passy, on Thursday May eighth early in the afternoon. "He looked worried," several of his students stated at the time of the inquest. But most of them added that he always looked worried.

He displayed, in fact, a disturbing combination of almost pathological nervousness, incompletely restrained anxiety, and a sweet, smiling lightness that had a great deal to do with the definite charisma that everyone agreed he possessed. In the most casual hallway conversation with a colleague, a student, or even a superior, he offered such easy chatty friendliness, full of casual and unexpected inventiveness, spontaneity, inconsequential humor, that he was liked by everyone, as one loves a child. . . .

Then, suddenly, the innocent smile would vanish from his lips, which would lose in a few seconds their attractive, sensuous lines to become hard and thin; his eyes seemed to sink deeper, his pupils darkened. . . . And he would turn around abruptly, as though he would thus come face to face with an enemy who had approached him behind his back, silently. . . . But there was no one, and Simon would slowly resume his previous demeanor, before his bewildered interlocutor. Bewildered himself, the young man seemed then to have fled thousands of miles, or even light years away. He would then take leave on a few vague, incoherent, barely audible words.

On Friday, May ninth, he did not show up at school. That caused no concern: his Friday class, scheduled at the end of the day, was the last of the week, and many students—especially in the spring—made it a point to consider attendance optional: it sometimes happened that young instructors did the same.

But on Monday the twelfth, he was not seen again either, nor on Tuesday. His room did not have a phone. On Wednesday, an assistant director asked the students whether one of them could stop by the rue d'Amsterdam in order to enquire about the health of "Ján," who might have been seriously ill and unable to notify anyone. The volunteer messenger said she found a closed door. There was no answer to her repeated rings or her calls. No sound came from within.

Thursday the fifteenth was Ascension Day. On Friday the sixteenth in the morning, school authorities alerted the police. Simon Lecoeur's door was broken in, in the presence of a police commissioner, that Friday around noon.

In the room as in the bathroom, the inspectors found everything in order, just as our agents (they, obviously, possessed a duplicate key) already had two days earlier. There was no evidence of a struggle, or of any untimely visit, or hurried departure. The ninety-nine typed pages (which we had been careful to replace after Xeroxing) soon became therefore the only element that could be considered a clue.

The interest of the investigators in that text only grew, as one can guess, when, on Sunday the eighteenth, around seven P.M., there was discovered in an abandoned workshop, near the Gare du Nord, the lifeless body of an unknown woman, about twenty years old. She hadn't been dead for more than an hour, perhaps even less.

The young victim was carrying no document that might help to identify her. But her physical appearance, her clothing, her exact position on the ground (as well as the location itself, besides) were exactly as described in Chapter Six of Simon's story. As he had indicated, the puddle of blood was not real blood. The coroner noted right away that the body showed no injury, no external trauma, the causes of death remaining therefore undiscovered. It appeared nevertheless almost beyond doubt that it was a case of murder, and not of natural death.

All investigations concerning the identity of the young woman have, so far, yielded no clues: no person answering her description has been reported missing anywhere in the country. Because of the proximity of the railroad station, investigations are now being directed toward Antwerp or Amsterdam.

Another point puzzles the police; the more than curious resemblance (general appearance, measurements, facial features, color of the eyes and the hair, etc.) that exists between the dead girl and Simon Lecoeur himself. The matter is so disturbing that it was believed for a while that they were one and the same person: the charming professor of the Franco-American School would have been a female transvestite. This attractive hypothesis was not however retained, for the school physician had given the so-called Simon a thorough physical some two weeks earlier, and he guaranteed that Simon did belong to the masculine sex.

That practitioner—Dr. Morgan—was treating Simon for eye problems, acute troubles, it seems, although they were probably of nervous origin. The missing man claimed, indeed, to have been experiencing with increased frequency sudden moments of diminished vision (decreased luminosity of the images on the retina), sometimes to the point of total blindness, lasting occasionally for several long minutes. Morgan, given to psychoanalysis, had immediately thought of an everyday Oedipus complex.

The patient had only laughed off the suggestion, saying he had nothing to do at Cologne. That absurd pun, linked to the theme of the disjointed paving stones, continued to plunge the physician into deep perplexity, and renewed his suspicions. It cannot be ruled out, of course, that our sometime blind man was an ordinary faker, but his motives aren't clear, since he wasn't asking his employer for any sick leave, nor the slightest change of schedule.

Of all the characters that appear in his story, one in any case—at least—does exist without any doubt: little Marie. Starting from the abandoned workshop, investigators had no trouble finding the café where they don't serve pizza. A policeman watched the establishment for several days. Little Marie, still in her

1880-style dress, walked in on the evening of the twenty-first (she was coming, as it will be learned later, to pay off an old debt). As she was leaving, the policeman tailed her. He followed her to the Vercingétorix dead end. About halfway down the long alleyway, some of our people stepped in. Having quietly intercepted that overzealous guardian of law and order, they brought him back, once more, to square one.

# LA MAISON DE
# RENDEZ-VOUS

Women's flesh has always played, no doubt, a great part in my dreams. Even when I am awake, its images constantly beset me. A girl in a summer dress exposing the nape of her bent neck—she is fastening her sandal—her hair, fallen forward, revealing the delicate skin with its blond down, I see her immediately subject to some command, excessive from the start. The narrow hobble skirt, slit to the thighs, of the elegant women of Hong Kong is quickly ripped off by a violent hand, which suddenly lays bare the rounded, firm, smooth, gleaming hip, and the tender slope of the loins. The leather whip, in the window of a Parisian saddle-maker, the exposed breasts of wax mannequins, a theater poster, advertisements for garters or a perfume, moist parted lips, an iron manacle, a dog collar, generate around me their provocative, insistent setting. A simple canopied bed, a piece of string, the glowing tip of a cigar, accompany me for hours, as I travel, for days. In parks, I organize celebrations. For temples, I establish ceremonies, command sacrifices. Arabian or Mogul palaces fill my ears with screams and sighs. On the walls of Byzantine churches, the slabs of marble sawed in symmetrical patterns suggest, as I stare, vaginas parted wide, forced open. Two rings set into the stone, in the depths of an ancient Roman prison, are enough to conjure up the lovely captive chained there, doomed to long tortures, in secrecy, solitude, and at leisure.

Often I linger to stare at some young woman dancing, at a party. I like her to have bare shoulders and, when she turns around, to be able to see her cleavage. The smooth skin glistens softly, under the light from the chandeliers. She performs, with a graceful diligence, one of those complicated steps in which she remains a certain distance from her partner, a tall, dark, almost recessive figure who merely indicates the movements in front of her, while her lowered eyes seem to watch for the slightest sign the man's hand makes, in order to obey him at once while continuing to observe the complicated laws of the ritual, then, at an almost imperceptible command, smoothly turning around, again offering her shoulders and the nape of her neck.

Now she has stepped back, a little to one side, to fasten the buckle of her sandal, made of slender gold straps which crisscross several times around the bare foot. Sitting on the edge of a sofa, she is leaning over, her hair, fallen forward, revealing more of the delicate skin with its blond down. But two people step forward and soon conceal the scene, a tall figure in a dark tuxedo listening to a fat, red-faced man talking about his travels.

Everyone knows Hong Kong, its harbor, its junks, its sampans, the office buildings of Kowloon, and the narrow hobble skirt, split up the side to the thigh,

132

*[handwritten marginalia: very specific scene set up around unspecified people / Characters]*

worn by the Eurasian women, tall, supple girls, each
in her clinging black silk sleeveless sheath with its
narrow upright collar, cut straight at the neck and
armpits. The shiny, thin fabric is worn next to the
skin, following the forms of the belly, the breasts, the
hips, and creasing at the waist into a sheaf of tiny
folds when the stroller, who has stopped in front of
a shopwindow, has turned her head and bust toward
the pane of glass where, motionless, her left foot
touching the ground only with the toe of a very high-
heeled shoe, ready to continue walking in the middle
of the interrupted stride, her right hand raised forward, slightly away from the body, and her elbow
half bent, she stares for a moment at the wax girl
wearing an identical white silk dress, or else at her
own reflection in the glass, or else at the braided
leather leash the mannequin is holding in her left
hand, her bare arm away from the body and her elbow
half bent in order to control a big black dog with
shiny fur walking in front of her.

The animal has been mounted with great skill. And
if it were not for its total immobility, its slightly over-
emphasized stiffness, its certainly too-shiny glass eyes
that are also too fixed, the excessively pink interior,
perhaps, of its gaping mouth, its exaggeratedly white
teeth, one would think it was about to complete its interrupted movement: to pick up the paw still stretched
out behind the other, prick up its ears evenly, open its
jaws wider to show its fangs in a threatening attitude,
as if some sight, on the street side, were disturbing it
or endangering its mistress.

Her right foot, advancing almost even with the

dog's hindmost paw, is touching the ground with only the toe of a very high-heeled shoe whose gilded leather covers only a narrow triangle at the tip of the toe, while slender thongs crisscross the rest of the foot three times and encircle the ankle over a very sheer stocking, scarcely visible, though of a dark shade, probably black.

A little higher, the white silk of the skirt is split laterally, revealing the hollow of the knee and suggesting the thigh. Above, by means of an inset zipper that is virtually indiscernible, the dress must open all the way to the armpit in a single stroke, along the naked flesh. The supple body twists from right to left, attempting to free itself from the slender leather thongs which bind ankles and wrists; but to no purpose, of course. The movements this posture permits are, moreover, of very slight scope; torso and limbs obey rules so strict, so constraining, that the dancer now seems quite motionless, merely keeping time with an imperceptible undulation of her hips. And all of a sudden, at a mute command from her partner, she turns around lightly, at once motionless again, or rather, swaying so slowly, so slightly where she stands, that she merely makes the thin fabric ripple over her belly and breasts.

And now the same fat, red-faced man intervenes again, still talking in a loud voice about life in Hong Kong and the elegant shops of Kowloon that sell the most beautiful silks in the world. But he has stopped in the middle of what he was saying, his red eyes raised, as though wondering about the gaze he sup-

poses fixed on himself. Strolling in front of the sh
window, the girl in the black sheath meets the gla
reflected in the plate glass; she turns slowly to l
right and continues walking with the same even g
past the buildings, holding on its taut leash the l
dog with the shiny fur whose half-open mouth drools
a little, then closes with a dry snap.

At this moment, down the street, parallel to the
sidewalk where the young woman with the dog is walking away with short, quick steps, a rickshaw passes by,
pulled rapidly in the same direction by a Chinese in
overalls and the traditional funnel-shaped hat. Between the two high wheels, whose wooden spokes are
painted bright red, the black canvas hood over the
single seat completely conceals the passenger sitting
there; unless this seat, which from behind remains
invisible because of the hood, is empty, occupied only
by an old flattened cushion whose split oilcloth, worn
to the buckram in spots, releases its kapok stuffing
through a rip at one of the corners; that would explain
the astonishing speed at which this apparently puny
little man can run on his bare feet, whose blackened
soles appear in mechanical alternation between the red
shafts, without his ever slowing down to catch his
breath, so that he has immediately disappeared at the
end of the avenue, where the deep shadow of the giant
fig trees begins.

The man with the red face, his eyes bloodshot, soon
looks away, after having—probably just in case—
offered a vague smile to no one in particular. He
heads for the buffet, still accompanied by his auditor

in the tuxedo who continues listening politely, without speaking a word, while he resumes his narrative, making abrupt gestures with his short arms.

The buffet has been stripped almost clean. It is easy enough to reach, but there is almost nothing left on the sandwich and cookie platters, irregularly strewn on the crumpled tablecloth. The man who has lived in Hong Kong helps himself to a glass of champagne, which a white-jacketed, white-gloved waiter serves him on a rectangular silver tray. The tray remains suspended for a moment over the table, about eight or twelve inches from the hand of the man about to pick up the glass, but who is now thinking of something else, having resumed his loud and rather hoarse tone in order to describe his travels to this same mute companion, toward whom he turns sideways, raising his head, for the other man is much taller than he. The other man, on the contrary, looks at the silver tray and the glass of yellow champagne in which tiny bubbles are rising, at the white-gloved hand, then at the waiter himself, whose attention has also just been drawn elsewhere: downward and a little to the rear, in an area hidden by the long table whose white cloth reaches to the floor; he seems to be looking at something on the floor, perhaps an object he has inadvertently dropped, or someone else has dropped, or else has deliberately thrown to the floor, an object which he will pick up as soon as the late-comer who had asked for a drink has taken his glass from the tray, which tilts at this moment in a manner dangerous to the sparkling liquid and to its crystal vessel.

But without paying any attention, the man continues talking. He is telling a classic story of white-slave traffic, the missing beginning of which soon becomes easy to reconstruct in its main outlines: a girl bought as a virgin through a Cantonese agent and then resold at three times the price, intact but after several months of use, to a newly arrived American who had settled in the New Territories, on the official pretext of studying the possibilities of growing . . . (two or three inaudible words). Actually he was growing Indian hemp and white poppies, but in moderate quantities, which reassured the British police. He was a Communist agent concealing his real activity under the more banal one of manufacturing and trafficking in various drugs, on a very small scale, just enough to satisfy his personal consumption and that of his friends. He spoke both Cantonese and Mandarin, and naturally frequented the Blue Villa, where Lady Ava organized special entertainments for some of her intimate acquaintances. Once the police appeared at her house in the middle of a party, but a perfectly ordinary one, probably arranged as a front, the vice squad called in on a false alarm. When the police in khaki shorts and white knee socks burst into the villa, they find only three or four couples still dancing, with dignity and restraint, in the big salon, a few officials or businessmen in sight, chatting here and there in armchairs, on couches, or standing in a window recess, merely turning their heads toward the door without changing position, leaning back against the window frame or resting a hand on the back of a chair,

137

a young woman breaking into a mocking laugh at the surprised expression of the two young men she is talking to, three gentlemen lingering at the buffet where one of them is being served a glass of champagne. The waiter in a short white jacket, who was staring at the floor at his feet, glances back to his silver tray, which he straightens in order to offer it horizontally, saying: "Here you are, sir." The fat man with the red face turns his head toward him, noticing his own hand still in mid-air, his half-curled fat fingers and his Chinese ring; he takes the glass, which he immediately raises to his lips, while the waiter sets the tray on the cloth and bends down to pick up something behind the table, which conceals him almost completely for several seconds. Nothing can be seen now except his curved back, where the short jacket has slipped up over the belt of the black trousers, exposing a strip of wrinkled shirt.

When he straightens up, he sets down beside the tray a small object he is holding in his right hand: a colorless glass ampoule of the common sort used by pharmacists, only one end of which has been broken, the liquid therefore removable only by means of a hypodermic syringe. The man in the dark tuxedo also looks at the ampoule, but it bears no label or trademark which might suggest what it has contained.

Meanwhile, the last dancers have separated, the music having come to an end. Lady Ava offers an elegant, polite hand to one of the businessmen who is taking his leave with ceremonious gestures. He is the only guest wearing a dark tuxedo (very dark navy blue, unless it is black); all the others, this evening, were in white dinner jackets or business suits of different colors, mostly dark of course. I approach the mistress of the house in my turn and bow, while she holds out her long fingers whose nails are a little too red. She repeats the gesture she has just made for my predecessor, and I bow ceremoniously in the same way, take her hand, raise it and brush it with my lips, the whole scene being repeated down to its slightest details.

Outside, the heat is stifling. Perfectly motionless in the sultry night, as though petrified within a solid substance, the delicately silhouetted foliage of the bamboos extends over the path, illuminated by the uncertain light from the villa's front doorstep and outlined against a completely dark sky, in the continuous and strident sound of the cicadas. At the gate of the grounds there is no taxi, but several rickshaws parked in a row along the wall. The runner first in line is a puny little man in overalls: he offers his services in an incomprehensible language which must be some kind of pidgin English. Under the canvas hood erected against the sudden showers, which are frequent at this time of year, the seat is fitted with a hard, sticky cushion whose cracked oilcloth releases its stuffing at one of the corners: a rough substance wadded into stiff damp clots.

The center of the city gives off, as usual at this hour, a sweetish smell of rotting eggs and overripe fruit. The Kowloon ferry affords no relief, and, on the other side of the water, the row of waiting rickshaws is identical, all painted the same bright red, with the same oilcloth cushions; still, the streets are broader and cleaner. The few pedestrians still circulating here and there at the foot of the buildings are almost all wearing European clothes. But a little farther on, in a deserted avenue, a tall, supple girl in a white silk sheath split up the side passes into the bluish circle of a street lamp. She is holding a leash, her arm extended, a very large black dog with shiny fur walking stiffly ahead of her. It disappears at once, and its mistress afterward, into the shadow of a giant fig tree. The feet of the little man running between the shafts continue, with a quick, regular rhythm, pounding the smooth asphalt.

So I am now going to try to describe that evening at Lady Ava's, to explain in any case what were, to my knowledge, the main events which characterized it. I reached the Blue Villa around ten after nine, by taxi. Thickly overgrown grounds surround the huge stucco house, whose ornate architecture, juxtaposition of apparently disparate elements and unusual color are always surprising, even to someone who has already observed it often, when it appears at the turn of a path in its frame of royal palms. As I have the impression of being a little ahead of time, that is, of finding myself among the first guests to cross the threshold, if not *the* first since I saw no one else on either the drive or the doorstep, I have decided not to go in right away and have turned to the left to take a stroll in this part of the garden, which is the pleasantest. Only the immediate environs of the house are illuminated, even when there is a party; very quickly, thick clumps cut off the light from the lanterns and even the blue glow reflected by the stucco walls; soon nothing is visible but the paths of pale sand, then, once one's eyes grow accustomed to the darkness, the general shape of the groves and the nearest trees.

The noise is deafening, produced by thousands of invisible insects which must be cicadas or a related nocturnal species. The noise is strident, uniform, perfectly even and continuous, coming from all sides at once, its presence so violent that it seems to be located at the very level of a man's ears. The stroller, nonetheless, may frequently be unaware of it, on account of the total absence of interruption, as of the slightest variation in intensity or pitch. And suddenly words are spoken against this background of sound: "Never! . . . Never! . . . Never!" The tone is touching, even a little theatrical. Although deep, the voice is certainly that of a woman who must be quite near by, probably just behind the tall clump of traveler's palms lining the path on the right. The soft earth here makes no sound, fortunately, when anyone walks on it. But among the slender trunks topped with their fan-shaped bouquet of fronds, nothing is discernible except other identical trunks, increasingly close-set, forming an impassable forest which probably extends for some distance.

Turning around, I have taken in the scene at a glance: two people frozen in dramatic attitudes, as though under the shock of an intense emotion. They

141

were hidden just now by a rather low shrub, and it is by advancing to the clump of traveler's palms, then climbing the slope of cleared ground, that I have reached this position from which it is easy to see them, in a haio of blue light from the house, all at once closer than the ground cover suggested, and in a suddenly open prospect at this very point. The woman is wearing a long dress, white with a bouffant skirt, her shoulders and back bare; she is standing, her body rather stiff, but her head turned away and her arms making a vague gesture of farewell, or disdain, or expectation: the left hand just in front of her body at hip level, and the right raised to her eyes, elbow half bent and fingers splayed apart, as if she were leaning against a wall of glass. About ten feet away, in the direction which this hand appears to be condemning—or fearing—stands a man in a white jacket who seems about to collapse, as if he had just been shot with a pistol, the woman having immediately dropped the weapon and remaining, her right hand open, dumbfounded by her own action, no longer even daring to look at the man who has merely sagged a little, his back bent, one hand clutching his chest and the other stretched out to one side, behind him, apparently groping for something to catch hold of.

Then, very slowly, without straightening his body or his knees, he brings this hand forward and raises it to his eyes (thus producing a perfect image of the expression "to veil one's face") and then remains as motionless as his companion. He stays frozen in the same attitude when she, with a sleepwalker's slow and regular gait, turns toward the house with its bluish halo and walks away, arms still in their raised position, left hand pushing away the invisible glass wall in front of her.

A little farther along the same path, there is a man sitting alone on a marble bench. Dressed in dark colors and resting under a fleshy plant with hand-shaped leaves that extend over him, his arms are spread on either side of his body, palms resting flat on the stone, fingers curved over its rounded edge; the upper part of his body is bent forward, head tilted in a fixed—or blank—contemplation of the pale sand in front of his patent leather dress shoes. Still farther on, a very young girl—wearing only a kind of tattered shift which reveals her naked skin at several points, parting over her thighs, her belly, her slight breasts, her shoulders—is attached to the trunk of a tree, her hands pulled behind her, her mouth parted in terror and her eyes dilated by what she sees appearing before her: a huge tiger only a few yards away, staring at her for a moment before devouring her. This is a group of life-size statuary carved out of wood and painted, dating from the beginning of the century and representing an Indian hunting scene. The artist's name—an English name—is cut into the wood, at the base of the imitation tree trunk, along with the statue's title: "The Bait." But the third element of the group, the hunter, instead of being astride an elephant or on top of a log platform, is merely standing a little distance away in the tall grass, his right hand clutching the handle-bars of a bicycle. He is wearing a white linen suit and a pith helmet. He is not preparing to fire; the barrel of his rifle, still in its sling, sticks out over his left shoulder. Moreover it is not the tiger he is looking at, but the bait.

Of course it is too dark, in this part of the garden, to be able to make out most of these details, which are visible only in daylight: the bicycle for instance, as well as the name of the statue and that of the sculptor (something like Johnson, or Jonstone). The tiger, on the contrary, and especially the girl tied to the tree, both of which are quite close to the path, stand out quite clearly against the darker background of the vegetation. Nearby, one can also admire, by day, various other statues, all more or less horrible or fantastic, of the type which embellish the temples of Thailand or the Tiger Balm Garden in Hong Kong.

"If you haven't seen that, you haven't seen anything," the fat man says about this as he sets his empty champagne glass down on the white, wrinkled cloth near a withered hibiscus flower, one petal of which is then caught under the crystal disk forming the foot of the glass. It is at this moment that the salon's main door suddenly opens, the heavy panel violently pushed from outside, letting in the three British policemen in their uniforms: khaki shorts and short-sleeved shirts, white knee socks and low shoes. The last one in closes the door behind him and remains on guard there, his legs slightly apart, his right hand resting on the leather holster of his revolver, against one hip. A second policeman crosses the room with determined steps toward the rear door, while

144

the third—who does not seem to be armed, but whose epaulettes have a second lieutenant's insignia on them —heads toward the mistress of the house as if he knew just where she was, although she is at this moment hidden from his gaze, sitting on a yellow couch in one of the columned recesses which correspond to the bay windows of the west façade. She is just saying: "Never. . . . Never. . . . Never. . . ." in an amused tone, more evasive than emphatic (but perhaps insinuating), to a blond young woman standing near her. As she speaks these words, Lady Ava has turned toward the window whose thick curtains are drawn. The young woman is wearing a white organdy gown with a long, bouffant skirt and a very décolleté top, revealing her shoulders and cleavage. She keeps her eyes fixed on the yellow velvet of the couch; she seems to be thinking; she says, finally: "All right. . . . I'll try." Lady Ava then glances at the pale face, once again with the same rather ironic smile. "Tomorrow, for instance," she says. "Or the day after. . . ," the young woman says, without raising her eyes. "Tomorrow's better," Lady Ava says.

Doubtless this scene has taken place another evening; or else, if it is today, it occurs, in any case, a little earlier, before Johnson's departure. It is in fact his tall dark silhouette Lady Ava indicates with her eyes, when she adds: "Now you'll go dance with him one more time." The young woman with the pink doll's complexion also turns then, but as though reluctantly, or apprehensively, toward the man in a black tuxedo who, standing a little apart, in profile, is still looking in the direction of the drawn curtains, as if he were waiting—but without attaching much importance to it—for someone to appear, suddenly, through the invisible window.

Suddenly the setting changes. When the heavy closed curtains, sliding slowly on their rods, part for the next scene, the stage of the little theater represents a kind of clearing in the forest, in which the habitués of the Blue Villa immediately recognize the general arrangement of the entertainment entitled: "The Bait." The position and the attitude of the characters has just been described, among the collection of bibelots decorating the mirrored salon, either in connection with the garden or with something else. Still, there is no tiger here, but one of the huge black dogs of the house, made still more gigantic by skillful lighting and also, no doubt, because of the diminutiveness of the young half-caste girl who is playing the part of the victim. (Most likely this is the girl, bought some time before from a Cantonese agent, who has already been mentioned.) The man playing the hunter has no bicycle, this time, but holds a thick braided leather leash; he is wearing dark glasses. There is no use adding further details to this scene which everyone knows. It is already quite late at night, once again. I hear the old mad king prowling up and down the long corridor on the floor above. He is looking for something in his memories, something solid, and he no longer knows what. So the bicycle has disappeared, there is no longer a carved wooden tiger, no dog either, no dark glasses, no heavy curtains. And there is no longer any garden, no blinds, no heavy curtains which slide slowly along their rods. Now there is nothing left but some scattered debris: bits of faded papers heaped by the wind in the corner of a wall, rotting scraps of vegetables it would be difficult to identify for certain, crushed fruits, a fish head reduced to its skeleton, splinters of wood (from some slat or broken crate) floating in the muddy water of the gutter where the front page of a Chinese tabloid drifts by, swirling slowly.

The streets of Hong Kong are filthy, as everyone knows. At dawn the little shops with their vertical signs, bearing four or five red or green ideograms, spread all around their displays of suspect produce the stale-smelling rubbish that eventually covers the whole sidewalk, overflows into the street, dragged in all directions by the clogs of the pedestrians in their black pajamas, soon turned sodden by the sudden torrential afternoon rains, then reduced to broad sheets by the wheels of the split-cushioned rickshaws, or else heaped into vague piles by the sweepers whose uncertain, slow, almost useless gestures are interrupted a moment while the slanting eyes glance up obliquely as the haughty Eurasian girls pass at nightfall, imperturbably strolling through the sultry heat and the gutter stench, walking Lady Ava's huge silent dogs.

An animal with shiny fur, advancing stiffly with a swift, sure gait, head high, mouth open a little, ears perked, like a police dog that knows where it is going without needing to nose about to the right or left in order to find its way, nor even to sniff the ground where the scents are blurred among the garbage and

147

the various stinks. Delicate spike-heel shoes whose gilded leather thongs crisscross three times around the tiny foot. A clinging dress, streaked at each step by slender shifting wrinkles across the hips and belly; the shiny silk gleams in the light from the shop lanterns like the dark fur of the animal walking six feet ahead, pulling just enough on the leash, held at arm's length, to keep the leather braid taut without forcing the girl to change the speed or the direction of her route, which passes straight through the crowd of pajamas as if the place were a deserted square, the young woman keeping her whole body motionless, despite the quick and regular movement of her knees and thighs under the hobble skirt, whose lateral slit moreover permits only tiny steps. The features of her face, under the black hair, accentuated by a red hibiscus flower over her left ear, also remain as motionless as those of a wax mannequin. She does not even glance down toward the displays of squid, green fish and fermented eggs, nor turn her head, right or left, toward the faintly illuminated signs whose enormous characters cover all the available space on the walls as on the square pillars of the arcades, or toward the newspaper and magazine vendors, the mysterious posters, the bright-colored lanterns. It is as if she sees nothing of all this, like a sleepwalker; nor has she any need to look at her feet to avoid obstacles, these seeming to disperse of their own accord to leave her path clear: a naked child sprawling among the orange peels, an empty crate which the hand of someone out of sight removes from her path at the last moment, a rice broom which brushes the pavement at random, unnoticed by a distracted municipal employee in over-alls, whose sleepy eyes soon abandon the leg's brief periodic appearances between the flaps of the slit skirt, turning back for a moment to his work: the bundle of rice straws whose tip, curved by use, sweeps toward the gutter a motley image: the cover of a Chinese tabloid.

*Circle start*

Under a horizontal heading in large, square-cornered ideograms, which fill the whole upper part of the page, a crude drawing represents a huge European salon whose walls, elaborately decorated with mirrors and stucco, must be meant to suggest great luxury; some men in dark clothes or cream or ivory dinner jackets are standing here and there, chatting in little groups; in the middle distance, to the left, behind a buffet covered to the floor with a cloth on which are arranged many platters filled with sand-wiches or cakes, a waiter in a white dinner jacket is about to serve a glass of champagne, on a silver tray, to a fat important-looking man who, his arm already ex-tended to take his glass, is talking to another guest much taller than himself, which obliges him to raise his head; in the background, but in an empty area which makes it possible to notice them at first glance—especially since it occurs in the center of the picture—a large double door has just opened, letting in three soldiers in battle dress (camouflaged green-and-gray parachutist uniforms), who, each one holding a ma-chine gun motionless at hip level, ready to fire, train their weapons in three divergent directions, covering the whole of the room. But only a few people have noticed their sudden appearance in the noise of the festivities: a woman in a long dress, directly threatened by one of the gun barrels, and three or four men very close by; a recoiling movement affects their heads and the upper parts of their bodies, while their arms are frozen in instinctive gestures of defense, or surprise, or fear.

Everywhere else in the room, local involvements are sustained as if nothing were happening. In the foreground, for example, to the right, two women quite close together and evidently linked by some momentary concern, although they do not seem to be in conversation, have still seen nothing and continue the scene they had begun, without concern for what is happening thirty feet away. The older of the two, sitting on a red velvet—or rather yellow velvet—couch, smiles as she looks at the younger one standing in front of her, but turned so that she faces in another direction: toward the tall man who was absently listening, just a moment ago, to the champagne drinker near the buffet and who, alone now, stands apart from the crowd, facing a window whose curtains are drawn. The young woman, after a few seconds, looks back toward the seated woman; her face, seen straight on, seems grave, exalted, suddenly resolved; she takes a step toward the red couch and very slowly, raising the hem of her gown a little with a supple and graceful gesture of her left arm, rests one knee on the floor in front of Lady Ava, who quite naturally and without concern, still smiling, holds out a sovereign or condescending hand to the kneeling girl; and the girl, gently taking the fingertips with their lacquered nails in her own, bends down to rest her lips on them. The bent nape of the neck, between the blond curls . . .

But the young woman straightens up immediately with a rapid movement and, standing now, turns away and walks boldly toward Johnson. Then things happen very fast: the various conventional phrases exchanged, the man bowing ceremoniously to the young woman whose eyes remain modestly lowered, the Eurasian servant girl, who enters by parting the velvet curtains, stopping a few steps away from them and stands watching in silence, her features, as motionless as those of a wax mannequin, betraying no feeling whatever, the glass falling to the marble floor and breaking into tiny, gleaming pieces, the young woman with blond hair staring at them blankly, the Eurasian servant girl moving like a sleepwalker amid the debris, still preceded by the black dog pulling on its leash, the delicate gold slippers vanishing along the dubious shop fronts, the rice-straw broom, completing its curving trajectory, pushing the illustrated cover of the magazine into the gutter, whose muddy water sweeps along the colored image swirling in the sunlight.

*Really completes the circle* [marginal handwritten note]

The street, at this hour of the day, is nearly empty. The air is sultry and heavy, even more oppressive than usual at this time of the year. The wooden shutters of the little shops are closed. The big black dog stops of its own accord in front of the customary entrance: a narrow, dark, very steep staircase which begins flush with the façade, with neither door nor hallway of any kind, and rises straight up into depths where the eye is confounded. The scene which then takes place lacks clarity. . . . The girl glances left and right, as though to make sure no one is watching her, then she climbs the stairs as rapidly as her long, clinging dress permits; and, almost immediately, she would come back down clutching to her breast a thick, bulging, brown paper envelope which seems to have been stuffed with sand. But what would have become of the dog this time? If, apparently, it has not gone up with her, has it waited calmly at the foot of the stairs, no longer needing to be kept on a leash? Or would she have attached it to some ring, bolt, or railing (but the stairway has no railing), some knocker (but there is no door), hook, or rusty old nail stuck in the wall here and clumsily twisted upward? But this nail is not very solid; and the unwonted presence of such an animal, clearly marking the house, would then unnecessarily attract the attention of possible observers. Or else the agent was standing in the shadows, almost at the bottom of the stairs, and all the Eurasian servant girl has had to do is walk up two steps, without letting go of the leash, and extend her hand toward the envelope—or the package—which the invisible person would hand her, in order to return without further delay. Or rather, there was actually someone at the bottom of the stairs and he was certainly there for an appointment, but all he has done was hold out his hand to take the end of the leash which the servant girl has given him, while she rapidly climbed the little staircase in order to reach the agent still in his room, or his office, or his laboratory.

Here the objection of the too obvious dog would recur, unfortunately, in full force. And in any case, the end of the episode is not suitable, since it is not an envelope which is being picked up, but a very young girl, who according to her face must be Japanese, moreover, rather than Chinese. Now they are all three on the glistening sidewalk near the entrance that is growing increasingly dark: the servant girl in the clinging dress with its slit skirt, the little Japanese girl in a black, full, pleated skirt and a white school-girl blouse, the kind of girl one meets by the thousands in the streets of Tokyo or Osaka, and the big dog that approaches the newcomer to sniff her at length, raising its muzzle. This part of the scene, in any case, leaves no doubt: the dog's muzzle sniffing the terror-stricken young girl, back to the wall against which she must submit to the contact of the disturbing muzzle from thighs to belly, and the servant girl watching her coldly, while giving the leather leash enough play to permit the animal to move its head and neck freely, etc.

I believe I have said that Lady Ava gave performances for habitués on the stage of the little private theater of the Blue Villa. It is probably this stage which is involved here. The audience is in the dark. Only the footlights are on when the heavy curtains part in the center, opening slowly on a new scene: the high wall and steep narrow staircase against it, descending straight from somewhere invisible in the shadows after ten steps or so. The wall of huge rough stones suggests a cellar or even an underground dungeon, given the meager limits imposed by the side walls on the left and right. The crudely paved floor is shiny in places with wear or moisture. The only opening is that of the narrow, arched staircase, breaking the rear wall at about a third of its length from the right corner. Here and there, irregularly scattered on the three visible walls of the cell, several iron rings are set into the stone at various levels. From some of them hang thick rusty chains, one of which, longer than the rest, reaches to the floor where it forms a kind of loose S. One of the rings, placed just to the right of the stairs, has been used to attach the free end of the dog's leash, the dog lying in front of the bottom step, head raised as though it were guarding the entrance. The spotlights gradually focus on the animal. When nothing more can be seen but the dog, all the rest of the scene being plunged into darkness, a rather bright but remote light comes on at the very top of the stairs, and it then appears that the staircase ends in an iron grille, whose unornamented pattern of vertical black lines is now silhouetted against the pale background.

The dog has immediately risen to its feet, growling. Two young women appear at this moment behind the grille, which one of them—the taller—opens in order to let both of them through while she pushes her companion ahead of her; the door is then closed once more with the metallic sound of creaking hinges, a bolt shot home, and chains rattling. Soon no one can be seen any more, the two girls having been swallowed up by the shadows, one after the other, from the legs up, as soon as they have begun coming down the staircase; they reappear only at the bottom, in the focus of the spotlights. They are, of course, the Eurasian servant girl and the little Japanese girl. The former immediately detaches the end of the leather leash—which she will hold throughout the scene—while the new arrival, frightened by the animal's threatening growls, takes refuge against the rear wall, in the area to the left of the stairs, where she backs against the stone. The dog, which has received special training for this purpose, must entirely undress the captive, whom the servant girl indicates with her free arm, pointing toward the pleated skirt; down to the last triangle of silk, its fangs rip off the garments, tearing them away in strips, gradually, without ever piercing the flesh. Accidents, when they occur, are always superficial and without importance; they do not lessen the interest of the act, quite the contrary.

The girl playing the role of the victim holds her arms out on either side of her body, pressing against the wall as if she wanted to become part of it in order to escape the animal; perhaps a realistic staging would instead suggest that she use her hands to protect herself. Similarly, when she turns around, face against the stone, still on the pretext of the unthinking terror she is supposed to be feeling (and which perhaps she really is feeling, tonight, since she is a beginner), raising her arms higher, elbows bent and hands near her hair, this mode of defense can be explained

155

only by an aesthetic preference for introducing some variety into the audience's view. The spotlights, whose rays are still focused on the dog's head, illuminate the area—hip, shoulder or breast—the animal is concerned with. But each time that the servant girl, who directs the operation by slackening the leash, considers that a particularly decorative stage of the undressing is attained—as a result of the new surfaces revealed, or of the rips that happen to be made in the materials—she tugs on the leather leash, murmuring a brief "Stand!" which hisses out like a whiplash; the animal draws back, as though reluctantly, into the shadows, while the circle of light, remaining on the prisoner, widens in order to reveal her entirely, either from the front or the rear, depending on the way she is facing the audience at that moment.

Among the audience of the little theater, some comments are then exchanged in low voices and in polite tones. When the actress is a new one, as this evening, she obviously enjoys special attention. Some blasé spectators nonetheless take this occasion to return to the subject that concerns them: the movement of ships, the Communist banks, life in Hong Kong today. "In the antique shops," says the fat man with the red face, "you still find those nineteenth-century objects Western morality considers monstrous." He then goes on to describe, as an example, one of the objects in question, but in a voice too low, whispering as he brings his mouth very close to the ear which his interlocutor offers him by bending down. "Of course," he says a little later, "it's not the way it used to be. With patience, though, you can get the addresses of secret brothels the size of palaces, whose special features, salons, gardens, secret rooms, defy our European imagination." Then, without any apparent connection, he begins describing the death of Edouard Manneret. "There was a character for you!" he adds by way of conclusion. He raises to his lips the champagne glass that is already three-quarters empty and finishes it in one swallow, throwing back his head with an exaggerated gesture. And he sets the glass down on the wrinkled white cloth near a faded hibiscus blossom the color of blood, one petal of which is caught under the crystal disk forming the foot of the glass.

The two men then cross the salon where the last guests seem to have been forgotten in little, irresolute groups; and they doubtless separate almost at once, since the following scene shows the taller of the two— the one called Johnson, or even often "the American," although he is English and a baron—standing near one of the large, curtained bay windows, in conversation with that blond young woman whose name is Lauren or Loraine, who a few moments before had been on the red couch beside Lady Ava. The dialogue between them is rapid, a little distant, reduced to essentials. Sir Ralph (known as "the American") never loses his almost scornful, in any case ironic, half-smile, while he stiffly bows to the young woman—one might say in mockery—and gives her brief indications of what he expects of her. Raising her large eyes, which she had hitherto kept stubbornly fixed on the ground, she suddenly turns toward him her smooth face with

157

its excessive, consenting, rebellious, submissive, blank, expressionless gaze.

In the next scene, they are climbing the enormous grand staircase, her eyes lowered once again, her neck bent, and holding in both hands, on each side, the hem of her white bouffant dress, which she gradually raises in order to keep it from sweeping at each step the red and black carpet whose thick brass rods are held at the ends by two heavy rings and terminate at each tip in a tiny stylized pineapple, he following slightly behind and watching her with an indifferent, enthralled, icy gaze which rises from the tiny feet on their high spiked heels to the bent neck and bare shoulders whose skin gleams with a satiny luster when the young woman passes under the bronze three-branched lingam-shaped sconces, which one after the other illuminate the successive flights of the staircase. On each floor, a Chinese servant stands guard, petrified in an improbable, twisted posture characteristic of the ivory statuettes in the Kowloon antique shops; one shoulder too high, one elbow forward, one arm bent with the fingers against the chest, or the legs crossed, or the neck twisted in order to look in a direction which the rest of the body resists, they all have the same slanting, nearly closed eyes insistently fixed on the approaching couple; and with a movement suggesting the efficient mechanism of a robot, one after the next pivots his waxen face very slowly from left to right in order to accompany the two persons who pass without looking at them, continuing their regular ascent toward the next landing between the successive sconces and the vertical balustrades supporting the railing, crossing from step to step the horizontal bars that attach the thick black-and-red striped carpet to each stair.

Then they are in a room whose decoration is vaguely oriental, dimly lit by small lamps whose shades shed a reddish glow here and there, most of the rather large room remaining in obscurity. Such is the case, for example, in the area around the entrance, where Sir Ralph has come to a stop after having closed the door behind him and turned the key in the massive lock with its baroque ornaments. Leaning against the heavy wooden panel as if he were forbidding access to it, he stares at the room, the canopied bed covered in black satin, the fur rugs and the various refined and barbarous instruments which the young woman, also standing but in a somewhat brighter zone of light, motionless and her eyes on the floor, tries not to see.

The fat man with the red face then doubtless begins to describe one of these instruments, but his voice is too low, and it is just at this moment that the performance continues on the stage, after a pause of several seconds. The Eurasian servant girl takes a step forward. An imperative "Go!", accompanied by a precise gesture of the left arm pointing toward the belly of the little Japanese girl, indicates to the dog the piece of cloth it must now rip away. And the lights focus once again on the designated spot. Henceforth nothing more can be heard in the silence of the theater but the brief hissing orders of the nearly invisible servant girl, the muffled growls of the black dog, and

159

at moments the victim's gasping breath. When she is entirely naked, but with a certain pause immediately after the widening of the circle of light cast by the spotlights, there is a spatter of polite applause. The young actress takes three dancing steps toward the footlights, and bows. This entertainment, traditional in certain interior provinces of China, has been, as always, highly appreciated this evening by Lady Ava's English or American guests.

However, the Eurasian servant girl (it is she, if I am not mistaken, who must be called Kim) has remained in place, without moving, as has the animal, when the last sounds of applause died down in the dark theater. She looks like a fashion mannequin in a shopwindow, holding on a leash a huge stuffed dog, mouth open, legs still, ears perked. Without one feature betraying the slightest emotion, she stares at the undressed girl who has returned to the stone wall, back to the audience this time, body slightly inclined, arms raised and hands lifting her black hair above the nape of her neck. From here, the servant girl's gaze gradually slides down to a fresh scratch which marks the amber-colored skin on the inner side of the left thigh, where a drop of blood is already coagulating. And now she is walking through the night along the great new apartment buildings of Kowloon, supple and rigid at the same time, free and enslaved, advancing behind the black dog that tugs a little harder on the leather leash, without turning her head to either side, without even glancing at the windows of the elegant shops, or, on the street side, at the single rickshaw passing as fast as its barefoot runner can manage, parallel to the sidewalk, behind the trunks of the giant fig trees.

The trunks of the fig trees conceal, at regular intervals, the slender fugitive silhouette, whose silk sheath dress glows faintly in the darkness. My hand, resting on the oilcloth cushion sticky from the sultry heat, again encounters the triangular rip through which a tuft of damp hairs protrudes. A fragment of a sentence suddenly, without any reason, has come to mind, something like: ". . . in the splendor of the catacombs, a crime with useless, baroque ornaments . . ." The runner's bare feet continued regularly thudding on the smooth asphalt, alternately showing the soles dirtied by the dust in a clear black pattern, like the sole of a shoe deeply notched on its inner side and ending in a fan of five toes. Clinging to the armrest, I have leaned out of the rickshaw to look back: the white silhouette had disappeared. I am almost positive that it was Kim, imperturbably walking one of Lady Ava's silent dogs. That is the last person I saw, that night, returning from the Blue Villa.

As soon as my door was closed, I wanted to reconstruct, point by point, the events of the evening, from the moment when I enter the villa garden, amid the shrill, continuous, deafening grating of the millions of nocturnal insects which infest the proliferating vegetation overhanging the paths, the branches touching the solitary stroller hesitating in the overly dense shade of the leaves shaped like hands, lances, or hearts, of aerial roots seeking some support to cling to, of flowers with a violent, sweetish, slightly rotten smell, suddenly illuminated at the corner of a grove by the blue light reflected from the stucco walls of the house. Here, in the center of a clearing, a tall man in evening clothes is talking to a young woman in a long, white, décolleté dress whose bouffant skirt touches the ground. At somewhat closer range, I easily recognize our hostess' new protégée, whose name is Lauren, in the company of a certain Johnson, Ralph Johnson, known as "Sir Ralph," that American recently arrived in the colony.

They are not speaking to each other. They are some distance apart: about six feet. Johnson is looking at the young woman, who continues to stare at the ground. He examines her slowly, from head to foot, lingering over her cleavage, her bare shoulders, and the long graceful neck slightly inclined to one side, contemplating each line of her body, each surface, with that indifferent expression which has probably earned him his British nickname. Finally he says, still with the same smile: "All right. It will be just the way you want it."

But, after a silence and while the man bows in a respectful salute, which can only be a mockery, by which he appears to be taking his leave, Lauren suddenly raises her head and holds out one hand in the uncertain gesture of a person asking for another moment of attention, or pleading for a last reprieve, or trying to interrupt an irrevocable action already being performed, saying slowly, in a very low voice: "No. Don't go. . . . Please. . . . Don't leave me right away."

Sir Ralph bows again, without changing expression, as if he always knew that things would happen this way: he is expecting this sentence, which he knows in advance down to the last syllable, every hesitation, the slightest inflections of the voice, and which merely takes a little too long to make itself heard. But now, already, the expected words are falling one by one from his companion's lips, who has doubtless followed the prescribed tempo, as she finally raises her eyes again. "Please. . . . Don't leave me right away." And it is only at this moment that he can leave the stage.

Some polite applause, from the audience, greets his exit, the applause, too, anticipated in the normal course of the performance. The lights in the theater come on again, while the curtain closes on the actress left alone on stage, seen in profile facing the wings where the hero has just vanished, apparently petrified by his departure, still holding her arm half extended and her lips parted as if she were going to speak the decisive words which would change the play's outcome, that is, on the point of yielding, of confessing herself vanquished, of losing her honor, or even of triumphing.

But the first act is over, and the heavy red velvet curtain, whose two halves have come together, now leaves the spectators to their individual conversations which have immediately resumed. After some brief comments on the new actress—who appears on the program as Loraine B—, everyone returns to the subject which preoccupies him. The man who has been to Hong Kong continues talking about the horrible

sculptures decorating the Tiger Balm Garden: after
the group entitled "The Bait," he begins describing
"The Rape of Azy," a monolith ten or twelve feet
high which represents a gigantic orangutan carrying
on its shoulder, where it holds her almost negligently,
a beautiful life-size girl, three-quarters undressed, who
struggles hopelessly, for she is absurdly small in relation to the size of the monster; her arched back
is resting on the blackish-brown pelt (the statue is
painted in bright colors, like all the others in the
park), and her long loose blond hair hangs down over
the animal's hunched back. Close by stands the final
episode in the adventures of Azy, the unfortunate
queen of Burmese mythology whose body . . . The
man standing next to the fat man with the red face
finally loses patience—especially since the spectators
in front of them have just turned around toward the
speaker again, in order to indicate their irritation—
and asks him to be quiet. The connoisseur of Oriental
sculpture then decides to watch the stage, where the
performance is continuing. The end of the first act
is approaching: the heroine, who had kept her mouth
closed and her eyes lowered throughout her partner's
entire speech (and up to the final sentence: "It will
be just the way you want it. . . . I'll wait as long as I
have to . . . and some day . . ."), finally looks up to
say, slowly and vehemently, staring the man straight
in the eyes: "Never! Never! Never!" The bare arm
of the young woman in the white dress makes a gesture of disdain, or of farewell, the hand raised level
with her forehead, the elbow half bent, the five fingers

parted and extended, as if the palm were pressing against an invisible wall of glass.

By approaching a few yards closer, on the soft earth which muffles the sound of my footsteps, I discover that the man whose face was partly concealed by a low-hanging branch is not Johnson as I had thought at first, deceived by the vague bluish glow reflected from the walls of the house, but that insignificant young man to whom Lauren is supposed to be engaged (although she usually treats him, with no concern for appearances, harshly or indifferently); the boy, moreover, can be here tonight only for that reason, since he is not a habitué of Lady Ava's parties. Under the effect of so categorical a dismissal, which has just been given him in a merciless voice, he now seems to crumble: his legs sag, his back hunches, his left hand tightens on his chest, his right hand, extended to one side behind him, seems to be groping for something to cling to, as if he feared losing his balance under the violence of the shock. Continuing on my way I meet, a little farther along the same path, a man sitting alone on a stone bench, motionless and leaning forward, staring at the ground under his feet. Since this bench is situated in a particularly dark area, under an overhanging clump of trees, it is difficult for me to identify the person with certainty; but if I am not mistaken, it must be the man familiarly known here as "the American." Since he seems lost in his thoughts, I pass without speaking to him, without turning my head toward him, without seeing him.

I arrive almost immediately in the region of the

monumental statues made by R. Jonestone in the nineteenth century, most of which recount the most famous episodes in the fabulous existence of Princess Azy: "The Dogs," "The Slaves," "The Promise," "The Queen," "The Rape," "The Hunter," "The Execution." I have been familiar with these figures for a long time and do not linger to look at them. Moreover it is too dark, in this whole part of the grounds, to distinguish anything among the vague silhouettes appearing here and there under the trees, and some of whom are also Lady Ava's first guests.

I walk up the steps to the door at the same time as a group of three people coming from the garden gate, a woman and two men, one of whom is none other than that same Johnson I thought I had glimpsed dreaming in solitude on a stone bench. So it was not he. Upon reflection, it could only be Lauren's fiancé swallowing his defeat, patching up the various fragments of his existence, now reduced to dust, perhaps modifying some detail in order to reach another, less unfavorable outcome, and even re-examining the points previously regarded as most positive in the new light of his sudden disgrace which casts both doubt and discredit upon them as well. In the large salon, Lady Ava is quite surrounded, of course, by the guests who, as soon as they come in, head immediately toward her in order to greet her, as I do myself. Our hostess seems smiling and relaxed, addressing to each guest a word of welcome which touches or charms him. Yet as soon as she sees me, she abruptly leaves all the others, walks straight up to me, pushing aside those

importunate bodies whose faces she no longer e'
notices, and draws me aside into a window recess. Her
face has changed: hard, reserved, distant. I have not
yet had time to venture a word. "I have something
very serious to tell you," she says: "Edouard Manneret
is dead."

I know this already, of course, but reveal nothing. I
pattern my attitude and my expression on hers and
ask her in a word how it happened. She speaks rapidly
in a toneless voice I do not recognize, which reveals
disturbance and perhaps even anxiety. No, she has
not yet been able to learn anything about the circumstances of the drama; a friend has just telephoned her,
and he too had no idea when and how it had happened. Lady Ava cannot, moreover, continue this conversation of ours any longer, sought after as she is by
all her guests. She turns swiftly toward an approaching pair of new arrivals and, relaxed, smiling, completely in control of all of her features, greets them
with a warm word of welcome: "Oh, I'm so glad
you came! I wasn't sure Georges would be back in
time . . . , etc." Probably there are other people in this
happy and carefree crowd who also know the news,
even some for whom no detail of the affair remains a
secret. But these, like the others, are chatting in
little groups about commonplace things: their cats or
dogs, their servants, their discoveries in the antique
shops, their travels, or even the latest gossip concerning the episodic love affairs of people not present, or
the arrivals and departures noted in the colony.

The groups form and dissolve as people happen to

meet. When I am once again in the presence of the mistress of the house, she smiles at me quite naturally and asks if I've had something to drink. "No, not yet, but I will in a minute," I answer lightly, quite innocently, and head toward the buffet of the large salon. There are waiters in white jackets serving the drinks tonight and not the young Eurasian servant girls employed for the more intimate parties. The immaculate white cloth covering the trestles and hanging to the floor is covered with many silver platters filled with different kinds of tiny sandwiches and cakes. Three men, in animated conversation, are taking little sips from the champagne glasses the waiter has just served them. The moment I come within hearing (they are speaking rather low), I make out several words of their dialogue: ". . . to commit a crime with useless, baroque ornaments, and it's a necessary crime, not a gratuitous one. No one else . . ." For a moment I wonder if these words could have any connection with Manneret's death, but this seems, upon reflection, quite improbable.

Moreover, the man who had made the remark has immediately stopped speaking. I could not even tell with any certainty which of the three men it was, so closely do they resemble one another in dress, height, attitude, expression. None of them says anything more. Together, they calmly drink their champagne, in little sips. And when they resume their conversation, it is to make some perfectly ordinary remarks about the quality of the wines recently imported from France. As they move away I ask for a glass in my turn: as a matter of fact, the champagne is very dry and sparkling, but without bouquet. Two other guests approach the buffet, waiting to be served. It is here that the scene occurs of the white-coated waiter leaning over to pick up an empty ampoule from the floor, putting it down beside him on the edge of the table.

The orchestra has begun playing again. The dancing has resumed. There are a number of couples, revolving in time to the music. There are many good-looking women, among whom I count, tonight, at least five or six who figure among Lady Ava's protégées. Lady Ava herself happens to be with a girl I have never seen before, a girl who has lovely golden hair, an attractive mouth and satiny flesh generously exposed by the décolleté of a dress revealing her shoulders as well as her back and cleavage. Standing near the red couch where the older woman is sitting, she looks like a diligent pupil listening to the orders of her schoolmistress. A tall man in a dark tuxedo walks up to them and bows to Lady Ava, who exchanges some casual remarks with him; then she indicates the young woman with her right hand, making some extended comment on her person, as her gestures suggest, her arm pausing at different levels while the man silently contemplates the girl in question, who lowers her eyes in modesty. Obeying a sign which has just been made to her, the girl turns around with a supple dancer's movement, but slowly enough so that there is time to see her from every side; once she has returned to her initial position, it seems to me (but it is difficult to be sure, at this distance) that her face has

169

reddened slightly; and, as a matter of fact, she turns her head a little to one side in what might be an expression of embarrassment or shame. Then Lady Ava must have asked her not to flinch that way, for she immediately faces straight ahead and even raises her lashes, revealing then two large eyes made larger still by skillfully applied mascara. And now Sir Ralph offers her his hand; it must be to ask her to dance, since they are walking together, now, toward the floor. I cross this part of the salon to reach the yellow couch in my turn—or rather the red-and-yellow striped couch, as I discover at closer range. Lady Ava is still turned, in profile, in the direction the couple has just taken. After waiting a moment, and since she has not stopped staring after them, I ask: "Who is that?" But she does not answer me immediately and even delays another moment before looking at me, finally saying, with an imperceptible narrowing of her eyes: "That is the question."

I begin cautiously: "Isn't she . . ." But I stop, my companion seeming, now, to be thinking about something else and no longer to be paying me any more than the most formal attention. This piece of music which has gone on for some time, perhaps even since the beginning of the evening, is a kind of cyclically repeated refrain in which the same passages can always be recognized at regular intervals. ". . . for sale?" Lady Ava says, continuing my question and then an-

t, although extremely evasively: "I already thing for her, I think."

better," I say. "Something interesting?"

"One of our regulars," Lady Ava says.

She then explains that she means an American named Johnson, and I pretend to learn this fact from her own lips (although I have known the story for a long time), and not even to know just who the person in question is. Our hostess therefore takes the trouble to describe him and to tell me briefly about the opium poppy fields under cultivation on the border of the New Territories. Afterward her head is again turned toward the dance floor, where neither the man nor his partner is to be seen. And she adds, as though to herself: "The girl was on the verge of marrying a nice boy, who wouldn't have known what to do with her."

"And then?" I say.

"And then it was over," Lady Ava says.

A little later, the same day, she also says: "You'll see her tonight in the play, if you come to the performance. Her name's Lauren."

But meanwhile there has been the episode of the broken glass whose fragments are scattered over the floor, and the dancers who have stopped, then parted slowly to form a ring, contemplating wordlessly, with dread, with horror, as if it were an object of scandal, the tiny sharp fragments in which the lamplight is reflected in a thousand sparkling icy-blue facets, and the Eurasian servant girl who passes through the circle without seeing anything, like a sleepwalker, making the debris crunch in the silence under the soles of her delicate sandals whose gilded leather thongs crisscross three times around her bare feet and ankles.

And the couples who continue, as if nothing had happened, the complicated figures of the dance, the girl standing quite far from her partner who directs her at a distance, without needing to touch her, makes her turn around, keep time, undulate her hips where she stands, and then—in a swift turn—look at him again, at that severe gaze which fixes on her intently, or which focuses beyond her, ignoring her, above the blond hair and the green eyes.

Then comes the scene of the shopwindow of an elegant establishment in the European section, in Kowloon. However it must not take place precisely at this point, where it would not be understandable, despite the presence of this same Kim who is also on the stage of the little theater where the performance, which continues, has now reached those few minutes preceding the murder. The actor playing the part of Manneret is sitting in a chair at his desk. He is writing. He writes that the Eurasian servant girl then passes through the ring without seeing anything, making the gleaming splinters of glass crunch in the silence under her delicate sandals, all eyes being immediately turned toward her and following her as if fascinated, and she moving like a sleepwalker toward Lauren, and stopping in front of the terror-stricken young woman, and standing there staring at her coldly for a very long time, too long, unendurably, and finally saying in a clear, impersonal voice which allows no hope of escape: "Come. You're expected."

In the vicinity the dancing follows its normal course, as if all this were happening at the other end of the world, the couples still swept along by the same slow but irresistible rhythm, much too powerful to be interrupted, even momentarily, or altered by such dramas, however violent and sudden they may be. However, accidents multiply on all sides: a glass that breaks on the floor, a girl who suddenly faints, a little ampoule of morphine that falls from a tuxedo pocket when a guest takes out his silk handkerchief to wipe his moist forehead, a long cry of pain that tears through the polite buzz of the salon, the silent entrance of one of the maidservants, one of the big black dogs that has just bitten a dancer's leg, a white silk handkerchief stained with blood, a stranger who suddenly stands in front of the mistress of the house and hands her, at arm's length, a thick, brown paper envelope that seems to be stuffed with sand, and Lady Ava who, without losing her composure, quickly takes the object, weighs it in her hand and makes it disappear, just as the messenger has disappeared at the same time.

It is just at this moment that the British police have burst into the large salon of the Blue Villa, but this episode has already been described in detail: the short harsh whistle blast which abruptly stops the orchestra and the murmur of conversation, the iron heels of the two soldiers in shorts and short-sleeved shirts that ring on the marble floor in the sudden calm, the dancers who have frozen in the middle of a step, the man standing with one hand extended in front of him toward his partner still half-turned away, or the two partners facing each other but looking in different directions,

173

one to the right and the other to the left, as if their attention had been attracted at the same moment by diametrically opposed events, other couples, on the contrary, keeping their eyes mutually fixed on their feet, or their bodies united in a motionless embrace, and then the careful search of all the guests, the long investigation of their names, addresses, professions, dates of birth, etc., until the final sentence spoken by the lieutenant, which follows the words ". . . a necessary crime, not a gratuitous one" and which concludes: "No one else could have anything to gain from his death."

"Surely you'll have a glass of champagne," Lady Ava then says in her calmest tone of voice. A few yards behind her, standing against the frame of a doorway, like a perfectly trained servant ready to answer the first summons, body rigid and waxen face fixed in that kind of impassive smile characteristic of the Far East, which is actually not a smile at all, one of the young Eurasian girls (the one, I believe, whose name is not Kim) stares unblinking at her mistress. Seeming to ignore the incident, she is, according to her habit, attentive and vacant, given up to dark thoughts, perhaps, behind her frank, level gaze, prepared at the slightest notice, effective, impersonal, transparent, lost all day long as well in splendid and bloody dreams. But when she looks at something or someone, it is always directly and with her eyes wide open; and when she walks, it is without turning her head right or left, toward the baroque setting which surrounds her, toward the guests she passes and most of whom, nonetheless, she has known for several years, or several months, toward the faces of the anonymous passers-by, toward the little shops with their variegated displays of fruit or fish, toward the Chinese characters of the signs and posters whose meaning she at least would understand. And when she arrives, at the end of her errand, at the appointed house, in front of that narrow steep staircase without a railing which begins flush with the façade, rising directly toward the dark interior, and which resembles all the other entrances of the long straight street, the servant girl abruptly turns left and unhesitatingly climbs the inconvenient stairs, not even suggesting the awkwardness caused by her narrow split skirt; in a few steps, she has vanished into the total darkness.

She climbs to the second floor without seeing anything, or to the third. She knocks softly three times at a door, and immediately goes in without waiting for an answer. It is not the agent who is here to receive her today, it is the man she knows only by a nickname: the "Old Man" (though he is probably only sixty), whose real name is Edouard Manneret. He is alone. His back is to the door by which she has just entered the room and which she has closed behind her, still leaning against it. He is sitting in a chair, at his desk. He is writing. He pays no attention to the young girl, whose arrival he does not even seem to have noticed, although she has not taken any special precautions to avoid making noise; but her movements are naturally silent, and it is possible that the man has really not heard anyone come in. Without doing any-

175

thing to indicate her presence, she waits for him to decide to look toward her, which probably takes some time.

But she is then (immediately afterward or a little later?) facing him, both of them standing in a dark corner of the room, motionless and mute; and it is the servant girl who is standing with her back to the wall, as if she had slowly retreated there out of mistrust or fear of the Old Man who, two steps from her, is at least a head taller. And now she is leaning over the desk from which he has still not moved; she has rested one hand on the green leather top whose worn surface disappears almost entirely under a clutter of papers, and with the other hand—the right one—she holds onto the brass rim that protects the edge of the mahogany surface; in front of her, the man, still sitting in his chair, has not even raised his eyes toward his visitor; he stares at the delicate fingers with their red lacquered nails resting on a manuscript page of business stationery only three-quarters covered with a very small, close, and regular handwriting without erasure or mistake; the word which the servant girl's forefinger seems to be pointing to is the verb "represents" (third person singular of the present indicative); a few lines lower, the last sentence has remained unfinished: "would tell, upon his return from a trip" . . . He has not found the word that came next.

The third image shows him standing once again; but Kim, this time, is half-reclining beside him on the edge of a bed with rumpled blankets. (Was the bed already visible, previously, in this room?) The girl is still wearing her sheath dress slit up the side in the Chinese fashion, whose thin white silk, doubtless worn next to the skin, makes a cluster of tiny fan-shaped creases at the waist, produced by the evident torsion of the long, supple body. One foot is touching the floor with the toe of the thonged sandal; the other, shoeless but still sheathed in its transparent stocking, rests on the far edge of the mattress, the leg, bent at the knee, emerging as far as possible from the split skirt through its side opening; the other thigh (that is, the left one) lies full length, up to the hip, on the rumpled covers while the upper part of her body is propped on one elbow (the left one) as it turns toward the right side. The open right hand is spread on the bed, palm exposed and fingers slightly curved. The head is tipped back a little, but the face has kept its waxen mask, its frozen smile, its wide eyes, its complete absence of expression. Manneret, on the contrary, has the strained features of a man observing the course of an experiment or a project with feverish attention. He moves no more than his companion whose indecipherable face he scrutinizes as though he were waiting for it to reveal at last some anticipated, or feared, or unpredictable sign. One hand is extended in a cautious gesture, ready perhaps to intervene. The other is holding a delicate, stemmed glass whose shape suggests that of a champagne glass, but smaller. There are the remains of a colorless liquid at the bottom.

In a final scene, we see Edouard Manneret lying on the floor, in his dark suit that shows no disorder, between the impeccably made bed and the desk where the manuscript page remains unfinished. He is lying at full length on his back, arms extended symmetrically a few inches away from his body. In the room around him, there is no trace of violence or struggle or accident. The cessation of all action continues in this way for some time, until the leather clock on the desk chimes out, in the silence, the even ringing of the alarm; the spectators, recognizing this conclusion, then begin to applaud and stand up from their chairs, one after the other, to proceed one by one or in little groups toward the exit door, toward the red-carpeted staircase, toward the large salon where refreshments are waiting for them. Lady Ava, smiling and relaxed, is quite surrounded, as is natural, everyone wanting to offer his thanks as well as his compliments to the mistress of the house, before leaving. Having caught sight of me, she approaches with her most open, ordinary expression, seeming to have lost all recollection of the serious words she spoke a few moments ago, as of the events which caused her anxiety, and saying in her polite calm voice: "Surely you'll have a glass of champagne." I smile in my turn, answering that I was just about to, and before heading toward the buffet, I compliment her on the success of the evening.

So it is here that the dialogue occurs, once again, between the red-faced fat man and his tall companion in the dark tuxedo who bends his head a little to hear the stories the other man is telling him as he raises his congested face, no longer paying any attention to the silver tray offered by the white-jacketed waiter. The fat man has one hand extended in that direction, but he seems to have completely forgotten the reason for his gesture, and even his hand, which remains suspended about six inches from the brimming glass which the waiter too is no longer watching, his attention elsewhere, and which is tilting dangerously.

The fat man's hand has in time closed a little, only the forefinger remaining extended and the third finger partially curved. On this finger, which is as thick and short as all the rest, he wears a large Chinese seal ring whose stone, skillfully carved in every tiny detail, represents a young women half-reclining on the edge of a sofa, one of her bare feet still resting on the ground, the upper part of her body propped on one elbow and her head tilted back. The supple body which twists under the effect of some ecstasy, or some pain, produces in the thin black silk of the clinging dress several series of tiny divergent creases: at the top of the thighs, at the waist, over the breasts, at the armpits. It is a traditional dress, clinging and severe, with long sleeves tight at the wrists and a low, stiff, close-fitting collar, but instead of being slit no higher than the knee, it is open to the hip. (There is doubtless an invisible zipper which runs up to the armpit and perhaps even runs down the inner side of the sleeve to the wrist.) The left hand, which is resting on the unmade bed, palm upward, still holds loosely under the thumb a tiny glass syringe with its needle attached. A last drop of liquid has dripped from the hollow beveled tip, leaving on the sheet a round spot the size of a Hong Kong dollar.

Manneret, who has not moved from his desk during the entire scene, merely turning his head to observe the bed (so there must have been a bed in the room), his right shoulder drawn back and his left hand resting on the right arm of the chair, then looks back at his manuscript page and his pen on the interrupted sentence; after the word "trip," he writes the words "made clandestinely" and stops once again. Kim, facing him, leaning over the mahogany desk covered with a jumble of manuscript pages, one hand with three of its long, bright red, lacquered nails resting on a tiny area of old and faded green leather still visible amid the clutter, the line of her hip—emphasized by her asymmetrical posture—silhouetted against the almost closed Venetian blind, Kim straightens up, holding in her other hand the thick, brown paper envelope which the man has just given her (or perhaps merely indicated to her on the table with a rapid gesture of his chin . . .). And without a word, without a greeting, without a gesture of farewell, she retires as silently as she had come in, closes the door behind her without a sound, crosses the landing, goes down the narrow, dark, inconvenient stairs which lead directly to the swarming overheated street smelling of rotten eggs and fermenting fruit, amid the crowd of men and women uniformly dressed in black cotton pajamas as shiny and stiff as oilcloth.

The servant girl is still accompanied by the big dog which tugs just hard enough on its leash to keep it

taut and straight between the leather collar and the
hand with lacquered nails holding the other end at
arm's length. In her other hand, there is the thick
brown envelope, bulging as if it had been stuffed
with sand. And a little farther on, there is again the
same municipal sweeper in overalls, wearing a light
straw hat in the shape of a flattened cone. But this
time he does not even glance up as the girl passes.
He is leaning against one of the big square pillars
of the covered gallery on which are posted a number
of very small signs; the broom handle stuck under
one arm, the sheaf of rice straw curved by use partially
covering one of his bare feet, he is holding in both
hands in front of his eyes the piece of mud-stained
magazine which he has picked up from the gutter.
Having sufficiently examined the many-colored scene
embellishing the cover, he turns the page; this side,
much dirtier than the other, is furthermore printed
only in black and white. The majority of the still-
legible surface is occupied by three stylized drawings,
one above the other, showing the same young woman
with high cheekbones and slightly slanted eyes, still
situated in virtually the same setting (a poor and
empty room furnished with a simple iron bed) in the
same costume (a black sheath dress, of traditional
cut) but increasingly faded.

The first of these drawings shows her half-reclining
on the edge of the bed with rumpled sheets (the upper
part of her body propped on one elbow, dress open
to the hip over the naked flesh, face tilted back with
an ecstatic smile, hand still holding the empty syringe,

etc.); but a second setting is superimposed on the first in the whole upper part of the frame, occupying what seems to be the girl's field of vision: here are many elements of a naive and ornate luxury, such as walls covered with ornamental moldings, carved columns, mirrors in baroque frames, bronze candlesticks cast in fantastic shapes, heavily draped materials, ceilings painted in the eighteenth-century manner, etc. In the second drawing, all this tawdry luxury has vanished: nothing is left but the narrow iron bed on which the girl is now chained by all four limbs, lying on her back in a twisted and awkward position, which must indicate her vain efforts to free herself from these bonds; in her convulsive movements, her dress has opened still more, the lateral slit now revealing a small round breast (so that one can tell, here, that the zipper extended all the way to the neck instead of running back down the inner side of the sleeve, as had first been supposed without much concern for probability). The third drawing is doubtless symbolic: the girl is no longer chained, but her lifeless, entirely naked body is lying at an angle on its side, half on the bed where the arms and bust are stretched out, half on the floor where the long legs, knees bent, are extended; the black dress is lying on the floor, near a pool of blood; a huge hypodermic needle, the size of a sword, pierces the body through, penetrating the breast and emerging behind, below the waist.

Each image is accompanied by a brief caption, whose large Chinese characters signify, respectively:

"Drugs are a Disloyal Friend," "Drugs are an Enslaving Tyrant," "Drugs are a Deadly Poison." Unfortunately, the sweeper cannot read. As for the short fat man with the red face and bald head who is telling the story, he does not understand Chinese; at the bottom of the last picture, he has only been able to make out some very tiny Western letters and numbers: "S.W.N. Tel.: 1-234-567." A far more scrupulous narrator, who seems to be unaware of the meaning of the three initials (Society for the War on Narcotics) and who insists, on the contrary, on the attraction of the illustrations to a specialist, he declares to his interlocutor—who is quite incredulous, moreover—that the drawings are an advertisement for some clandestine establishment in the lower part of the city, where habitués are offered forbidden and monstrous pleasures which are not those of morphine and opium alone. But the white-jacketed waiter, who has straightened the tray in order to extend it horizontally, then says, at last: "Here you are, sir." The fat man turns his head and for an instant considers his own hand still in midair, the jade ring squeezing the middle finger, the silver tray, the glass full of a pale-yellow liquid in which tiny bubbles slowly rise to the surface; having finally realized where he is and what he is doing there, he says: "Oh! Thank you!" He picks up the glass, empties it in one swallow, sets it down again clumsily, without paying any attention, too close to the edge of the tray still held toward him. The glass pitches over and falls to the marble floor where

183

it breaks into a thousand splinters. This passage has already been reported, hence it can be passed over quickly.

Not far from here, Lauren happens to be reattaching her sandal, whose thongs have come undone during the dance. Pretending to be unaware of Sir Ralph's gaze, the young woman has sat down on the edge of a couch, where her long bouffant skirt spreads around her. She remains leaning forward, almost to the floor, so that both hands can reach the foot just visible under the white material. The delicate shoe, whose upper is no more than a narrow triangle of gilded leather which scarcely conceals the tips of the toes, is held in place by two long thongs which crisscross over the instep and around the ankle, above which a tiny buckle fastens them together. As she concentrates on this delicate operation, Lauren's blond hair falls forward and further exposes the curved nape of her neck and the delicate skin whose down is even paler than the blond hair, which falls forward and further exposes the curved nape of her neck and the delicate skin whose down is even paler than the rest of the curved nape and the delicate skin which curves further and the skin . . .

It is as if everything has come to a stop. Lauren reattaches the gilded thongs of her sandal. Johnson watches her, standing a few yards behind her, in a curtained window recess. The fat man with the red face lost the thread of his story when the champagne glass broke on the floor, and now he raises his bloodshot eyes—filled with something like panic, or despair

—toward the tall American whose silent face is bending over him, no longer even trying to conceal the fact that for some time now he has been thinking about something else altogether. Edouard Manneret, at his desk, carefully erases the word "clandestinely" so as to leave no trace of it on the sheet of paper, then he writes instead the words "to foreign parts." Lady Ava, sitting alone on her varicolored couch, suddenly looks worn, faded, tired of struggling to keep up appearances which no longer deceive anyone, knowing all too well in advance what will happen: the abrupt collapse of Lauren's marriage, her fiancé's suicide near the clump of traveler's palms, the discovery by the police of the little heroin laboratory, the venal and impassioned liaison between Sir Ralph and Lauren, the latter insisting on remaining an inmate of the Blue Villa and agreeing to meet him only in one of the rooms upstairs reserved for such transactions, where she has given herself to him for the first time, and he finding at first only an additional pleasure in this situation and contriving to pay more and more for more and more exorbitant services, and she lending herself exultantly to everything, but never failing to ask afterward for the sums due according to their agreements and according to the rates in effect in the house, thereby insisting on her status as a prostitute each time, although she also refuses—always, moreover, according to the same agreements—all the other propositions formally made by Lady Ava, in whose roster she nonetheless remains as one of the girls at the disposal of any rich client, and Sir Ralph, far from complaining about this, savoring it as something humiliating for his mistress, something excessive and cruel. But now he asks her to renounce this as well, to abandon a situation which is merely a pretext, to give up everything in order to leave with him. He must return to Macao on business and can no longer do without her, even for a single day, if only in the reception rooms of the Blue Villa, on the occasion of dances, or on the stage of the little theater where she continues to play the role of the heroine in that play of Jonestone's entitled: "The Murder of Edouard Manneret," and to act in several other dramas, sketches, or *tableaux vivants.*

So he wants to take her to Macao, to have her live with him, in his own house. But she refuses, of course, as he doubtless expected: "What reason would I have for leaving?" she asks, lowering her darkened eyelids a little over her green eyes. She is happy here. He should leave if he wants to. There are plenty of old millionaires in Kowloon and in Victoria to replace him. In any case, she has no desire to bury herself in that provincial little town where you bore yourself to death playing Russian roulette, and where everyone speaks Portuguese. She is lying on her back on the furs and the black satin of the canopy bed and stares, above her, at the mirror set in the canopy in which her body is reflected, keeping throughout the scene the exact pose of "Maya," a famous painting by Manneret and the goddess of illusion. Sir Ralph, who has finished what he had to say, strides up and down the big room, alternately passing the square bed on the right and left side without even glancing at the object of his demands, exposed there nonetheless in all her pink and blond luster. Occasionally he speaks a few more words, but to no purpose: arguments he has already employed ten times, reproaches meaningless in their mutual situation, promises he knows perfectly well he cannot keep. She is no longer listening. She draws a fold of black silk over one of her hips, the top of her thighs and half of her belly, as if she were cold, although the heat in the room tonight is overpowering. Sir Ralph, who is still wearing his tuxedo and tie, seems on the verge of exhaustion. "Then you don't love me at all?" he asks, at the end of his resources. "But," she says, "there's never been any question of that."

Then he offers her money, a great deal of money. With a smile she asks how much. He will give her whatever she wants. "All right," she says, and immediately sets the figure, with the calm assurance of someone who has long since calculated what this acceptance was worth. And to seal the bargain, she insists further that the sum be paid this very night, before daybreak. It is a considerable amount, much higher than what he can get hold of in so little time. Yet Johnson does not protest. He abruptly stops walking and finally glances toward the bed, as if he were discovering the young woman's presence there, at that moment. He stares at her in silence, but it seems as if his gaze passes through her without seeing anything. Lauren has turned her head toward him, though she does not lift it from the pillows. Very slowly, with a supple and graceful hand, she slides the black silk over her hip and shoves it completely to one side, doubtless wanting her lover to reach a knowledgeable decision and to be able, among other things, to appreciate the value of the marks still visible on her flesh.

Sir Ralph's gaze, however, remains motionless and blank, still seeming to pass through Lauren and to focus, beyond her, on some fascinating object, some imaginary scene. Then he says: "I'll do it," without its being quite clear whether he is speaking of the payment and its terms, or else of some other project; then, emerging from his reverie, he finally meets her huge, green, burning, intense, icy, irrational eyes. He tries for a moment to regain control of himself but, suddenly determined, he commands in a voice that admits of no appeal: "Wait for me here," heads for the door, turns the key, flings open the door, leaves the room.

And now he is striding through the dark grounds, now he is in a taxi driving too slowly toward Queens Road, now he is climbing a steep narrow staircase in the dark. And now he is leaning across a desk covered with a clutter of papers, toward a Chinese of no particular age sitting in front of him, or rather below him, whose wrinkled face preserves a polite calm before this fanatic in a tuxedo who is talking so fast, gesticulating and threatening. Now Sir Ralph again climbs a staircase identical to the first, leading from one floor to the next in a single straight flight, without a railing to hold onto despite the narrowness and steepness of the steps. And now he is in a taxi driving too slowly toward Queen Street. And now he knocks on the wooden door of a very tiny shop on which can be read, in the pale light of a street lamp, the word "Exchange" written in seven languages. He pounds furiously with both fists, making the empty street echo faintly with the sound, at the risk of arousing the whole neighborhood. When no one answers, he presses his mouth to the crack of the door and calls: "Ho! Ho! Ho!", which is perhaps the name of the person he is trying to awaken. Then he pounds again, but already less violently, like someone whose hope is fading.

Moreover, nothing has stirred in the neighborhood, despite the racket, no sign of life has been made; this setting, too, would be empty, without depth, with no more reality than a nightmare; that would explain the muffled artificial sound made by the pounding on the wooden door. Johnson, at this moment, notices an old man in black cotton pajamas sitting in a recess of the façade next door. He immediately goes toward him, runs toward him, more exactly, and shouts several words of English, asking if there is anyone in the shop. The old man begins to give long explanations in a slow voice, in a language which must be Cantonese, but which he pronounces so indistinctly that Johnson does not grasp a single sentence. He repeats his question in Cantonese. The other man answers with the same slowness, the same fullness; this time, what he says sounds more like English, though only the word "wife" is recognizable, actually recurring several times. Johnson, growing impatient, asks the old man what his wife has to do with it. But the Chinese then launches into a new series of incomprehensible comments, from which this word has entirely disappeared. No gesture, no expression of his face manages to explain the obscure meaning of his words. The man remains seated on the ground without moving, his back to the wall, his hands clasped around his knees. There is something hopeless in his voice. The American, exasperated by this flood of lamentations, begins shaking his interlocutor, leaning over him to seize him by the shoulders. The old man leaps up at once and utters piercing shrieks with an unexpected energy, while, just at that moment, the siren of a police car is heard a few streets away; the howling quickly draws nearer, rising and falling in a cyclical modulation which repeats the same shrill notes.

Johnson lets the old man go and quickly walks away, soon beginning to run, pursued by the shrieks of the Chinese standing in the middle of the road, making huge gestures with both arms in his direction. According to the sound of the siren, the police car must certainly be coming from there. Johnson turns around as he runs and sees the yellow headlights as well as the flashing red beacon on the car roof. He turns sharply up a steep street, with the evident hope of reaching a stairway before being overtaken by the car which could not then pursue him any farther. But the car, having taken the turn immediately after him, has already caught up. Adopting the manner, although a little late and not very naturally, of the innocent bystander, he stops at the first command to do so; three

British policemen jump out and surround him; they seem surprised and favorably impressed by his evening clothes. They are in khaki shorts and short-sleeved shirts, low shoes and white knee socks. Johnson thinks he recognizes the lieutenant as the one who burst into the large salon of the Blue Villa this very evening; the two policemen accompanying him are also, probably, the ones who disturbed the party's end. Asked to show his papers, Johnson offers his Portuguese passport which he takes out of an inside coat pocket.

"Why were you running?" the lieutenant asks.

On the point of answering mechanically: "To keep warm," Johnson catches himself in time, thinking of the tropical temperature, his heavy black tuxedo, his sweating face. "I wasn't running," he says, "I was walking fast."

"It seemed to me you were running," the lieutenant says. "And why were you walking so fast?"

"I was in a hurry to get back."

"I see," the lieutenant says. Then after a glance up the street where the broad stairs littered with garbage vanish between increasingly wretched wooden shop fronts, he adds: "Where do you live?"

"Hotel Victoria."

The Hotel Victoria is not situated in Victoria, nor even on the island of Hong Kong, but in Kowloon, on the mainland. The officer leafs through the passport; the residence indicated there is in Macao, of course. The officer also looks at the photograph and then stares at the American's face for nearly a minute.

"Is this you?" he says at last.

"Yes. It's me," Johnson answers.

"It doesn't look like you." He is speaking of the picture, of course, and not of Johnson's face.

"Perhaps it's not a very good photo," Johnson says. "And it's not very recent."

The lieutenant, having again considered for a long time the face and the photograph, then the detailed information which he reads with the help of his pocket flashlight and subsequently compares with the model, finally hands back the passport, but declaring:

"This isn't the way to the Hotel Victoria, you know. The ferry's in the other direction."

"I don't know the city well," Johnson says.

The lieutenant stares at him a moment longer without a word, shifting the flashlight beam across his forehead, his eyes, his nose, thereby changing their outlines and expression. Then he remarks in an indifferent tone (in any case, it is not a question): "You were at Madame Eva Bergmann's just now." Johnson, who has been expecting this remark from the start of the interview, is careful not to deny it.

"Yes," he says, "as a matter of fact I was."

"Are you a habitué of the house?"

"I've gone several times."

"People enjoy themselves there, it seems."

"That depends on your tastes."

"Do you have an idea what the police were looking for there?"

"No. I don't know."

"Why was that old man shouting in the middle of the street?"

"I don't know. But you could ask him."

"Why were you taking an uphill street, if you wanted to get back to the harbor?"

"I told you, I was lost."

"That's no reason to look for a boat on top of a mountain."

"Hong Kong's an island, isn't it?"

"Yes, of course, so is Australia. Have you walked from Madam Bergmann's house?"

"No, I came by taxi."

"Why didn't the taxi let you off at the dock?"

"I had him stop on Queens Road. I wanted to walk a little."

"The party was over long ago. How many hours have you been walking?" But without waiting for an answer, the lieutenant adds: "At the rate you were going, you must have come a long way!" Then in the same tone of voice which attaches little importance to all this: "Did you know Edouard Manneret?"

"Only by name."

"Who have you heard talking about him?"

"I don't remember."

"And what did they say?"

Johnson makes a vague gesture with his right hand, accompanied by a shrug of uncertainty, ignorance and unconcern. The lieutenant continues:

"You didn't happen to have dealings, more or less indirectly, with him?"

"No. Certainly not. What business is he in?"

"He's dead. Did you know?"

Johnson feigns astonishment: "No! I certainly

didn't. . . . How did he die?" But the policeman goes on:

"You're sure you never met him at the Blue Villa, or in other such places?"

"No. No. . . . I don't think so. But how did he die? And how long ago?"

"It was tonight. He committed suicide."

The officer knows, apparently, that it was not a suicide. Johnson detects the trap and makes no remark which might suggest that this version seems contestable to him, even for psychological reasons, because of Manneret's character. Johnson decides to say nothing and to withdraw into a kind of abstraction, which he considers suitable for the occasion. One thing especially disturbs him: why did the police car head straight for him, instead of stopping where the old man was shouting, which happened to be on its way? Besides, since this lieutenant seems to be so involved with the Manneret case, what has he been doing between his departure from the Blue Villa and this unexpected patrol, still in the company of the same two soldiers? One of the latter has returned to sit behind the wheel during the first questions of the interrogation, doubtless deciding that the suspect was not dangerous. The other has remained at attention two steps from his chief, ready to intervene if the occasion arose. The lieutenant, after a rather long silence, then says (and his voice is increasingly indifferent, detached from what it is saying, as if he were talking to himself about a very old story): "Ralph Johnson, that's a funny name for a Portuguese from

Macao. . . . There's a Ralph Johnson who lives in the New Territories, but he's an American. . . . He's been growing Indian hemp and opium. . . . Small amounts. . . . Have you ever heard of him?"

"No, never," the American says.

"Lucky for you. He's been involved recently in a nasty white-slave case, and he's a Communist agent. . . . You should have the photograph on your passport changed to one that looks more like you. . . ." Then, abruptly changing his tone, he asks with no transition, raising his eyes: "At what time tonight did you arrive at the house of the woman you call Lady Ava?"

Without stressing the fact that Lady Bergmann has not yet been designated by this name during their entire conversation, Johnson, who has had time to prepare himself for this question, immediately begins the account of his evening: "I arrived at the Blue Villa around ten after nine, by taxi. Wooded grounds surround the enormous stucco house, whose elaborate architecture, the exaggerated repetition of ornamental, nonfunctional motifs, the juxtaposition of disparate elements, the unusual color—are always a surprise when the house appears at the turn of a path in its frame of royal palms. Since I had the impression I was somewhat ahead of time, that is, among the first guests to arrive, if not *the* first, since I saw no one else, I decided not to go in right away, and I turned to the left to take a stroll in the pleasantest part of the garden. Only the immediate environs of the house are illuminated, even during parties; very soon, thick clumps of trees cut off the light from the lanterns, and even the blue glow reflected from the stucco walls. Soon nothing more can be distinguished than the general shape of the . . . , etc."

I also skip the sound of the insects, already alluded to, and the description of the statues. I come immediately to the scene of Lauren's breakup with her fiancé. And when the lieutenant asks me the name of this person, who has not yet been mentioned, I answer quite at random that his name is Georges.

"Georges who?" he says.

"Georges Marchat."

"And what does he do?"

I answer quickly: "Businessman."

"Is he French?"

"No, Dutch, I think."

He is sitting alone on a white marble bench, under a clump of traveler's palms whose leaves shaped like broad leaves shaped like broad hands hang in a fan around him. He is leaning forward. He seems to be staring at his patent leather shoes, a little darker against the background of pale sand. His hands are resting on the stone bevel on each side of his body. Coming closer, as I continue along the path, I notice that the young man is holding a pistol in his right hand, his forefinger already on the trigger, but the barrel aimed at the ground. This weapon, moreover, will cause him considerable inconvenience, a little later, during the general search of the guests by the police.

Afterward nothing notable occurred, until the moment when the mistress of the house informs me—

or rather believes she is informing me—that Manneret has just been murdered. She asks me what I plan to do. I tell her that the news takes me by surprise, but that, quite likely, I shall be obliged to leave the British territory of Hong Kong and return to Macao for some time, perhaps even permanently. The evening nonetheless continues as planned. People talk about one thing or another, dance, drink champagne, break glasses and eat candwiches. At eleven-fifteen, the curtain rises on the stage of the little theater. In the audience, almost all the red plush chairs are occupied—chiefly by men—about thirty people in all, doubtless carefully chosen, since tonight the performance is for habitués. (Most of the guests at the party have left, not even knowing that something is supposed to happen on the floor below.) The performance begins by a strip tease in the Su-Chuan manner. The actress is a young Japanese girl whom the habitués have not yet seen; consequently she excites the curiosity of the public. She is, moreover, excellent from every point of view, and the act, although traditional, receives considerable applause; no one, as a matter of fact, disturbs the ritual, as happens all too often, by annoying comings and goings or inopportune chatter.

The program then includes an entr'acte in Grand Guignol style, which is called "Ritual Murders" and draws heavily on fake devices: knives with spring blades, red ink spread on the white flesh, screams and contortions of the victims, etc. The setting has remained the same as for the first scene (a huge vaulted dungeon into which a stone staircase descends); it re-

197

quires only a few accessories such as wheels, racks or trestles; the dogs, on the other hand, play no part in it. But the high point of the evening is indubitably a long monologue spoken by Lady Ava herself, alone on stage throughout the number. The term monologue is not, moreover, quite suitable, for few words are spoken during this little dramatic fragment. Our hostess plays herself. In the costume she has just been seen wearing during the party, she makes her entrance, now, at the rear (through the large double door), in an extraordinarily realistic setting which perfectly reproduces her own bedroom, located like the rest of her private apartments on the fourth—top—floor of the huge house. Greeted by sustained applause, Lady Ava bows briefly to the footlights. Then she turns back toward the door, whose handle she has not released, closes it, and remains there a moment, listening to some sound from outside (imperceptible to the audience), one ear toward the decorated panel, but without pressing her cheek against the wood. She has heard nothing disturbing, probably, since she soon abandons this posture to approach the audience, which she henceforth no longer sees, of course. Then she takes a few increasingly uncertain steps to the left, seems to think twice, to change her mind, turns back to the right, heads obliquely toward the rear of the room, to return almost at once toward the audience. She is evidently in distress, her face is tired, worn, older, all the party's urbanity suddenly vanished. Having stopped near a small round table covered with a green cloth that falls to the floor all around, she begins mechanically removing her jewelry: a heavy gold necklace, a charm bracelet, a ring with a large stone, earrings, which she sets one after the other in a crystal cup. She remains there, standing despite her fatigue, one hand on the edge of the table, the other arm hanging alongside her body. One of the young Eurasian servant girls then enters noiselessly from the left and stands motionless some distance from her mistress, whom she contemplates in silence: she is wearing bronze silk pajamas more clinging than is usual in the case of such garments. Lady Ava turns her face toward the girl, a tragic face with eyes so exhausted that they seem to rest on things without seeing them. Neither woman speaks. Kim's features are smooth and inscrutable, Lady Ava's so weary that they no longer express anything. There may be hatred on either side, or terror, or envy and pity, or pleading and scorn, or anything else.

And now the servant girl—though nothing has stirred in the interval—withdraws as she has come, lovely and mute, supple and silent. The lady has not made a movement, as if she had not even seen her leave. And it is then only after a notable lapse of time that she herself continues her comings and goings in the room, wandering from one piece of furniture to the other without deciding on anything at all. On the open desk, among the white sheets of manuscript, there is the heavy brown paper envelope, apparently stuffed with sand, which has been handed to her this evening; she weighs it in her hand, only to set it down again at once. Finally she goes over and sits down on a little round seat, with neither arms nor back, which looks like a piano stool, in front of the mirrored dressing table. She stares at herself in the mirror with deliberate attention—full face, three-quarters from the right, three-quarters from the left, full face again—then begins removing her makeup carefully, back to the audience.

When she has finished and again reveals her face, she is transformed: from a woman of no particular age, merely too heavily made up, she has become an old woman. But she looks less exhausted on the other hand, less remote, almost calm again. More decisively, she returns to the desk and with the blade of a pocket-knife opens the heavy brown envelope, which she empties out onto the scattered sheets: a large number of tiny white sachets, all alike, fall out pell-mell; she begins counting them rapidly; there are forty-eight. She picks up one of the sachets at random, tears open a corner and, without opening it further, taps some of the contents out of the orifice thus effected onto one of the manuscript sheets which she is holding in her other hand. It is a white powder, fine and shiny, which she examines carefully, raising it to her eyes, but pulling her head back a little at the same time. Satisfied by her scrutiny, she pours the grains of powder back into the sachet through the narrow opening, curling the sheet of paper into a summary funnel. Then, to close the white sachet, she folds the torn corner over, several times. She puts this sachet in one of the little inner drawers of the desk. She places the others back in the brown envelope, counting them once more, and replaces the envelope on the desk, where she found it. The sheet of paper she has just used remains slightly curved from the operation. Lady Ava rolls it in the opposite direction, in order to restore it to its original flatness; then her attention is drawn to what is written on the sheet, of which she rereads several lines.

Holding the sheet in one hand and continuing to read, she now walks toward the bed, a huge square canopy bed situated in an alcove at the other end of the large room, and she rings. The young servant reappears, in exactly the same costume as before, making as little noise and standing motionless in the same place. Lady Ava, who is half-sitting, half-leaning on the edge of the bed, inspects her in detail from head to foot, lingering over her breast, her waist, her hips in the clinging supple silk, then looking back up at the golden face, as smooth as porcelain, with its tiny lacquered mouth, its almond-shaped eyes of blue enamel, the black hair drawn over the temples to show the delicate ears and form, on the nape of the neck, a thick, short, shiny tress loosely braided so that it will come free, in bed, once the tiny ribbon that encircles the end is pulled. If the mistress' expression has focused, becoming insistent, in fact, the servant girl's has not changed since a moment ago; it is still just as impersonal and blank as before.

"You saw Sir Ralph, tonight," Lady Ava begins. Kim merely gives an almost imperceptible nod—doubtless affirmative—for an answer, the lady continuing her monologue without taking her eyes from the girl, but indicating no surprise at not obtaining the slightest word, even when a question is asked quite categorically: "Did he seem normal to you? Did you notice how haggard he looked? Loraine will eventually drive him quite mad, if she keeps on giving in to his ideas. It's all set now. As it is, Sir Ralph can only live on her account. Things will simply have to follow their course, now." The girl again fails to show the slightest sign of agreement or interest; she might as well be deaf and dumb, or understand only Chinese. Lady Ava seems not at all affected by this (perhaps she herself has forbidden the young servant girls to answer) and continues, after a pause: "At this very moment, he must be running around trying to get hold of the money she asked for. And he'll be ripe for our advice . . . suggestions . . . directions. All right. I don't need you tonight. I'm old and tired. . . . You can sleep in your own bed."

The Eurasian girl has vanished again, like a ghost. Lady Ava is once again standing near the desk, where she sets down on the flat surface, among the other papers, the sheet she had picked up to reread. She takes the brown envelope which contains the forty-seven sachets of powder; she could have noticed, on Kim's second entrance, that the girl had seen the package: if the hiding place was in the room itself, the envelope would have been put away long since, the servant girl has thought, Lady Ava thinks, the red-faced narrator says, who is telling the story to his neighbor in the little theater. But Johnson, who has other matters on his mind, lends only half an ear to his fantastic stories of Oriental travels, with go-between antique dealers, white-slave traders, over-skillful dogs, brothels for perverts, drug traffic and mysterious murders. He also bestows no more than a rather vague, wandering, interrupted gaze on the stage where the performance is taking place.

Meanwhile, Lady Ava, in her room, has worked the secret combination which she alone knows (the Chinese workman who installed the machinery died shortly afterward), in order to open the panel of the invisible safe on the wall opposite the double door. This sliding panel forms, with the adjoining door of the bathroom, a double door identical to the entrance door opposite it; the visitor has the impression that the right-hand section—which is actually the door to the safe—is merely a false panel there for the sake of decoration, for symmetry. Lady Ava puts the brown paper package on one of the shelves, and begins counting the boxes piled in rows on the shelf below.

Meanwhile the American returns to Kowloon by one of the night boats, whose huge rooms lined with benches or chairs are almost empty at this late hour. He has had some difficulty getting rid of the police; the lieutenant has even insisted on escorting him to the dock and making him get on the first ferry to leave. Johnson has not dared get off immediately (as he had first thought of doing), fearing to find himself once again facing the police car, which has remained there as if to observe him. He therefore disembarks on the other side of the water. The only taxi on duty is taken, at the very moment he himself reaches it, by another customer who appears at the opposite door. Johnson decides to get into a red rickshaw whose sticky oilcloth cushion leaks its rotting hair out of a triangular rip; but he consoles himself by thinking that the taxi, a very old model, can scarcely be any more comfortable. The runner advances, moreover, as fast as the car, which heads in the same direction along the broad deserted avenue overhung, from one sidewalk to the other, by the branches of the giant fig trees whose thick and delicate aerial roots dangle vertically like long hair. Between the huge knotty trunks appears at moments—soon caught up with and then passed—a girl in a white sheath dress who was walking rapidly along the house fronts, preceded by a big dog she was holding on a leash. The rickshaw stops at the same time as the taxi in front of the monumental door of the Hotel Victoria. But no one gets out of the car, and Johnson thinks he glimpses, glancing back as he steps into the revolving door, a face staring at him through the rear window which has remained closed, despite the heat. Then that would be a spy the lieutenant ordered to follow the suspect to Kowloon, to see if he was really staying in this hotel, and if he returned there at once without making further detours.

But Johnson has stopped at the hotel only to ask the porter if any message had been left for him in the course of the evening. No, the porter has nothing for him (he checks the message box to make sure); he merely received, a short while ago, a telephone call from Hong Kong asking if a certain Ralph Johnson was staying at the hotel, and how long he had been there. This was the lieutenant again, of course, who was certainly making his investigation obvious, unless the very obviousness is deliberate, in order to make an impression on him. It does not keep him, in any case, from leaving the lobby at once through the other revolving door, which opens at the rear of the building onto a square planted with traveler's palms, on the other side of which is the street. Here there is a taxi stand, with as usual one car waiting, of a very old model. Johnson gets in (after checking that no one, in the vicinity, is watching his departure) and gives the address of Edouard Manneret, the only person who, on this side of the bay, can help him in his urgent need. The taxi starts at once. The heat, in such close quarters, is stifling; Johnson wonders why all the windows are closed to the top, and he tries to open the one on his side. But it resists. He struggles with it, suddenly filled with a terrifying suspicion caused by the resemblance of this old car with the one which has just . . . The handle comes off in his hand, and the window remains hermetically closed. The driver, hearing the noise behind him, turns around toward the glass which separates him from his passenger, and the latter has just time to assume a sleepy expression likely to mask his agitation. Was it not this face with its tiny slanting eyes which Johnson has seen at the wheel of the first car, at the ferry dock? But all Chinese look alike. It is too late, in any case, to change his destination; Manneret's address has been given, and written down by the driver. If it is the driver's mission to . . . But why

205

did the spy who was watching him behind the closed window, at the hotel door, get out of the car? Where could he have gone? And how could a policeman cover his assignment in a cruising taxi? Unless, of course, this was a false taxi, also summoned by telephone from the island of Hong Kong and driving on purpose to the ferry dock to pick up the colleague and follow his orders. And, at this moment, this colleague himself is searching Johnson's room in the Hotel Victoria from top to bottom.

Behind the giant trunks of the fig trees, a girl in a sheath dress calmly, rapidly passes by the elegant shops with their dark windows; a huge black dog precedes her, exactly like the girl of a little while ago, who wasn't walking in this direction however and would have had difficulty covering all this distance in the interval. But Sir Ralph has more urgent problems which keep him from thinking about this one. If the lieutenant's spy really got out of the car at the Hotel Victoria, although with a short delay (he might have been looking for change, or waiting for Johnson to leave him a clear field), this taxi could also be a real taxi. What reason, then, did the driver have for parking behind the hotel, as though to check all the exits? The car, meanwhile, has reached the address given. The driver has opened the glass between himself and the passenger to tell the latter the cost of the trip; he takes advantage of this situation to take the window handle, which the passenger is still inadvertently holding, and replaces it on its pivot with the dexterity conferred by habit, ready to play the same trick on a new passenger. After which he exclaims, in Cantonese: "American goods!" and bursts into shrill laughter. Johnson, while handing him a ten-dollar bill (of Hong Kong currency, of course), takes advantage of this joke to start up a conversation, attempting to clear up the mystery of the first spy. He says, in Cantonese: "English cars aren't much better!"

The other man winks, with a sly expression full of complicity, answering: "Right! And what about the Chinese ones?" The man is probably one of the many propaganda agents who have come as refugees from Communist China, recently invading the Colony and taking over certain jobs—as taxi drivers and hotel porters in particular. But Johnson, following his own ideas, then asks: "Weren't you just parked in front of the ferry dock, where I just missed you by a few seconds?"

"Yes, sure!" the man says.

"And you drove someone to the Hotel Victoria?"

"Check!"

"Did he get out of the car?"

"If he didn't get out, he wouldn't have taken the cab, would he?"

"All right. But once he did, why did you drive around the building to the square behind, instead of staying at the stand in front of the hotel?"

The Chinese again winks slyly, exaggeratedly, a little alarmingly: "The tail," he says. "The police tail!" And he bursts into his high-pitched laugh.

The American gets out of the car and walks away, vaguely stunned. He dares not go straight up to Man-

neret's—though he has given his number quite clearly
—on account of the taxi which has not yet driven
away, still parked next to the curb. When he risks a
glance in that direction to see what the driver is waiting for, he sees the front door of the car open and
the little man stick out his head and one arm to show
him the right doorway, gesturing politely, doubtless
fearing that he will get lost in this dim avenue where
the numbers on the buildings are not all visible. Johnson then decides not to walk around the block, as he
had first thought of doing, and he rings at the outer
door, which opens automatically. Inside the lobby, he
easily finds the button for the light in the stairwell,
where the coolness of the air conditioning revives his
strength.

Edouard Manneret is at home, of course, and he
soon comes to open his door himself. There are no
servants at this hour; Manneret is usually up all night.
But tonight he has obviously taken a stronger dose
than usual, and his half-conscious state is a bad omen.
He is wearing rumpled pajamas; he hasn't shaved for
several days, so that his goatee and mustache, instead
of standing out clearly against his glabrous cheeks, are
lost in a grayish blur of hair growing in all directions.
His eyes are shiny, but with the abnormal luster
caused by drugs. At first he doesn't recognize Johnson,
whom he takes initially for his own son, and compliments him on his fine appearance and his elegant
clothes; with a fatherly gesture, he pats the tuxedo
sleeve and straightens the bow tie. Johnson, whose last
hope is in this old man, lets him proceed, determined

to treat him considerately. He nonetheless introduces himself, his voice gentle but firm: "I'm Ralph Johnson."

"Of course!" Manneret says, smiling with the expression of a man accommodating himself to the wiles of a child or a madman. "And I'm King Boris." He settles into a cushioned rocking chair and vaguely points to a chair for his visitor. "There," he says, "sit down!" But the visitor prefers to remain standing, racked by his desire to be understood; he points his forefinger at his own chest and repeats, syllable by syllable: "Johnson. I'm Ralph Johnson."

"Of course! Forgive me," the other man exclaims in a polite tone. "A name, you know. . . . What does a name mean? And how is Mrs. Johnson?"

"There is no Mrs. Johnson," the American says, losing patience. "Come on now, you know who I am!"

Manneret seems to think it over, lost in dim thoughts which the image of the intruder evidently disturbs. He rocks gently in his chair. The face with its feverish expression, its gray, disorderly beard, regularly rises and sinks in a slow, periodic oscillation. Finally he says, without interrupting his rocking movement which it is enough to watch for a few moments to grow dizzy: "Of course. . . . Of course. . . . But you must get yourself a wife, my boy. . . . I'll speak to Eva about it. . . . She knows so many fine girls."

"Listen to me," Johnson says vehemently. "I am Ralph Johnson, Sir Ralph, the American."

Manneret stares at him, squinting suspiciously.

"And what do you want with me?" he says.

"Money! I need money. I need it right away!" Johnson realizes that such a tone is not at all appropriate to his request. He had, of course, prepared quite another approach. Discouraged, he slumps into a chair.

But the old man, who has begun rocking back and forth again, immediately recovers his original smile and kindliness: "Listen, my boy, I gave you another fifty dollars this morning. You spend too much. . . . Is it on girls?" He winks lewdly, then adds, his voice suddenly mournful: "If your poor mother were still alive. . . ."

"Enough of this!" Johnson shouts, beside himself. "For the love of God, forget about my mother, my wife, and my sisters! I need your help. I'll write you a formal I.O.U. that will guarantee you a lien on the Macao property. . . ."

"There's no need for that, my boy, there's no need for that between us. . . . You mentioned your sisters, just what are they doing now?"

Johnson, who can no longer endure the movement of the rocking chair from which he cannot tear his eyes, stands and strides up and down the room. He is wasting his time with this old addict, who will soon fall asleep anyway. There is more to be done on the other side of the water, in Victoria, among the rich moneylenders in the miserable stalls on Queens Road. His mind suddenly made up, he crosses the apartment, slams the door behind him and dashes down the stairs, ignoring the elevator.

Outside the air is hot and sultry again, all the more surprising after leaving an air-conditioned house. The old taxi is still there, waiting for him, parked at the curb. Without considering the strangeness of such solicitude on the part of the driver (the passenger he had brought here half an hour ago was quite likely to be going home at such a late hour and not to be leaving again before morning), Johnson automatically walks over to the car and is about to get in, as the Chinese holds the door open for him.

"He's an old con man, isn't he?" the latter says in English.

"Who is?" Sir Ralph asks sharply.

"Monsieur Manneret," the driver says, giving his accomplice's wink.

"But who are you talking about?" the American asks, pretending not to understand.

"Everyone knows him," the driver says, "and only his windows are still lighted now." At the same time, he points at a large bay window on the fifth floor, where behind the transparent curtains, the figure of a man is silhouetted against the luminous background, staring out at the deserted avenue, with only an old taxi parked at the curb, the polite driver who closes the door behind the passenger who has just climbed into the back seat, then gets into his own seat in turn, starts up without too much difficulty, and drives off at the speed of a rickshaw.

Edouard Manneret then turns back toward the room and leaves the window, rubbing his hands. He smiles to himself with satisfaction. He feels like telephoning Lady Ava to describe the interview. But she must be asleep by now. Passing the air-conditioning control, he turns it down one notch. Then he returns to his desk and continues writing. Having covered, with her quick regular strides, the considerable distance from the dock, the young Eurasian servant girl will soon be returning with the dog. It is, as it is not difficult to guess, one of Lady Ava's big black dogs; and the girl is named Kim. So it was not this girl, but the second servant girl (who resembles her, moreover, as perfectly as if they were twins, and whose name may also be written Kim, and is pronounced quite similarly, the difference imperceptible except to a Chinese ear), so it was not this girl who was to spend the night with their mistress. Unless it was actually the same girl, who—as soon as she was liberated by Lady Ava's last-minute decision—had left the Blue Villa with the dog, walking directly to the Victoria dock, taking the ferry, where she notices Sir Ralph's presence, but being careful to keep him from catching sight of her, and quickly disembarking first, upon arrival at Kowloon, continuing her nocturnal promenade under the hanging roots of the giant fig trees, soon caught up with and passed by a taxi closely followed by a rickshaw, then a little further on caught up with again by the same taxi—alone this time—of a very old model, easily recognizable by its slowness and its closed windows. It is once again this same taxi, for the third time, that she passes (it is now coming toward her) just before reaching her destination.

Besides Kim, Johnson, and the spy following him on the orders of the police lieutenant in Hong Kong, there was also on this same ferry—which is not surprising, for there are very few crossings in the middle of the night—a fourth person who deserves to be identified: Georges Marchat, Lauren's ex-fiancé who has been wandering around for a long time, constantly ruminating on his lost happiness and his despair. Having left the party very early, where his presence was no longer justified, at first he too has walked through this residential neighborhood with its large estates concealed behind walls or bamboo fences, then he has returned for his car parked near the Blue Villa, and has taken the road around the island, stopping in all the bars and casinos still open on the coast, drinking whisky after whisky. Beyond Aberdeen, on a little beach where there is a middle-class beach club, he has picked up a rather pretty Chinese prostitute, and continued driving while trying to tell her his story, of which of course the woman has understood nothing, so blurred has the young man's diction become and so incoherent his presentation of events. She has nonetheless offered him her services, to help him forget his unhappiness, but he has rejected her with expressions of outraged virtue, saying that he was not trying to forget but on the contrary to understand, that besides he no longer wanted to have anything to do with women, that existence itself had become meaningless, and that he was going to throw himself over a cliff into the sea. The prostitute has decided to get out of the car rather than be mixed up in this troublesome case; he has therefore let her out precisely where they were, that is, nowhere in particular, far from any village, and he has given her a fifty-dollar bill for the

213

price of her company; she was still thanking him ceremoniously, assuring him that for such a sum she could
have . . . etc., when he had already continued on his
way. Driving straight ahead, faster and faster, showing
less and less caution around the countless curves of the
coastal road and passing through the villages, he has
finally reached the outskirts of Victoria, where he is
soon arrested by a police patrol, for the behavior of
his car obviously revealed the driver's drunkenness.
He has shown his papers to the lieutenant at the station, who has immediately recognized in this Georges
Marchat, Dutch businessman, one of the most suspicious guests among those he had interrogated at Eva
Bergmann's party this evening: the one who was carrying, at the time of the search, a loaded revolver, with
one bullet in the barrel. Questioned as to what he had
done since leaving the Blue Villa, the fiancé has given
the names of the places where he had been drinking
(at least those which he could remember) but he has
said nothing about the Chinese prostitute. The lieutenant has written the addresses in his notebook; since
the businessman's status in town was known and consequently easy to trace, he has let him go, advising
him to drive slower, after having merely issued him
a ticket for driving in a state of intoxication. Marchat,
to recover from this incident, has made another stop
in a harbor bar in order to have a few drinks; then he
has driven his car onto the ferry. Neither Kim nor
Johnson could meet him on board, for he has fallen
asleep at his wheel once he managed to get his car onto
the boat, one way or another. Wandering on the decks,

he would not have been in danger of firing his revolver at the American in any case, since the weapon had been impounded some hours earlier, at the Blue Villa, by the police.

When the boat lands at Kowloon, Georges Marchat is still asleep, slumped over his wheel. The sailors on board supervising the disembarkation of automobiles shake him to wake him up; but for an answer they obtain only snores, then incoherent words, among which perhaps figure the words "whore" and "kill"; still, in order to identify them among the vague syllables which do not manage to leave his throat, one would have to be aware of the young man's misfortunes. The sailors have no time to waste on explorations of this kind: the car is blocking those behind it, which are already indicating their impatience by blowing their horns. They therefore shove Marchat away from the wheel, in order to be able to maneuver it through the lowered window while the big car is pushed off the ferry, a maneuver accomplished without much difficulty, since the dock is on a level with the deck. The sailors then push Marchat and his car a little farther, alongside a closed depot. The businessman has slid across the seat and is snoring drunkenly.

Johnson and his spy, whose respective vehicles have left several minutes ago, could not have observed the incident. As for Kim, first to disembark of all the passengers—who step back with timid and reproving expressions, caused by the growling of the black dog— she is already far away. She has no special reason to go to Manneret's tonight; moreover she has been assigned no particular mission by her mistress, who thinks she is sleeping in her little room. Yet the girl, without having anything to do here, walks on as decisively as if she were feeling—as is more and more often the case—an absolute necessity to see the Old Man; and she is sure that he is expecting her too. She does not even wonder about the purpose of the experiments he makes on her, during each of her visits: she is not concerned to know if the drinks and injections he gives her are actually drugs he is testing, or magical philters which alienate the subject's will in order to leave her defenseless in the power of a third person, or of the experimenter himself. The latter, moreover, has not abused his powers hitherto, at least insofar as she can discover in her moments of complete consciousness. Of the hours she has spent in the modern Kowloon apartment, which looks like a fashionable clinic, some seem to her to have lasted very long; but there are others of which she has no recollection at all.

So that night, Kim finds Edouard Manneret seated at his desk; his back is to the door, as has already been said, and he does not even turn around to see who is coming in. So it is true, probably, that he knew she would come at this very moment. In any case it has been reported that she knocks at the apartment door and enters at once without waiting for an answer. Does she have her own key to get into the apartment or had Manneret left his key in the lock—or simply pushed the door closed, without latching it—in order not to have to get up again? But hasn't Johnson, a moment before, been obliged to wait for Manneret to come and open the door? Then it would be Johnson who had left the door not completely closed upon his departure: this is, as a matter of fact, what sometimes happens when a door is slammed too hard and the bolt reopens immediately, in the recoil of the impact. . . . All these details are probably of no importance, especially since the images of this visit have already appeared, in what precedes, apropos of the brown envelope containing the forty-eight sachets of powder, which the servant girl had collected for Lady Ava. The only question that remained was what she had done with the dog: she could not have brought it into the house, since these delicate animals cannot endure air-conditioned premises, or at least too great variations of temperature between the street and indoors. (Is this the reason why the Blue Villa, their habitual domicile, is still equipped with only prewar ventilators?) The solution of this problem now seems easy: Kim has left the dog in the building's vestibule, between the outer door to the street and the double glass door which leads to the stairway or to the elevators. With a customary gesture she has attached the end of the leash to a ring which seems to be here for this purpose, but whose presence she had not noticed upon her last visit. She would obviously have done better to keep the dog as a bodyguard until the third floor (or until the fifth?); this is what she thinks a little later, like every other time, while she retreats toward the corner of the room, the Old Man advancing slowly, matching step for step, with a face that frightens her, gradually gaining on her, his head towering over her now, motionless, the thin mouth, the carefully trimmed goatee, the mustache that looks like cardboard and the eyes gleaming with criminal madness. He is going to kill her, torture her, cut her up with a razor. . . . Kim tries to scream, like every other time, but, like every other time, no sound leaves her throat.

At this point in the narrative, Johnson stops: he thinks he has heard a scream, quite close, in the silence of the night. It is on foot that he has returned to the dock, from the hotel to which he had been driven back by the taxi with the closed windows. Taking his key from the rack, the Communist porter has informed him that a police inspector has just searched his apartment, though he has discovered no trace of this in the living room nor in the bedroom nor in the bathroom, so skillfully has the investigation been carried out. This discretion has disturbed him more than the too obvious surveillance of which he has hitherto been the object. Without taking time to change, he has merely armed himself with his revolver, which was still in its place in the shirt drawer, and has gone back downstairs. It was pointless to call a car: the scheduled departure of the next ferry left him plenty of time to get there by walking at an ordinary pace. Perhaps Johnson more or less consciously thought he could thereby avoid the indiscreet or disturbing comments of the persistent driver. But when he passed through the revolving door, he saw at once that the taxi was no longer there. Had it been parked in the square planted with traveler's palms behind the hotel?

Or had it, despite the hour, found another passenger? The American has subsequently observed nothing unusual around him, until the moment when, walking out onto the dock, he has heard that scream, a kind of gasp, or a moan which was not strictly a call for help, or some kind of a low and rather hoarse voice, or any sound from the nearby harbor, filled with junks and sampans that house whole families. Johnson has accused himself of being too nervous. On the dock as in the streets that led there, there was not a living soul; access to the ferry was open, but not attended, and for the moment neither passenger nor car was embarking. The waiting room was also empty and the ticket window seemed abandoned. In order to pass the time until the employee's return—there was no emergency—Johnson has gone back out onto the dock.

Now he has noticed the businessman Marchat's big car parked in front of the depot, a red Mercedes, probably the only one in the whole Colony. He has wondered what it was doing there and walked over to it, having nothing else to do. At first he has supposed that there was no one in the car, but after bending over on the driver's side, where the window was lowered, he has seen the young man lying on the seat: his temple was broken, the eyes out of their sockets, the mouth open, the hair sticky in a little puddle of already coagulated blood. From all appearances he was dead. On the floor of the car, near the emergency brake, there was a revolver. Without touching anything, Johnson has rushed to the telephone booth which stands against the glass wall of the waiting room outside. And he has called the police. He has given the description of the car and the exact point where it was parked, but he has decided not to name the victim; and he has hung up without having given his own name either. When he has returned to the ticket window the employee was still not there; he has appeared only about thirty seconds later and has given him a token without looking at him. Johnson has gone aboard through the automatic turnstile, after having dropped the token into the slot. The boat was almost empty; it left immediately afterward, when the sound of a police car's alternating siren could be heard in the distance. At Victoria, Johnson has taken a taxi, which has been driven rapidly, so that he has reached the Blue Villa early, around ten after nine more precisely.

Upon entering the large salon, he has been approached by that bald, stocky man whose skin is shiny and whose complexion is so red that he seems in constant danger of suffering a fit of apoplexy. The American, who had no reason to refuse, has accompanied him to the buffet to drink a glass of champagne, thereby making himself a party to interesting comments on the latest fraudulent intrigues devised by the importers of non-distilled alcoholic drinks. The fat man has thus monopolized him longer than Sir Ralph had feared; a good part of his life had been spent in remote countries and he described all kinds of scandalous situations, which he intended to cite as profitable examples for his friends and acquaintances; this evening, for example, apropos of illegal beverages, he has begun describing in detail the methods employed somewhere to make young girls, selected for their beauty in the street or even at parties, lose all desire for resistance, the girls then being imprisoned in special brothels in the city in order to serve the needs of thrill-seekers and sexual perverts. He was beginning to tell how a father had one day, quite by accident, recognized his own daughter in one of these houses, when the American, tired of his indiscreet chatter, had at last found an excuse to interrupt this over-resourceful narrator, or at least to stop listening to his stories: he had gone off to dance. For this purpose his choice had fallen on a partner whom he had never seen before this evening: a blond young woman in a décolleté white dress who moved gracefully. He found out later that her name is Loraine, that she had recently arrived from England, and that for the moment she was living at Lady Ava's.

A little later in the evening, a macabre piece of news had spread among the guests: one of the people who was expected today, a young man named Georges Marchand, known in town as such a serious boy, had just been found murdered in his own car. A Chinese prostitute, who was supposed to have spent part of the evening in his company (they had been seen together in a club, near Aberdeen), had been closely questioned by the police; although the victim's wallet had disappeared, it was thought to be a morals case rather than just a matter of theft. From this point on, comments and suppositions developed copiously, sometimes seasoned with quite preposterous details

by which Marchand himself would doubtless have
been astonished. The theatrical performance, scheduled for eleven, has occurred in spite of everything:
this Marchat, or Marchand, was not a habitué of the
house, and it was almost by accident that he had been
invited this time. No one in the audience, moreover,
knew him except by name; most people had never
even heard of him.

The main item on the program was a brief traditional comedy in two acts, with three characters: a
woman is caught between two men, engaged to one,
she begins to fall in love with the other, etc. The
part of the young woman is played by Loraine, and
that is the play's sole interest. In the middle of the
first act, selecting a moment when the stage is almost
in darkness and consequently reflects no light into
the darkened theater, I stand up furtively and reach
the little exit door, which I find by groping my way.
But I must have come to the wrong door in the darkness, for I do not recognize the place to which the
corridor I have followed leads. It is a kind of filthy
courtyard, lit by huge oil lamps, which must be used
to store props, for parts of the sets are strewn here
and there in great confusion. Against a half-dead
clump of banana trees is leaning a huge plywood panel
whose painted surface represents a stone wall, huge
rough-cut slabs which protrude irregularly, with iron
rings set at various heights, to which are attached old
rusty chains, the whole thing painted in rather clumsy
*trompe-l'œil*. A little farther away, in front of the
gable end of a shed, I also make out in the dim light

a fashionable shop front seen from the street: in the window under its English lettering, a mannequin in a clinging dress holds a big black dog on a leash. Without footlights and thrown here pell-mell, the whole thing no longer produces any sense of depth. I also discover some pieces of furniture which must belong to the opium den scene, as well as several door frames, windows, sections of stairs, etc.

Besides these pieces of stage sets, the courtyard is encumbered by a quantity of discarded objects: a dilapidated rickshaw, old rice-straw brooms, dismantled trestles, several plaster statues, many open crates in which are heaped the debris of dishes or broken glasses; in particular, there is a crate full of broken, chipped, footless champagne glasses, some even reduced to tiny, unrecognizable slivers. As I look for a way out of this chaos, I pass through regions which are not lit at all. I bump into piles of things which I afterward guess, from touching them, to be piles of thick magazines, on smooth paper, the size of the Chinese tabloids. Groping with one hand, I then touch something cold and moist which makes me recoil quickly. But, in a similar direction, and with the hope, still, of discovering a way through the increasing number of piles of paper, I stumble over other similar objects— flat, cold, rather sticky objects—whose nature I finally gather, from the stronger smell given off here: a huge number of big fish, probably regarded as inedible.

At this moment, I hear a voice behind me and turn around, more quickly than the situation demands. There is someone else in this courtyard: a man standing, motionless, whom I had taken for a statue; he points his arm in one direction, saying in awkward English: "It that way." I thank him and follow his advice. But it is not an exit he was pointing to, as I had thought; it is the toilet, also lit by an oil lamp, also filthy, its whitewashed walls covered with graffiti. There are chiefly Chinese inscriptions, most of them pornographic and indicating more imagination than is customary in such places. I also make out one sentence in English: "Funny things go on in this house," and a little lower, in the same careful though clumsy handwriting: "The old lady is a slut." I come out again only after having remained inside long enough not to disappoint my guide, in case he is still watching. But I am then filled with doubts concerning what he was pointing out to me just now, for I am now in front of an exit I didn't suspect, a passage through dense flowering hibiscus bushes, and suddenly I am back in the villa's grounds. I soon realize I am in the area of the groups of statuary I have mentioned several times, but tonight I see here a subject I am not yet familiar with and which probably wasn't here before, for it would have attracted my attention by its location at the intersection of two paths as well as by the dazzling whiteness of the new marble; it is doubtless a new acquisition of Lady Ava's. The surrounding earth, moreover, seems to be trampled in places, freshly spaded in others, as if a team of workmen had been working quite recently to install the piece. The pedestal has been buried so as to place the two figures on the same level as the people passing by, and they are life-size as well. This piece is called: "The Poison"; this word is clearly legible despite the darkness (to which my eyes are growing accustomed), for it is carved in large capital letters on the horizontal surface of the white marble, each letter underlined by a line of black paint. A man with a goatee and a monocle, dressed in a kind of frock coat, who is holding a little bottle in one hand and a stemmed glass in the other (a doctor?), is leaning over a girl entirely naked, her mouth open, her hair loose, who is squirming on the ground two steps away from him.

A little farther along the same bamboo-lined path, I glimpse the scene already described in which Lauren, having already exclaimed: "Never! Never! Never!", fires a pistol at Sir Ralph, who is standing about ten feet from her, the young woman having immediately dropped her weapon and remaining with her fingers spread, her arm half-extended forward, stunned by her own action, not even daring to look any longer at the wounded man, who has merely slumped a little, his back hunched, one hand clutching his chest and the other stretched backward, seeming to grope for something to cling to, before falling to the ground. But this scene no longer has much meaning now. And I continue on my way to the house. The entrance hall is empty, as is the large salon. Everyone must still be in the little theater, where the performance is probably not yet over; I walk down the red-carpeted stairs that lead to the theater.

But the theater is empty too, though Lady Ava is still on stage, performing alone before the empty chairs. Is this merely a rehearsal for a coming performance, which she is perfecting after the audience has left, tonight's play being over? (If I am not mistaken, at least, in supposing there has been a performance tonight.) Choosing at random, I sit in the middle of a row of chairs. Lady Ava has just worked the mechanism which closes the panel concealing the secret safe. She turns back toward the footlights and continues, still in her weary, broken, discouraged, scarcely audible voice: "There. Everything's ready. . . . Once again, I'll have settled the way things are arranged around me. . . ." Then, after a very noticeable pause: "There's nothing else to do." At this moment she stands perfectly still, very straight, at the very edge of the stage, precisely in the center. And the heavy velvet curtain begins closing, its two halves—one on each side—falling slowly, obliquely, from the flies. Instinctively I begin applauding. The actress bows, once, as the curtain goes up again, and I applaud more vigorously. But my solitary energy does not manage to generate much volume, this thin, stubborn sound, on the contrary, making the theater's emptiness all the more apparent. Hence the curtain, coming down a second time, closes for good as the lights come on in the theater. I walk to the exit, surprised nonetheless by the absence of an audience.

After the double swinging door, with its traditional pair of round windows, I meet Lady Ava coming from the wings, without having changed her costume or her make-up. She smiles at me sadly. "It was nice of you," she says, "to stay to the end. The play's absurd. And

I'm an old actress no one cares about. . . . They all left, one after the other." I've offered her my arm and she has leaned on it to climb the stairs. She was heavy and clumsy, as if she had suddenly been suffering from rheumatism in all her joints. I have feared she would never reach the top of the stairs. She has stopped halfway up to rest, and has said: "Won't you stay and take a glass of champagne?" I haven't dared refuse, for fear of seeming to abandon her in my turn.

We have settled down in the little mirrored salon, where there are all the Chinese *bibelots* in cases. There could be no question of ringing for a servant at this hour, of course, so that I have had to get a bottle myself, from the bar refrigerator, in the next room. But I have found only a few chipped glasses, which had probably been put aside to be thrown away afterward. Lady Ava had no more idea than I where the others were kept. Since these were clean, I have selected the two glasss in best condition and returned to the little salon. I have uncorked the bottle, and we have drunk in silence. On the little table, beside our glasses, was the photograph album. I have picked it up in order to leaf through it, more for something to do than out of genuine curiosity, since I have already looked at it a hundred times. And it has fallen open by chance to a very blond and beautiful girl I didn't know. Taken at full length, standing facing the camera, she is wearing only a black lace corset and a pair of openwork stockings; she has no shoes; a slender black velvet ribbon encircles her neck. She is holding her arms up, hands hanging limp, wrists crossed, just over her forehead. Her weight rests on her right hip, her left leg is a trifle bent, the knee ahead of the right one. "Her name's Loraine," Lady Ava says after a rather long pause.

Then she talks about her professional problems; and, apropos of the risks of being betrayed to the police or of even swifter retaliatory measures, she tells me once again about the death of Edouard Manneret. He was in the habit of leaving his apartment door open at hours when he was likely to receive visits, not wide open, but the bolt lying outside the lock, so that the door could be pushed open without his even noticing it, since he usually worked in an office at the other end of the hallway. The murderer was, apparently, well-informed as to the house, since he even knew where the safe was and how it worked. . . . I interrupt Lady Ava to ask her about this Manneret whom she has already mentioned to me several times. She answers that he was the putative father of those twin girls—whose mother was a Chinese prostitute—now in her employment, supposedly as servants, but whom she actually regards as her adoptive daughters. To say something agreeable, while appearing to take an interest in her stories, I tell her about the rather different relationship which gossip has suggested between the servants and their mistress. But Lady Ava objects more vehemently than the subject seems to me to require. "People will say anything," she says finally, her voice full of bitterness. Then, changing the subject abruptly, she adds: "Our telephone number's been changed. Now it's one, two hundred thirty-four, five hundred sixty-seven."

"Fine," I say. "At least that's easy to remember." This time, I have determined to leave. I stand up to say good-by, but I make the mistake of coming a little too close to one of the glass cases, where I glance distractedly at the shelf which holds the ivory statuettes. Lady Ava, who evidently is afraid to be left alone and is desperate for something to talk about, tells me that these come from Hong Kong, and she asks me if I've been there. I answer that of course I have; everyone knows Hong Kong, its harbor and the hundreds of tiny islands in the area, the sugar-loaf hills, the new airport on its promontory, the double-decker buses from London, the pagoda-shaped sentry boxes in which the policemen direct traffic at the intersections, the ferry which plies between Kowloon and Victoria, the big-wheeled red rickshaws whose green hoods form a broad shield over the passenger, without completely sheltering him from the sudden torrential rains which do not even diminish the speed of the barefoot runner, the throng in black canvas pajamas which closes its huge parasols, under which it took shelter from the sun a moment earlier, to seek refuge now in the arcades, the long streets with their covered galleries whose massive square pillars are covered, from top to bottom, on all four sides, by vertical posters with enormous ideograms: black on yellow, black on red, red on white, white on green, white on black. The sweeper steps back a little farther under the arcade, against the pillar, the water dripping from the upper floors (where the balconies are covered with drying laundry) is beginning to penetrate his shallow cone-shaped hat; the page of the magazine he is holding is already soaked through. Since he has looked at it enough, and can learn nothing more from the illustrations now, he decides to get rid of it; with an indolent gesture, he lets it drop back into the gutter.

The gutter is now inadequate to hold the water which continues falling from the sky; and it is the whole roadway, transformed into a stream from one sidewalk to the other, which carries the various rubbish accumulated since morning, while the intrepid rickshaw, drawn at a rapid gait by a coolie, raises in passing little fountains of muddy liquid. All the pedestrians, on the other hand, have taken shelter under the gallery, already so crowded by the encroaching displays of fruit or fish that there is almost no room to move. And it requires the huge black dog, whose low growls frighten the bystanders, for Kim to be able to make her way to the narrow stairs which, easily pivoting to her left, she begins to climb without . . . No, now the irritating problem of the dog arises again in all its acuity. It has been said somewhere that the servant girl left it in the vestibule between the door to the street and the lobby where the elevators are, but this is surely a mistake, or else it referred to another time, another moment, another day, another place, another building (and perhaps even another dog and another servant girl), for there are neither elevators nor lobby here, nor street door, but only a steep narrow staircase, without light or railing, flush with the façade of the building without any kind of door and rising in a single flight, without any intermediate landing on which to rest between floors.

Kim glances around to see what she can do with the bothersome animal. The next time, certainly, she will leave it behind, if there is a next time. Meanwhile, she must find a place for it somewhere. She does not see the smallest ring in the wall, even a rusty nail to which she could fasten the loop of the leash; and the unprepossessing way the animal behaves with strangers—Chinese or white—makes it quite impossible to entrust it to one of these unoccupied little men waiting here for the rain to stop, and who before that were perhaps waiting for it to begin, sitting on the ground in the corners or else standing, leaning against piles of crates or against the square pillars, staring through half-closed eyes at the young Eurasian girl who has just stopped in front of them, accompanied by her thoroughbred dog, and whom they immediately assimilate into their dreams.

The dog, meanwhile, not having the same scruples as its mistress and taking advantage of the latter's momentary confusion on its account, has tugged sharply on the leash, whose free end has surreptitiously slid out of the hand with its lacquered nails; and the dog has dashed into the stairway whose first flight it has covered in several bounds, disappearing in a second into the darkness, its presence then indicated only by the sound of its paws on the steps, which the curved claws scratch in their haste, and by the slapping noise of the leather leash that flies after it, snapping like a whip at the walls and the floor. There is, after all, no reason not to let it run upstairs. The only thing the old lady forbids is taking her precious beasts into air-conditioned buildings, which could scarcely be the case in this old house without any comforts and open to weather. Kim has only to follow the dog: in her turn she climbs the steep, narrow, wooden steps, a little more slowly, of course, and doubtless with a little more difficulty despite her apparent ease, the lateral slit of the tight dress not permitting her legs enough freedom, and the absence of light constituting a further obstacle for eyes accustomed to the bright sun outside.

On the second floor, at the top of this straight staircase as steep as an attic ladder, which rises perpendicularly to the street, there is a tiny rectangular landing off which open three doors: one to the right, one straight ahead, one to the left. No plaque indicates the name of the tenants who live here, nor, as is also possible, the modest firms which might have their offices behind these plain wooden doors, all three painted the same color brown, and now peeling. After having hesitated a moment, the servant girl decides to knock at the first door, the one on the right. No answer reaches her ears. Her eyes gradually becoming accustomed to the dark, she checks to see whether the door frames reveal any buzzer, or bell pull, or knocker. Then she knocks again, but still softly. As a final expedient, she tries to turn the filthy wooden handle, worn by use. It does not even turn on its axis; it would seem this door is no longer used.

Kim then tries the second door: the one in the middle. Seeing no buzzer here either, she knocks, without any better result. But this time the handle (in every point identical with the first) works, and the bolt slides out of the lock. The key had not been turned inside. Kim pushes the door open and finds herself on the threshold of a room so small that she has no need to step inside to take in at a glance the unpainted wooden table almost invisible under the stacks of files, the walls covered with pigeonholes whose crude planks, nailed roughly together, contain a considerable number of the same files, and the floor on which are lying in disorder, in every corner, still more files, always made in the same fashion (two pieces of canvas-bound cardboard held together by a strap misshapen by wear), and some of which disgorge a part of their contents: heavy manila folders of various colors, each bearing a huge black ideogram, drawn by hand with a thick brush. Behind the table, there is an ordinary chair with a straw seat. From the ceiling hangs a bare bulb, not lighted, the daylight entering the room by a tiny square opening, without a pane of glass but screened, set above the pigeonholes in the wall facing the door. There must be another means of access to this room, on the left or right side, for the servant girl is now faced by a man, whereas no one was in the room—neither on the chair nor elsewhere—at the moment she opened the door from the landing. He is a middle-aged Chinese, whose expressionless face is made still more impersonal by the absent gaze of myopia, behind steel-rimmed glasses. Dressed in a suit of European cut made of some thin, shiny material, his body is so slender—even nonexistent, it would seem—that the coat and trousers, though not extravagantly tailored, seem to float around a simple wire armature. The two persons say nothing, each seeming to think it the other's obligation to speak first: the Chinese because he is the one being disturbed, the girl because she hopes to have nothing to ask, from the moment that she is expected and that the man with whom she has an appointment obviously knows why she has come. Unfortunately she sees that the latter shows no intention of speaking, nor of letting her in without an explanation, nor even of encouraging her by a word or a gesture to indicate the purpose of her visit, which would however have facilitated her speaking. She therefore finally decides to say something on her own initiative. Very rapidly, she stammers a quite incoherent phrase, asking if this is where the agent lives, if the gentleman to whom she is speaking is the one she is supposed to meet here, if the merchandise is ready for her to take away, as planned. . . . But no sound can have come from her mouth, for the little man in the empty suit continues staring at her exactly as before, still waiting for her to make up her mind to speak. It was, as a matter of fact, impossible for her to have broached so many questions in so few words (moreover she does not even know what words were involved). Everything has to be begun all over again.

The servant girl now tries to imagine herself pronouncing several words. She realizes that this is easy, but that it does not lead anywhere. She must think of something else. She supposes that, in the street, the deluge is over, as suddenly as it had begun: the sun, as it warms the roadway, draws from the black and shiny asphalt strewn with little shapeless piles—a gray debris whose composition and origin are no longer discernible—a thick white steam which evaporates, accumulates, lingers like smoke, rises in spirals that quickly disappear. Men and women in shiny black pajamas emerge from under the gallery and again put up the big black parasols to protect themselves from the scorching rays, thus making movement easier along the crowded booths among which Kim advances with a determined gait, holding in one hand the paper on which is clearly written the address of the agent to whom she is going, and in the other the little rectangular purse embroidered with gilded beads, which she uses as a handbag and which bulges as if it had been stuffed with sand. . . . No, this remark does not concern the purse, which is actually quite flat, since Kim can hold it between two fingers as she turns unhesitatingly into the narrow staircase, which she climbs with a continuous, rapid, easy, uniform motion. Having reached the landing on the second floor, she knocks at the center door, that is, the one facing the stairs. A Chinese of about forty, in European clothes, immediately opens the door. "Mr. Chang?" she says in English. His face remaining impassive, he answers: "Yes. I am Mr. Chang." She says: "I'm here for the sale."

"I sell nothing," Mr. Chang says.

The servant girl is speechless. All the trouble she

has just taken, and for nothing? "But," she says, ". . . why?"

"Because I have nothing to sell."

"Nothing to sell today?" the servant girl asks again.

"Not today or ever," Mr. Chang says.

The servant girl explains: "It's for Madame Eva."

What is happening? The Eurasian girl is perplexed. It must be another Chang. The almost translucent little man in front of her has not spoken a friendly word, nor smiled since the beginning of their dialogue. No gesture, no change in the position of his body, no movement of his face has altered his immobility: he stands in the hallway, his lifeless eyes resting on this importunate visitor (whose height obliges him to keep his head raised) whom he ostensibly forbids to proceed any farther. But she persists:

"Do you know Madame Eva?"

"I do not have that honor."

"Then it's a mistake. . . . Excuse me. . . . I was looking for a Mr. Chang."

"I am Mr. Chang," Mr. Chang says.

"But you don't sell anything."

"No," Mr. Chang says, "here, we do appraisals."

"And do you know if there is anyone else in this house named Chang?"

"No doubt," Mr. Chang says. And he closes the door in Kim's face, leaving her standing for some time on the darkened landing, wondering what she should do now. Once again she consults the square of paper she is still holding in her hand: since she knows the text by heart, she needs no light by which to reread it; the address is quite plain. As she turns around, the servant girl notices, at the bottom of the stairs, at a much greater distance than she expected, the bright rectangle enclosing a bit of the sidewalk, occupied by many little persons clustered on the threshold of the building; they seem to be speaking to each other animatedly, making gestures with their hands and swinging their arms, while looking up toward the top of the stairs in the direction where she herself is standing, as if they had begun a great argument about her. Some even seem to be about to climb the stairs. Although she is certainly not visible from the other end of this dark passageway, Kim, vaguely uneasy, quickly knocks at the third door, the one to the left, from which she no longer sees the street. The door opens at once, as promptly as if someone were standing behind it, ready to intervene. It is the same Chinese with the steel-rimmed glasses, swimming in his narrow suit. He stares at the servant girl with the same neutral expression whose imaginary hostility cannot be strictly localized except in the delicate frame of the glasses. Kim is disturbed and glances around her, in order to make sure that in her haste she has not knocked at the same door as a moment before: not only is it not the same one, but this one is opposite the previous one, and the next flight of stairs, between the two, separates them without risk of confusion. In a voice less and less assured, the girl begins: "Excuse me . . ."

"Still nothing to sell," Mr. Chang says, interrupting her harshly. And he closes the door in her face, exactly like the first time.

Having no further recourse but to leave, Kim is about to go back down the stairs. She takes one step to the side and notices again, at the bottom of the steep stairs, the little men moving about, increasingly numerous and threatening to rush up the stairs. She quickly draws back out of their hypothetical field of vision, to begin climbing the next flight of stairs which is exactly the same as the first but rising in the opposite direction. On the landing of the third floor there are only two doors, the first of which is barred by three slender wooden laths nailed one on top of the other across the frame, to form a cross with six branches: two horizontal and four oblique (along the diagonals of the rectangle). The second door is wide open: this is the source of the vague light which made climbing the last steps easier. In a rather long room, where the light enters through a screened bay window opening onto a balcony covered with drying laundry, about a hundred people—mostly men—are sitting on benches arranged in parallel rows; they are all listening closely to an orator delivering a speech, standing on a little dais at one end of the room. But his speech is a mute one, consisting entirely of complicated, rapid gestures in which both hands play their part, and which is doubtless intended for deaf-mutes.

But now steps can be heard coming up from the lower part of the staircase, quick yet heavy steps, belonging to several individuals running at different rates of speed. They approach so quickly that the decision cannot await any further reflection. Since the stairs go no higher than this third floor, Kim quite casually enters the lecture hall where, with the assurance and naturalness of someone who had come here on purpose to attend this event, she sits down on the empty end of one of the benches. Yet some heads turn toward her and are perhaps surprised by her presence; her neighbors make signs to each other with their fingers, analogous to those of the speaker: it is not mostly men who are around her, but only men. She wonders what can be the subject of the meeting for which they are gathered; there are so many problems which do not concern women, or which at least cannot be discussed in front of them (which would make her situation all the more awkward). In any case, the question of discovering whether this is a speech in English or Chinese should not come up. (Is this certain?) Two new arrivals appear in the doorway (do they seem out of breath from climbing the stairs too rapidly?) who glance around the room, looking for empty places, that are rare and difficult to determine because of the absence of individual seats. Once they have noticed two located side by side, they hastily occupy them. Is it their steps which were heard echoing up the wooden staircase? And was it deaf-mute gestures which the little men on the sidewalk were making to each other, in the rectangle of light?

Now it is a British policeman in a short-sleeved shirt, khaki shorts and white knee socks who is framed in the doorway. Legs apart, hand resting on his revolver holster, he gives the impression of being stationed here on duty. Is this meeting a political one?

239

Could some Communist propaganda session have concerned the central commissariat of Queens Road more than the others? That is highly unlikely. Or could some criminal have concealed himself among the audience in order to escape his pursuers? Nothing has changed, however, in the behavior of the orator on the dais, nor in that of the audience on their benches. Kim is suddenly convinced, without any particular reason, that this abrupt intervention of the police has some relation to the death of the Old Man; she decides as a result that it is wiser to keep this belated protector of the peace from discovering her own presence in the house. First she takes the wise precaution of tearing into tiny fragments, which she gradually and secretly scatters on the floor, the piece of paper bearing the compromising address. Then taking advantage of the fact that the policeman has turned the other way, his back to the room, she stands up quietly and heads toward the other end of the long room, off which opens a double door, each panel of which has a small round glass window in it. Although this exit, judging by its traditional windows as by its swinging doors, seems to be the normal means of access to any meeting hall or auditorium, a notice is attached to it, showing a red ideogram printed on a white background, signifying that this is not an exit. Kim pushes one of the panels gently, it yields with no effort, and she slides through the gap. Before the door, which shuts automatically, is entirely closed behind her, she has time to see through the narrowing opening all the yellow faces which have turned toward her with a single movement. The two edges of the gap immediately come together.

At the end of a complicated, dark hallway which abruptly changes direction several times, the girl, walking faster and faster, comes out onto a staircase which she hurriedly descends; the narrowness and unaccustomed steepness of the steps accelerates her passage still further: she leaps down the steps two at a time, three at a time, she misses some which completely escape her count, she has the painful sensation of flying. This staircase is not straight, as she had thought at first, but constructed in a very steep spiral. On her way, she notices a calling card fastened to a door by four tacks: "Chang. Agent," in English of course. She continues her descent.

Now she is in a tiny office crowded with files. She has lost something. She searches feverishly among the colored cardboard folders, without relying on the misleading labels that have been written on them; or else the labels correspond accurately to the theoretical contents of the folders, but she is looking for a document that has inadvertently been put in the wrong place, or rather been hidden on purpose, in a file concerning matters bearing no connection to what she is looking for. Then she is in a courtyard where various discarded objects have been left: pieces of marble, iron beds, stuffed animals, old crates, mutilated statues, odd collections of pornographic Chinese magazines . . . (this episode, already past, no longer has its place here). Now we see the young Eurasian girl backed into the corner of a luxurious room, near a lacquer chest whose lines are emphasized by bronze ornaments, all escape cut off by a man in a carefully trimmed gray goatee who is towering over her. But now the big black dog comes on the scene; attached to a ring in the lobby of the building on the ground floor, it must have sensed, suddenly, that its mistress was in danger, and it has tugged so violently on its leash that a leather thong has yielded at once, near the collar; after having easily pushed open the glass panel opening onto the staircase, the animal, which has not had the slightest hesitation as to which direction to take, has reached the sixth floor in a few bounds.

As usual, Manneret had left the door of his apartment open. Before he has had time to turn around, the dog has leaped on him from behind and broken his neck with a single crunch of its jaws. Edouard Manneret, killed on the spot, then lies on the floor of his bedroom (or his study?), stretched out at full length, etc., while the servant girl, who has not made a move, stares at him with the same anguished expression she had had at the beginning of the scene, before the dog's arrival. If this expression is anguished, it is purely a matter of imagination, since none of its features betrays the slightest emotion. Similarly, when the girl is standing stiffly in front of the unpainted table, etc., with a Chinese of uncertain age seated opposite her; this is obviously the agent, whom she has therefore finally managed to reach and who moreover resembles, feature for feature, the false Mr. Chang, the appraisal man, except of course for the perpetual

Eastern smile—which is not a smile—appearing on this countenance. The servant girl takes out of the gilded-bead purse the money Lady Ava has given her. Mr. Chang counts the bills with a rapid finger and says: "That's right." After which, he indicates, with an almost imperceptible movement of his hand, a little side door whose existence she had not yet noticed. This door opens onto a tiny anteroom whose sloping ceiling must correspond to a mansard roof, which is quite impossible given the location of the room and the general structure of the building; this anteroom leads into a second office, quite similar to the other but empty of furniture and papers. It is here that the young Japanese girl (named Kito) is being guarded by the dog. Without having to return the way they had come, all three go out directly onto the landing by the door located opposite the one by which the servant girl remembers having originally come in, a door painted the same color brown and fitted with the the same worn and dirty wooden handle. The little anteroom thus passed under the sloping flight of stairs to the third floor. There is only one floor to walk down in order to be back in the covered arcade of Queens Road, deserted at this hour. Some inconsistencies remain in the foregoing; it has nonetheless happened, in every point, in this manner. The rest has already been reported.

I continue and conclude. Kito—as has been understood—is destined for the third-floor bedrooms of the Blue Villa. She will then be given by Lady Ava to an American, a certain Ralph Johnson, who raises opium poppies on the border of the New Territories. The story of the little Japanese girl having no other connection with the account of this evening, there is no use relating its various vicissitudes in further detail. The important thing is that Johnson, on that day . . . There's a lot of noise, up there, a lot of noise. It's getting louder, the rhythm is growing more insistent. The old mad king has an iron-tipped cane with which he accompanies his steps along the floor of the hallway, a long corridor that runs through the apartment from one end to the other. Have I said that this old king was named Boris? He never goes to bed, since he no longer manages to fall asleep. Sometimes he merely stretches out in a rocking chair and rocks for hours, banging the floor with the tip of his cane at each oscillation, to maintain the pendulum movement. I was going to say that on that evening, Johnson, who had happened to be the immediate witness of Georges Marchant's tragic end, found dead in his car in Kowloon, not far from the dock where the American arrived a few moments later to take the ferry to Victoria, that Johnson, then, had upon his arrival at the Blue Villa described the suicide of the businessman, whose action he attributed, along with everyone else, to an excess of commercial scruple, in a deal in which his partners had shown much less integrity. It seems, unfortunately, that his account—as lurid as fertile in emotions—has dramatically affected a young blond girl named Laureen, a friend of the mistress of the house and even, some say, her protégée, who came here precisely to marry this unfortunate young man.

From that day on, Laureen changed her life and even her character altogether; formerly docile, studious and reserved, she flung herself, with a kind of desperate passion, in pursuit of the worst depravities, the most degrading excesses. This is how she became an inmate of the de luxe brothel whose madam is none other than Lady Ava. And it is the latter who, showing the album of girls available to Sir Ralph, comments by this grim anecdote on the photograph in which her latest acquisition appears in the traditional black corset and openwork stockings, with nothing else below or above.

Sir Ralph carefully examines the picture being shown him. He regards the proposition as an interesting one, though the price seems very high. After some additional information of an intimate nature, followed by a moment's reflection, he announces his acceptance, on approval. Lady Ava replies that she was, for her part, certain of his answer and that he would have nothing to complain of. The introductions are to be made during a party that very evening, whose course has constituted the object of several detailed descriptions. It is this same Ralph Johnson, whose too frequent comings and goings between Hong Kong and Canton had finally attracted the attention of the political authorities of the British concession. Hence he was almost always followed by plain-clothes men, third-rate spies dissatisfied with their pay, who recorded without any conviction some of his movements with the sole purpose of filling up their notes, actually taken to indicate their own activity during

245

the day rather than to give any exhaustive information
as to that of the suspect under their surveillance. Most
of these contractual employees of the British secret
services worked clandestinely for private organiza-
tions, which they served with no more zeal or intelligence, but whose wretched investigations nonetheless
occupied a great part of their time. The less narrow-
minded of them had, moreover, been secretly rehired
by the many emissaries from Formosa or Red China,
among whom Johnson himself probably had to be in-
cluded; so that the schedule of his evening—estab-
lished by such observers—did not even involve a visit
to the Blue Villa: he had quite simply returned to the
Hotel Victoria for dinner and had not left it again. It
is the night porter who has furnished the information,
for a large tip.

Johnson occupies in this hotel—once luxurious but
long since out of fashion—a suite consisting of a foyer,
a living room, a bedroom, bathroom and terrace. He
has returned to it at seven-fifteen, noticed that the
monthly search of his papers had been made, with
the customary clumsiness, in the drawers of the desk
and the filing cabinet, and he has gone to take his
shower. He has then looked at his mail. The letters
from Macao, delivered during the afternoon, contained nothing particular. Johnson knows, in any case,
that no important matter can be discussed by mail,
since the secret service opens his correspondence before it is delivered to him. He finishes dressing (in a
light suit of white poplin), while making notes on the
proof sheet of an advertising poster he has to send

back once it is corrected. The bother of having to put on a silk shirt and his excessively heavy tuxedo, in such heat, has made him decide not to go to Lady Bergmann's party; he rereads the invitation card, with the printed words "cocktails, dancing," and the words "theatrical performance at eleven" added by hand (for only a certain number of the guests) ; he tears it across, then tosses it in the basket. He will telephone tomorrow to give the excuse of a migraine for his absence. Dining on tasteless meat and boiled vegetables in the huge, almost empty dining room, he glances through the *Hong Kong Evening*. It is here that he happens to see the headline announcing the death of Edouard Manneret.

The article is very brief, of the last-minute newsflash variety. Nothing is said as to the exact nature of this so-called accident; and there is not, of course, any reference to Kito. Nonetheless, we must now return to Johnson's relations with the little Japanese girl. The American has used her very little for his personal pleasures, since—as has been said—his senses found their employment elsewhere: the girl served only as a supernumerary, a secondary character, in some compositions in which Laureen always played the leading part—if not the gentlest one. This was during the time when Kito was an inmate of the villa; if Johnson subsequently removed her, it was with a quite different intention—to subject her to experiments on which he based his future wealth, which he saw as already considerable. (His present income, based on well-established enterprises in Macao and Canton, was of more modest dimensions.) It should be mentioned here that the cultivation of toxic plants which he had recently undertaken, on the other side of the border, involved many species besides poppies, hemp and erythroxylum: as a matter of fact Johnson sold, in the Chinatowns of the world, from the Indian Ocean to San Francisco, all kinds of remedies, poisons, youth potions, love philters, aphrodisiacs, whose effects—described in alluring terms by illustrated prospectuses, or by the advertisements of shops with a special clientele—did not involve the vendor's imagination exclusively. His latest idea, which would surpass the fame of the too famous "Tiger balms," was a preparation half derived from the science of plants and half from magic, whose formula he had discovered in the recent edition of a religious book of the Chou period. But Johnson was neither a magician nor a pharmacist nor a botanist. He merely possessed certain commercial gifts which he often exercised at the expense of his associates: he had joined forces, for example, under cover of one of the many companies he was constantly founding, with a young Dutchman of good family, named Marchant, who had ultimately committed suicide for reasons still undisclosed, but certainly linked with their mutual enterprises, apropos of which he himself had never felt the slightest embarrassment. The man he needed this time, for the development and testing of the potion, simultaneously a physician, a chemist, and something of a fetish expert, was the famous Edouard Manneret, who further possessed—it was said—a colossal fortune and probably had no lucrative expectations from the exercise of his talents. He was addicted, on the other hand, to both vampirism and necrophilia, so that the death of Kito, on whom the new product proved its efficacity by the absolute mastery it left to the beneficiary, must soon have passed into the losses and gains of the association.

The police are not concerned about the disappearance of a prostitute, even one underage; especially since the little Japanese girl, secretly arrived from Nagasaki on a smuggler's junk, did not figure on any official list or immigration form. Her bloodless body, marked only by a tiny wound at the base of the neck, just above the clavicle, was sold to be served with various sauces in a well-known Aberdeen restaurant. The Chinese cuisine has the advantage of making its contents unrecognizable. It is obvious, nonetheless, that the meal's origin was revealed—with proofs to support the matter—to certain customers of either sex with depraved tastes, who consented to pay high prices in order to consume this kind of meat; prepared with particular care, it was served to them in the course of ritual banquets whose setting, as well as the various excesses to which these celebrations gave rise, necessitated a private dining room located apart from the regular rooms. The fat man with the red face describes with delighted precision some of the perversions committed under such circumstances, then continues his story. Manneret, who had thus rid himself quite ingeniously of a bothersome piece of evidence, had made the mistake of coming to participate in one of these ceremonies. Under the effects of the euphoria induced by wine, a guest (a disguised policeman who had become a member of the group only in hopes of deriving some dishonest profit by doing so) was able to hear from his own lips, toward the dinner's end, certain remarks which, though not precisely clear, nonetheless gave the indiscreet inquirer the desire to know more. A skillful investigation, conducted among the servants and neighbors of the Kowloon apartment, revealed that he had not been wrong to follow this trail, one branch of which then led him to the New Territories plantation and to the American, Ralph Johnson.

When the policeman knew enough about Kito's death, he obviously wanted to blackmail Manneret, since on the one hand the latter's responsibility in the crime was quite direct, and on the other he possessed enough to pay a high price to get off free. Johnson's turn would come later. What then happens has remained confused. Doubtless Manneret, out of pride and defiance, refused to buy a silence which nothing, moreover, could guarantee. Or did he pretend to agree, in order to draw his blackmailer into a trap and get rid of him in another fashion? The fact remains that, at the moment when the officer appears in the millionaire's residence, in that ultramodern luxury apartment building with its labyrinths of mirrors and its sliding panels, Edouard Manneret makes him open the door and receives him in his office, offering him a chair and treating him cordially, though speaking of other matters, as is his habit in such cases. He asks his visitor if he has been in the Colony long, if the country agrees with him, if he endures the climate easily despite the difficult profession in which he is engaged, etc. While speaking, and without paying much attention to the fact that the other man answers only in monosyllables (embarrassed, annoyed, suspicious?), he takes the trouble to serve him an *apéritif* with his own hands, even apologizing for having to turn his back a few seconds while he is doing something at the little bar.

A moment later, they are sitting opposite each other; the crooked policeman in an armchair made of steel tubes, and beside him (on the narrow tray attached to the arm) the stemmed glass of delicate crystal containing a liquid the color of sherry, and Manneret himself in his rocking chair, where he rocks, smiling, while he continues the conversation. Twice his taciturn interlocutor grasps the engraved base of the glass and raises it to bring the liquid to his lips; but each time, he sets it down again on the tray, on the excuse of listening more closely to what his host is saying, so that the latter decides to be silent; and he stares at the policeman as if he were trying to disconcert him, in hopes that he will take a drink at last to gain assurance. Indeed, the man again begins his gesture that has already been interrupted twice, but, at the last moment, his gaze meets—above the carefully trimmed goatee and the slender, arched nose —the too brilliant eyes with their slightly squinting lids which are staring at him with what seems to him to be abnormal intensity. Does he suddenly remember

251

the disturbing products Johnson raises? Is he realizing that his host's *apéritif*, of which the latter has already drunk several mouthfuls, does not look quite the same as his own? He makes a sudden movement with his left hand, the movement of a man trying to drive off a mosquito (an absurd pretext in this air-conditioned house, whose windows cannot be opened to admit insects) and the glass he is holding in the other hand slips and falls to the marble floor, where it breaks into a hundred pieces. . . . The splinters which glitter amid the spilled liquid, the drops spattered in all directions around a central star-shaped puddle, the foot of the glass still almost intact and now bearing, instead of the goblet, only a triangle of curved crystal, pointed like a dagger—all this has long since been known. But I ask Lady Ava why the blackmailer has not, upon his arrival at Manneret's that evening, discussed his intention of obtaining payment of a first installment at once, since matters had reached this point.

"He probably said why he was there," she answers; "the Old Man must have pretended not to hear the remark and he covered it up with his chatter about hard work, the climate, and the drinks. The other man preferred not to make the conversation difficult, since he was certain of having all the trump cards in his own hand and thought he would lose nothing by a few minutes' chat, which left his man time for thought."

"Hadn't Manneret already had several days to think?"

"No," she says, "that's not certain. His friendliness

at first was the result of the fact that he still didn't know precisely what it was this man wanted, whom he had met once at a dinner in Aberdeen, and who had turned up on some excuse or other—something to do with the building, for example."

"Manneret had his office to deal with such matters. Even his checks were signed by his attorney. He no longer bothered to deal in person with anything except very big deals; and even then, not before they had gone through the hands of his advisers, who studied them in detail and then gave him the results of their calculations."

Lady Ava reflects on this aspect of the problem, which takes her a little unawares, for no reference has yet been made to Manneret's professional activities. But she quickly recovers herself: "Well," she says, "the excuse could have had some more intimate nature: with him, there was no lack of reasons."

"So it was an intimate reason, but with no connection to Kito's death?"

"Yes, that's it: he was selling little girls, or heroin, or something."

"Yet if Manneret hadn't had good reasons to think he was in danger, he wouldn't have tried to poison his visitor right away, or drug him, or something of the kind."

"Who says that's what he did?"

"That detail of filling the glass with his back turned, and with a liquid which didn't have quite the same color as the real sherry from the bottle?"

"Oh no! That could be just the crooked policeman's imagination, or his bad conscience. Such people are suspicious on principle. And in any case, he didn't risk anything by getting rid of the drink once he suspected it, even slightly."

"Right. Let's say things went just as you say: the man comes, supposedly to sell dope, Manneret talks about one thing and another, trying to sound him out, and see whether he's dealing with an *agent provocateur* or a blackmailer. Right. . . . Then what did that remark about his visitor's 'hard job' mean?"

"I don't know. . . . Perhaps the other man had said straight off that he was in the police, to inspire confidence."

"Let's say he did. Then the policeman explains the real purpose of his visit, and demands money. Does he name a figure?"

"No. At first he must proceed by allusions: 'Don't you think it would be in your interest, my dear sir, to keep it from being discovered how you . . .' You see?"

"All right. And Manneret pretends he hasn't heard a word, he sips his sherry and goes on rocking and keeps talking—about one thing and another. Maybe he really hasn't understood what the man wants, if the insinuations were too obscure. The other man isn't in any hurry: he figures he has time and that he will finally make his point. . . . Then why did he kill Manneret, a few minutes later?"

"Yes," she says, "that's the question."

"And a second question is about the kind of glass— you don't serve sherry in a champagne glass. Besides, the pointed splinter that sticks up from the base, the one that could also serve as a 'dagger,' doesn't correspond to the wide curve of the glass."

"No, obviously not. It must have been something longer than it was wide, and conical rather than round at the bottom: what they call a 'flute'. . . ."

"And the crystal surely wasn't as thin as the kind in a champagne glass or a flute, if it was used as a weapon—and a mortal one into the bargain."

"But actually," she says, "that isn't the weapon that killed him. It was all a setting intended to camouflage the crime as an accident. The murderer used a Chinese stiletto with a spring blade covered with poison—once it's telescoped, it's easily concealed in any little pocket, or even in the hollow of the palm. It was afterward that he arranged the body on the fragments of the broken glass, as if the wound at the base of the neck had been produced by the crystal point still attached to the stem: 'Manneret must have fallen with a glass in his hand . . .', etc."

The murderer had added some elements to complete the scene: a little empty ampoule that had contained morphine, intended to explain the millionaire's unsteadiness at the moment of his strange fall: a sliding glass panel, half closed—almost invisible—against the edge of which he must have crashed; finally, the alarm clock on the other side of this plate glass, on the desk, with the alarm hand set at the precise moment of the death. . . . The alarm rang; to shut off this irritating noise, Manneret has stood up from his rocking chair, holding his glass of sherry in one hand; in his addict's clumsiness and haste, he hasn't seen that the glass partition is sliding across his path, barring his way. More concerned with decoration than verisimilitude, the theater director also removes the corpse's shoes and puts them back on inversely: the right shoe on the left foot, and the left shoe on the right foot. A final detail before leaving the stage: with deceased's pen and ink, on the very page´ he had been writing, after the last, hesitant words—about half a line at the end of a long interrupted paragraph which already descends to the middle of the page: "to foreign parts, and not gratuitous" —he concludes, imitating the uncertain calligraphy: "but necessary"; then he draws an oval fish, with its three fins, its triangular tail and its big round eyes.

It is in this state that Kim finds matters when she enters the apartment, having merely had to push open the door whose bolt was not fastened, which has surprised her. She stops in the middle of the foyer, her ear cocked. Not a sound can be heard throughout the house. She decides that Manneret is still at his desk, in the office. She walks in this direction, silently as usual. In the den, separated from the office by a glass panel which is half shut, she sees the Old Man lying at full length on the floor, on his belly. Only his head is turned to one side, the left hand still holding the stem of a broken glass which has slashed his throat in his fall. All around him are fragments of crystal, the spilt sherry, and blood, but in quite small quantities. Kim approaches with tiny, muffled steps, as if she were afraid of waking the dead man, on whose face she keeps her eyes fixed. Noticing the delicate wound and the point of glass piercing it, the young servant girl cannot help raising her hand to her own neck, at the place where, just above the left clavicle, her fingers encounter the still recent little scar. Then her mouth opens gradually and she begins screaming, without taking her eyes off the corpse, and this time her scream fills the whole apartment, the whole house, the whole street. . . .

No, it is still the same mute scream, which cannot escape her throat as she dashes down the stairs, two at a time, three at a time. As she passes, the doors open, dark figures are framed in the doorways, silhouetted against the bright light of the foyers, which makes it impossible to make out the faces. Yet it is evident from their clothes that it is men who appear on each landing and fling themselves in pursuit. They must have seen the Old Man's body, or the blood dripping down through the floor, and they think she has killed him. There are more of them on each floor. She leaps down the steps four at a time, five, six, but her delicate gilded shoes make no sound on the elastic surface of the stairs, and the others too, behind her, run faster and faster on the padded stairs. . . . Yet they do not seem to be gaining ground on the fleeing murderess, for when she turns to look behind her, she sees only the empty and silent staircase.

Then, without her having realized it, there is someone quite close to her, already descending the last flight that leads to the landing where she herself has just come to a halt. The place, fortunately, is very

257

dimly lit. Cautiously, Kim draws back into an even darker corner, where she presses against the wall. Her dark dress will help her to remain unnoticed. . . . Fortunately, for the person who is approaching is doubtless looking for her; he is a tall man wearing a goatee and carrying a metal-tipped cane. Elegantly dressed in a suit of severe cut, he walks with a firm yet supple gait: the cane must be merely an ornamental or offensive accouterment. When he comes opposite her, Kim, for a second, has the impression that he is the Old Man, but then she remembers that she has killed him. So it is only someone of the same age and who looks like him. He looks to the right, then to the left, in order to discover the criminal's hiding place; yet he passes oblivious in front of the servant girl crouching in the corner, frozen with terror and about to faint from holding her breath so long. He moves away a little, leans on the railing and bends over it, to examine the lower part of the staircase. Certain that she will be discovered soon, Kim raises and puts into her mouth the piece of paper containing the compromising address; she moistens it with saliva, nibbles it and rolls it under her tongue, chews it carefully so as to swell it into a slippery wad which is immediately transformed into a gluey, tasteless paste which she swallows with disgust. But the almost imperceptible sound of her lips on the little piece of still stiff paper, at the beginning of the operation, must have attracted the pursuer's attention: he turns around and inspects the landing in every direction. Then he walks stealthily toward one of the doors, and brings his cheek close to the varnished wood to listen to what is going on inside; he probably hears nothing of interest, for he returns to the equidistant, parallel and vertical iron rods which support the railing. He also rests his ear on this, as though in hopes of registering the metal's revealing vibrations. Obtaining no further result here, apparently, he begins descending the next flight.

But after three or four steps, he stops again and seems to change his mind: inspired by some suspicion, he is about to climb back up. Kim notices, then, that the door which is closest to her hiding place is not quite closed. She pushes it open gently, without making the hinges creak, just wide enough to slip inside. Once the door is back in its original position, the darkness of the place is complete. Immediately, Kim feels herself brushed by hands, two huge hands which grope their way, caressing the smooth, thin silk of her dress. She bites her lower lip to keep from crying out, while the caresses become more precise and insistent. Outside, the man has returned to the landing: he too has noticed the door which is not quite closed. (Is this because of Kim's movements?) She hears him scratching with his nails, as if he were trying to discover some device whose functioning would open the way to him. Silently she leans harder against the door, in order to press it closed and make the man believe the bolt is fastened. But the pressure increases, at the same time, from the other side. The young woman arches her body and strains all her muscles, while the two huge hands continue to explore her armpits, her breasts, her waist, her hips, her belly, her thighs. She persists, pressing with all her weight, all her strength, so that finally the beveled bolt shoots home of its own accord, entering the lock with a dry click, like a shot which echoes throughout the house.

At the same time, the light goes on. In the foyer, Edouard Manneret comes toward her. It is he who has flipped the switch. The young Eurasian servant girl catches her breath. "I found the door open," she says. . . . "I came in. . . ." The Old Man still has the same half-smile and too shiny eyes. He says: "And you were right. You're welcome here. . . . I was expecting you." Then, after a pause, during which he stares at her with an embarrassing insistence: "Have you been running? . . . Didn't you take the elevator?" She answers that she did not, that she has merely been walking fast, and that she walked up because of the dog. And, when he asks her where the dog is, Kim explains that she has left it, as usual, attached by its leather leash to a ring, in the vestibule. We know that the animal will manage to free itself, sensing that its mistress is in danger, etc.

If Manneret has already just been murdered, this scene takes place earlier, of course. And now it is Mr. Chang, the agent, who comes to meet Kim, in the little room she has just entered. (The sound of the bolt clicking, when she has pushed the door closed, is still in her ears.) Mr. Chang still shows the same half-smile so widespread in the East, where it is probably no more than a sign of politeness. He asks her if she has been running. Silent as usual, she merely shakes her head. He does not question her about the dog. It is on this day that the agent hands her the heavy brown paper envelope stuffed with forty-eight sachets of powder. She immediately walks downstairs and finds herself back in the middle of Queens Road, in the noisy, sun-drenched swarm of rickshaws, shiny black oilcloth pajamas, vendors of fish and spices, porters with shoulders bent under the long, traditional yoke, on the ends of which are hung the reed baskets. When Kim returns to the house, the old lady, alone in her room, does not notice that the white silk dress is quite rumpled, crushed, soiled with grayish stains that cover wide areas where the material's sheen has entirely disappeared. The pretty servant girl will merely be punished for having let the black dog go into an air-conditioned building.

As a matter of fact, the girl has been forced to confess her mistake. In order not to say that she has simply attached the precious beast to a ring somewhere, she still prefers the version—which she considers less dangerous—of the sweeper standing at the foot of the stairs: she has entrusted the dog to him, but he has let the end of the leash get away from him, out of laziness, and the animal has dashed upstairs to join his mistress, dragging the leash which flies behind him and whips the wooden steps. The municipal employee in a Chinese hat then lowers his arm, which is no longer holding anything, toward the broom handle. A vague smile hovers around his mouth and his eyes. He has nothing else to do but go on sweeping. At the end of the rice-straw sheaf, curved by use, appears a new example of the same illustrated magazine; it is at least the twelfth he has picked up since he has started working. (When?) This is certainly last week's issue. Although he has exhausted all it contains, since he cannot read and must be satisfied with the pictures, he leans down nonetheless to pick up this one in its turn. And once again he stares at the elegant party taking place in the huge salon filled with mirrors and gilded moldings.

Under the sparkling chandeliers, young women in low-cut evening dresses are dancing in the arms of partners in dark tuxedos or white dinner jackets. In front of the buffet covered with silver platters, a little fat man with a very red face is talking, head tilted up, to an American much taller than he, who has to lean over to hear what he is saying. A little way off, bending down to the marble floor, Lauren knots the gilded thongs of her sandal around her ankle and instep. Off to one side, near the window recess with its heavy, drawn curtains, Lady Ava is still sitting on her colorless sofa; her tired eyes stray along the walls whose various panels are decorated with pictures of various sizes, all of which show her as a young woman standing at full length and resting one hand lightly on the back of an armchair, or else seated, or reclining, or on horseback, playing the piano, or merely her head and bust, enlarged to giant proportions. She is wearing feather boas, veils, huge plumed hats; elsewhere she can be seen bareheaded, with ribbons in her hair, or with corkscrew curls that fall to the hollow of her shoulders, against the white flesh. There are also statues in their niches, between columns of red or green porphyry, representing her in active poses, making huge vague gestures with her round arms and turning to one side, or else toward heaven, with an exalted expression. Voluminous vaporous materials float around her body, scarfs of *mousseline,* trains of tulle, veils of bronze and stone. I walk past all this without stopping: I have had a hundred occasions to examine these sculptures, these paintings, these pastels, which I know down to the very signatures, almost all of famous names: Edouard Manneret, R. Jonestone, G. Marchand, etc. The huge room is made still more impressive by the absence of any living person, whereas I am accustomed to seeing it full of people, agitation, noise; there is no one here tonight except an innumerable, mute, motionless, inaccessible woman who multiplies her studied, grandiloquent, exaggeratedly dramatic poses, and who surrounds me on all sides, Eve, Eva, Eva Bergmann, Lady Ava, Lady Ava, Lady Ava.

After the large salon, I walk through other empty rooms. It seems the servants themselves have vanished; alone, I climb the grand staircase up to the room that belongs to the mistress of the house. She is lying on her huge canopy bed, attended only by one of the Eurasian servant girls standing near her, who silently leaves as soon as I arrive. I ask Eva how the doctor has found her, how long she has slept, if she feels better this evening. . . . She answers with a remote smile of her gray lips. Then she looks away. We remain that way for a moment, without saying another word, she staring at the ceiling and I still standing at her pillow, unable to keep from staring at her wizened face, the deepening wrinkles and her hair that has turned white. After some time—a long time, probably—she begins talking, saying that she was born in Belleville, near the church, that her name is neither Ava nor Eve, but Jacqueline, that she has not married an English lord, that she has never gone to China; the fancy brothel, in Hong Kong, is merely a story people have told her. In fact she wonders now if it wasn't actually in Shanghai, a huge baroque palace with gaming rooms, prostitutes of all kinds, fine restaurants, theaters with erotic performances and opium dens. It was called "Le Grand Monde" . . . or something of the sort. . . . Her face is so blank, her gaze so remote, that I wonder if she is still quite conscious, if she is not already a little delirious. She has turned her head toward me, and suddenly she seems to notice me, for the first time; she fixes her reproving eyes on me; her face is severe now, as if she were noticing me with horror, or with incredulity, or with astonishment, or as though I were an object of scandal. But her pupils begin to drift, gradually, to turn back toward the ceiling. She has also been told that meat was so rare there, and children so numerous, that little girls who didn't find a protector or a husband soon enough were eaten. But Lady Ava does not believe that this detail is true. "It's all stories," she says, "invented by travelers."

"Who knows?" she says again after a long silence, without taking her eyes from the white surface above her, whose stains she has once again begun to inspect. Then she asks me if it is dark yet. I answer that it has been dark for some time. I was going to add that night falls quickly in these latitudes, but I refrain. Raising my head, I notice in my turn the reddish stains with complicated, precise outlines: islands, rivers, continents, exotic fish. It is the lunatic who lives upstairs who, when he had a fit one day, spilled something on his floor. Today it seems to me that the damaged area has grown even larger. And here is Kim, whose footsteps can never be heard, returning now toward the bed, carefully carrying a champagne glass filled to the brim with some golden-yellow medicine which from a distance resembles sherry.

And meanwhile, Johnson is still pursuing the money he cannot find, from one end of Victoria to the other: Wales Road, Wishes Road, Queens Road, Queen Street, Lucky Street, Goldsmith Street, Taylor Street, Edouard Manneret Street. . . . And in the middle of the night, he keeps running into closed doors, locked gates, chains. And even if the banks were open, what bank would accept the terms he offers? He must, however, think of something or someone, before daybreak, who will rescue him; Lauren has not given him any more time, and it would not be wise for him, in any case, to remain a day longer in the British concession, waiting for the police to arrest him for good. At the ferry dock, arriving from Kowloon, there was only one rickshaw at the stand, which was lucky, given the hour. Johnson has refused to ask himself questions about this unhoped-for piece of luck, as about the amiability of the runner who seems disposed to take him wherever he wants to go for the rest of the night and who is patiently waiting for him where he stops, when at least he manages to go in somewhere, as is presently the case at the house of that Chinese agent where he has seen a light; he has not even had to pound very long, with his fists, against the wooden shutter that walls up the booth on the street side: hurried steps are heard on the stairs, and an old woman in a black European gown has opened the door. She has nonetheless pointed out that he could have pushed the door open himself, since the screws had been removed in preparation for his arrival. Since she grabbed him by the lapel of his jacket to lead him faster up to the second floor (by a steep, straight, narrow staircase), overwhelming him with lamentations in a piercing voice, in a mixture of crude English and a northern dialect he could grasp only in fragments, but in any case describing her husband's health, he has finally understood that she took him for the doctor whom she had sent a neighborhood child to fetch. Without telling her the truth, still in hopes that the sick man might nonetheless do something for him, Johnson has followed her to a rather large room on the second floor occupied by several pieces of French furniture of 1925 style, placed regularly along the walls and which seem to have been conceived for a tiny attic, so that considerable space is left between each piece. The man is lying on his back, arms and legs extended across the damp and wrinkled sheets of a varnished wooden bed whose entire surface he covers, although he himself is puny enough. On account of the heat, which is quite unaffected by the tiny electric fan set on a cane chair, he is wearing only a pair of white cotton drawers which reach to his knees. His skinny body and his worn face have the same greenish-yellow color as the wallpaper.

Johnson asks the woman what disease her husband is suffering from. As she stares at him in astonishment, he suddenly recalls that he is the doctor, and he immediately corrects himself: "I mean: where is the pain?" But the old woman has no idea. She must be beginning to wonder why he has neither bag nor stethoscope, if she is used to Western medicine. Or else she has hitherto had dealings only with Chinese practitioners, and it is in desperation that she has sent for an Englishman this time; if that is the case, she cannot be surprised by anything, not even at seeing him in evening clothes. Johnson also tells himself that the real doctor will soon interrupt this farce, and that he will have to hurry, before his arrival, to broach the matter of a deal with the agent, if the latter is still in a state to discuss loans and collateral. The man has not moved since the American has come into the room, not even flickered his eyelids, although his eyes are as wide open as those of a Chinese can be; nor do the skinny sides of his chest seem to be rising and falling; and when he is asked what kind of pain he feels, he does not even seem to have heard. Perhaps he is dead already. "Look," Johnson begins, "I've got to have some money, a lot of money. . . ." But the old woman begins uttering new shrieks, scandalized this time, at the sight of a practitioner who does not hesitate to demand his fee before beginning the consultation, as if he were afraid he might not be paid afterward. Johnson tries to explain his situation to her, but she does not listen to him, runs toward a little wardrobe closet and returns with a bundle of ten-dollar bills which she tries to make him put in his pocket. The American finally takes some bank notes and puts them on the night table, no longer daring to continue his doubtless futile request. Moreover, it is absurd to think that this petty moneylender, even willing and in good health, could obtain the enormous sum he needs in time. Suddenly abandoning his efforts, Johnson hurriedly runs back down the stairs, pursued by the old woman's imprecations.

The next scene takes place on the nighttime quay of a fishing port, Aberdeen probably, although it takes a long time to get here in a rickshaw. The setting is visible only in part, under the meager lighting of some lanterns, each of which sheds its yellow light only on the objects in its immediate proximity, so that nothing can be discerned in its entirety, but merely disconnected fragments: a cast-iron mooring post from which extends a taut halyard, other ropes coiled and forming a kind of loose collar on the wet cobbles, half of a ragged girl sleeping on the ground against a huge empty basket, two thick iron rings set about a yard apart and at the same level in a vertical field-stone wall, with a chain linking them in a slack curve, hanging freely on each side, wooden crates piled up and huge metallic fish with spindle-shaped bodies arranged neatly in the top one, water rippling in silver wavelets between sampans and boats anchored in all directions, the plank pier which runs to first one and then another, rising and falling, leading from the shore to a junk moored a little farther out. Coolies, each carrying a huge bulging sack of jute on his shoulders, follow these rocking catwalks which yield under their bare feet and sway alarmingly, without ever casting one of the porters who follow each other at an interval of four or five feet into the black water or the boats. Since they cannot pass each other on the narrow pier, they all return together, unloaded, six short men in Indian file, making the flexible planks dance all the more vigorously; and they return to pick up a new load in a dark zone where some truck, buffalo cart or wagon must be parked. An older man with a sparse long beard, wearing blue overalls and a skullcap, watches them go by and notes the number of sacks they carry in a notebook much longer than it is wide. It is to him that Johnson speaks, asking in Cantonese if the junk being loaded is Mr. Chang's. The man does not answer, still watching the movement of the little men in shorts who are continuing their operation. Taking his silence for acquiescence, Johnson asks the sailing time and the boat's destination. Still obtaining no reply, he adds that he is the American who is to be taken as far as Macao. "Passport," the supervisor says without taking his eyes off the improvised catwalk; and he merely glances at Johnson, who, rather astonished by this official formality with regard to a clandestine passage, nonetheless holds out the document. "Departure this morning at six-fifteen," the overseer says, handing back the passport. As he replaces it in his inside right pocket, Johnson wonders how the man will be able to recognize his passenger, whom he has not once attempted to examine. But now there is nothing left in the silence but the water washing between the sampans, the bare feet slapping in cadence on the cobbles, or on the wet planks which bump against the gunwales.

Afterward, there is the opium den, already described: a bare white décor consisting of a series of tiny cubical rooms, without furniture, entirely whitewashed including the dirt floor, on which customers in black pajamas are lying everywhere, against the walls or in the middle of the rooms, which communicate by rectangular openings in the thick walls, without doors of any kind and so low that Johnson must bend double in order to pass through. What does he hope to find here? The habitués do not seem to be in a position, judging from their clothes, to furnish him the money he wants, nor from their behavior to discuss obtaining it for him.

Then we see Johnson at an intersection in the center of town, probably, for under a street lamp sharp black shadows extend from people and things alike. He is talking with another man, a European apparently, wearing a light suit and a raincoat with the collar up, and a felt hat with its brim pulled down over his eyes, who is showing him on the rear part of a bank façade—whose name appears in huge letters above the principal entrance: "Bank of China"—a small fire escape leading to a window of the second floor which is not fitted with an iron grille, unlike all the others on the upper floor as well as on the ground floor. There is no one else in the field of vision, no car driving in the vicinity or parked along the curb; the rickshaw itself is no longer visible. The man in the raincoat must be trying to explain some piece of mischief to the American; but the latter, estimating the likelihood of success of such an enterprise, makes a grimace of doubt, expectation, or even refusal, even clearer in the close-up which follows.

This face is soon followed by a scene in a little bar. (Are there bars still open at this hour of the night?) Two customers, sitting beside each other on tall stools, are seen from behind, leaning over the counter on which they have set their champagne glasses. They seem to be talking to each other in low voices. To the right, a Chinese waiter in a white jacket, in a slightly higher position between the counter and the racks where the bottles are lined up in closest rows, watches them out of the corner of his eye, one hand stretched out toward a telephone in a niche.

Then the images follow one another very rapidly: Johnson and Manneret in an interior setting difficult to identify (was it these two who were talking in the bar, where they had arranged to meet?), now making broad gestures, which it is quite impossible to interpret. Then Edouard Manneret in his rocking chair and the American facing him, saying: "If you don't, you better be careful what happens to you!", and to the left, in the foreground, Kito telling herself: "Now he's threatening to kill him!" Then Johnson and Georges Marchat drinking champagne in a garden, near a flowering hibiscus bush. Then Johnson striding away from a big Mercedes parked in front of a closed depot in the Kowloon harbor (the name "Kowloon Docks Company" appears above the iron shutters), and glancing back as he hurriedly leaves the scene. Johnson in conversation with a fat man in front of a buffet covered with silver platters, at an elegant party. Johnson presenting his passport to a police lieutenant, in a steep alley that leads to a staircase not far from a small open military car, behind the wheel of which is sitting another policeman, the lieutenant saying: "A bartender saw you with him, you were making a proposition, and a Japanese prostitute heard you. . . ." Johnson in his hotel room discovering that his papers have been searched again, and deciding to add, for the benefit of the secret service agents on their next visit, a forged document which he begins to write at once, imitating Marchat's handwriting: "My dear Ralph, I'm writing you this brief note to reassure you about your situation: everything will be all right, you'll have the money you need in plenty of time; so there's absolutely no use going to Manneret, or borrowing the money from anyone else." Signed: "Georges." And in a postscript underneath: "It's still not known who owned the heroin laboratory the police have discovered. In my opinion, it must belong to those Belgians from the Congo who want to buy the Hotel Victoria to turn it into some kind of brothel. I hope they arrest every one of those drug merchants who are messing up the Colony."

After having put this paper among the letters recently received, inside a green folder in the top left-hand drawer of the desk, Sir Ralph goes into the bathroom to take a shower; then he puts on a dress shirt and his tuxedo, carefully tying his dark-red bow tie. He still has time to have dinner somewhere before going to Lady Bergmann's party. In the hotel lobby, as he hands his key to the porter, Sir Ralph gives him a wink of complicity; and he leaves by the rear door that opens onto the little square planted with traveler's palms, for it is on this side that he has the best chance of finding a taxi. A car, as a matter of fact, is parked at the curb; he gets in and is driven to the ferry. Since the heat in the back seat is stifling, he lowers the windows on both sides: although the air from outside is not much cooler, the car's movement makes it endurable nonetheless, and it thus becomes easier to watch the women strolling in front of the brightly lit shopwindows under the giant fig trees.

Once Sir Ralph is on the boat, he notices a girl in a tight fitting dress, slit very high up the side, who is holding on a leash a huge black dog with pointed ears; she is strolling along the covered deck, her gait supple and regular, beside the water that is invisible in the darkness but making the sound of ripping cloth against the side of the ferry. Her body moving under the thin silk gives her a provocative look, despite her reserved attitude. When she tries to restrain the dog pulling a little too hard on the taut leather leash, the young woman makes a short, sharp, almost imperceptible cobra hiss between her teeth. Several times, during the twenty-minute crossing, Sir Ralph, passing her

273

on the deck, meets her blue eyes, which calmly return his stare. But he does not speak to her, after all, perhaps because of the dog which growls when strangers approach. At the Victoria landing there are still many taxis; the American selects one, of a recent model, to drive to the little harbor of Aberdeen, where he will be dining in a well-known restaurant, floating in the middle of the roadstead.

There are not many people, this evening, in the large square room with a pool in the center, in which many huge blue, violet, red or yellow fish can be seen. A slender girl in a close fitting silk dress, probably a Eurasian girl who resembles the passenger on the ferry, dips them out one after the other with a long-handled net which she manipulates with grace and skill, offering them alive, wriggling, their shiny bodies caught in the meshes of the net, to the customer seated at his table, so that he can choose the one he wants to eat. Returning to shore on a lantern-lit sampan rowed by a slender girl in a close fitting dress, etc., with a gait both provocative and reserved, etc., etc., who manipulates the long gondolier's oar with grace and skill, making undulating movements that slide the thin, shiny silk over her skin . . . (that's enough, up there! the sound of steps, and the iron-tipped cane which repeatedly pounds the floor . . .), Sir Ralph notices, in the dim light of the harbor lanterns, a row of coolies carrying on their bent shoulders sacks stuffed with some (clandestine?) merchandise to a huge junk —without lights—moored to the quay by a long cat-walk which zigzags from gunwale to gunwale through the flotilla of little boats. A third car then takes him to the Blue Villa, where he arrives at ten after nine, as planned.

Shortly after he enters the large salon, where some couples are already dancing self-consciously, he is taken aside by the mistress of the house. She has some serious news to tell him: Edouard Manneret has just been murdered by the Communists, on the—obviously false—pretext that he was a double agent in the Formosan service. Actually, the murder was the conclusion of a much more confused, much more complex affair. In any case, Johnson is among the immediate suspects, whom the police have to arrest: perhaps it is only by a kind of diplomatic courtesy toward Peking that they haven't done so already. Lady Ava asks him, then, what he plans to do. Johnson answers that he will leave Hong Kong that night, on a junk, for either Macao or Canton.

The evening then passes in a normal fashion, in order not to raise any suspicions, but other guests are certainly on their guard, for something strained is apparent in the atmosphere: the least glass that breaks on the floor petrifies everyone, as though they were expecting an event whose imminence is beyond question. Sir Ralph stands in the recess of a bay window, listening through the thick, closed curtains for the sound of a car arriving. Georges Marchat does not leave the buffet, where he has been served, one after the other, six glasses of champagne which he has drunk in succession. In the little music room, Lauren, Marchat's fiancée, is playing the piano for some silent guests, a modern composition full of breaks and pauses which she punctuates with nervous, abrupt, brief laughs, indicating the wrong notes which only she can identify. Kito, the young Japanese servant girl, has just cut her arm—a little below the elbow, on the inner side—by picking up the fragments of a broken glass too hastily; and she remains where she is without moving, still on her knees on the floor, staring blankly at the thread of bright red blood that slowly runs over her dull skin and falls, drop by drop, at long intervals, on the marble strewn with glittering splinters. A few yards away, behind an armchair on whose back is leaning with an indifferent expression, to conceal her real feelings, though her head is turned toward the preceding scene with a fixed stare which is unmistakable, a lovely Eurasian girl who answers to the American name Kim, contemplating the little kneeling Japanese girl, the pale arm with its slender red line and the drops of blood which form a constellation of scattered points on the floor, concentrating around an axis like the perforations of bullets on a target. And now, slowly, her eyes fixed on the wounded servant girl, Kim's right hand leaves the back of the chair to rise to her own left clavicle, in the hollow of which the young woman is marked by a faint, bright pink scar—two oblongs close together—which no one would have noticed without her furtive gesture, but whose unusual shape, once attention has been drawn to them, makes one wonder how they were made.

Some distance from the rest of her guests, Lady Ava waits too, still sitting on her sofa whose velvet has faded with age. Standing beside her is Lucky, Kim's twin sister who resembles her in every feature, but who is wearing a white silk dress instead of the black one that would be more suitable, in her recent bereavement. (Have they not both lost their father?) She has just handed Lady Ava a brown paper envelope stuffed with documents, which Lady Ava has immediately put out of sight.

Everywhere in the vicinity, then, occur abrupt or mechanical movements, sidelong glances, gestures suddenly frozen, immobilities which are too long or forced, an abnormal silencing of all sounds, against which stand out, at moments, short sentences which sound unnatural: "When does the performance begin?" "May I have the next dance?" "Won't you have a glass of champagne?" etc. And for everyone, it is almost a relief when the police in British uniforms finally make their appearance. Moreover the silence was complete for several seconds, as if the precise moment of their entrance had long been known to everyone. The scenario then takes its course in a mechanical fashion, like a well-oiled, precision mechanism, each person henceforth knowing his role to perfection and able to play it without being a second off, without a jolt, without the slightest faux pas that might surprise a fellow actor: the musicians in the orchestra all laying down their instruments or letting them fall back gently, the bow alongside the body, the flute on the desk, the trumpet between the thighs, the sticks across the skin of the drum, and Kito the servant girl who gets to her feet, the Eurasian girl who looks straight ahead again, the fat man with the red face who sets down his empty glass on the silver tray held out by the waiter, the soldier taking his post at the main door, the other soldier who crosses the salon in a straight line between the pairs of motionless dancers, without having to make the slightest detour to avoid anyone on his way, and who will guard the exit at the other end, the lieutenant, finally, who heads unhesitatingly toward the window recess where Johnson is standing, to proceed with his arrest.

But one thing disturbs me now: wouldn't the lieutenant actually be walking toward the mistress of the house in that resolute way of his? Isn't it more logical to arrest her, in the first place? As a matter of fact, Lady Ava hasn't made any secret, during a conversation with Kim—during a monologue, more exactly (for there is no point playing with words), delivered in the latter's presence, it will be recalled, while the old lady is preparing to go to bed—she has made no secret, I say, of her deliberate intention of inducing Johnson, by means of Lauren's exorbitant demands— a classical method, it appears, for this kind of recruiting—of inducing Johnson to become a secret agent for Peking, which would imply a previous commitment on the part of Lady Ava in this matter. One solution of the problem would perhaps lie in the ignorance of the British police, or in its diplomatic fair play policy, which here prefers to deal with the Communist organization known under the names of "Free Hong Kong" or the S. L. S. ("South Liberation Soviet")— whose role is nonexistent and whose claims are rather contrary to the Chinese interests (to such a degree that many regard it as no more than a front for some drug or white-slave traffic)—rather than put a brutal end to the activities of the real spies.

In any case, when the police lieutenant presents himself before Lady Ava, and makes the usual salutations, the latter offers the new arrival a drink in her worldly tone of voice, which leads to nothing. Another question: have not the terms "soldiers" and "police" been used somewhat carelessly to indicate the British officers? Were they plain-clothes inspectors, or actual soldiers in combat uniforms with camouflage patterns? Furthermore, various essential points remain to be settled, for example: did the patrol's arrival take place before or after the theatrical performance? Perhaps it was even in the middle of the performance, at the moment when Lady Ava, having counted, then put away the sachets in the secret safe, and classified in order the papers on the desk, exhausted, pale, staggering, finally goes to her bed and lies down. Then comes the knocking at the main door with its elaborate moldings, once, twice, three times. . . . Who is the unexpected visitor who keeps knocking without receiving an answer? The audience is obviously unaware of what is happening in the rest of the house. But the door opens, and it is a great surprise to see Sir Ralph suddenly come in. He rushes toward the bed. . . . Is he too late? Has the poison already done its work? The spectators are in suspense.

Sir Ralph bends toward the agonized face, holding the dying woman's hand. Lady Ava, without seeing him, eyes fixed on the void, in some remote recollection which she cannot recapture, speaks disconnected words, her inflections low and hoarse, among which appear, now and then, fragments of more comprehensible phrases: about the place where she was born, about her marriage, about the countries she has visited, or which she has never known, except by hearsay. She is talking about things she has done, or she would have liked to do, and saying that she has always been a bad actress, and that now that she is an old woman, she no longer interests anyone. Sir Ralph tries to comfort her, assuring her that she was, on the contrary, splendid on stage tonight, right to the end. But she no longer hears him. She asks if he could stop the noise, over her bedroom. She hears the sound of a cane. She says that someone should go up there to see what is happening. Doubtless someone is sick, or hurt, and calling for help. But she changes her mind immediately: "It's old King Boris," she says, "rocking on his ferryboat. . . ." Her diction is so uncertain that Sir Ralph is not sure he has heard her properly. Then she seems a little calmer, but her face has become still more haggard, still grayer. It seems as though all the blood, all the flesh is draining away inside. After a longer silence, with a sudden perfect and unexpected lucidity, she then says: "Things are never where they belong for good." Then, without moving her head, her eyes widen excessively, and she asks where the dogs are. These are her last words.

And now Ralph Johnson, known as the American, returns again to the new part of Kowloon, to Manneret's apartment. He will try his luck again, since there is no one else, in the entire territory of the concession, capable of furnishing him the sum he needs to buy back Lauren. He will use any means to convince the millionaire, if need be. Without thinking of taking the elevator, he walks up the seven flights. The door of the apartment is ajar, the apartment door is wide open, despite the late hour, the apartment door is closed—what does it matter?—and Manneret himself comes to open it; or else it is a Chinese servant girl or a sleepy young Eurasian girl whom the bell, whom the insistent electric buzzer, whom the thumps of fists against the door have finally roused from her bed. What does all that matter? What does it matter? Edouard Manneret has not yet gone to bed, in any case. He never goes to bed. He sleeps fully dressed in his rocking chair. He hasn't managed to sleep in a long time, the strongest soporifics having ceased to have the slightest effect on him. He is sound asleep in his bed, but Johnson insists that he be wakened, he waits for him in the living room, he shoves aside the terrified servants and enters the bedroom by force; all this comes to the same thing. Manneret first takes Johnson for his son, he takes him for Georges Marchat or Marchant, he takes him for Mr. Chang, he takes him for Sir Ralph, he takes him for King Boris. It comes down to the same thing, since ultimately he refuses. The American insists. The American threatens. The American begs. Edouard Manneret refuses. Then the American calmly takes his revolver out of the inside right (or left?) pocket of his tuxedo, that revolver which he had removed a while ago (when?) from the wardrobe or the chest in his hotel room, between the starched, white, carefully pressed shirts. . . . Manneret watches him and remains impassive, still smiling as he rocks slowly in his chair with a regular rhythm. Johnson removes the safety catch. Edouard Manneret is still smiling, without moving a muscle in his face. He looks like a wax figure in a museum. And his head rises and sinks, still in the same cadence. Johnson puts a bullet in the barrel and with a calm gesture raises the weapon toward the body which alternately rises and sinks, like the moving targets in carnival shooting galleries. He says: "Then the answer is no?" Manneret does not even answer; he does not seem to believe that all this is really happening. Johnson carefully aims at the heart, his hand following the oscillations of the rocking chair, rising, sinking, rising, sinking, rising, sinking. . . . How easy it is, once in time with the chair. Then he squeezes the trigger. He fires five times in a row: down, up, down, up, down. All the shots have found their target. He puts the still hot revolver back in his inside pocket, while the rocking chair continues its periodic movement, which will gradually die away, and he dashes for the stairs. In the darkness, it seems to him that doors are opened, on each landing, as he passes, but he is not sure of this.

In front of the building, on the avenue, parked along the curb, there is the old taxi with closed windows, waiting for him. Without saying anything to the driver, Johnson opens the rear door and gets in. The car immediately starts up, to deposit him a few minutes later at the ferry dock. The boat is about to leave the quay; Johnson, whom a company employee vainly tries to hold back, has just time to leap on board, where he suddenly finds himself among a silent crowd of short men in blue overalls or black pajamas who are going to their jobs, though day has not yet broken. During the crossing, Johnson calculates that he has exactly enough time to reach Aberdeen harbor before six-fifteen, in order to get on board the junk. But when he gets off the ferry, in Victoria, and into a taxi, he has himself driven in the opposite direction, toward the Blue Villa: he cannot leave Hong Kong without seeing Lauren again. He will try once more to persuade her to leave, although he has not been able to keep his promise. She may have done all this only to test him. . . .

He crosses the grounds, walking fast, guided by the blue glow from the house, in the steady, strident shrilling of millions of nocturnal insects; he crosses the vestibule, he crosses the abandoned large salon. All the doors are open. It seems that the servants themselves have vanished. He climbs the grand staircase. But he walks more slowly at each step. Passing in front of Lady Ava's bedroom, he finds its door wide open too. He enters without a sound. The old lady is lying in the huge bed framed by two torches which give her a funereal aspect. Kim is at her bedside, still standing motionless; has she spent the whole night there? Johnson approaches. The sick woman is not asleep. Johnson asks her if the doctor has come, and how she is feeling. She answers calmly that she is dying. She asks if it is dark yet. He answers: "No, not yet." But she then begins thrashing about again, moving her head with difficulty, as if she were looking for something, and saying that she has some important news to tell him. Then she begins saying that they have just arrested the Belgian drug merchants recently arrived from the Congo who had set up a heroin factory . . . , etc. But she gradually loses the thread of what she is saying and soon breaks off altogether, asking where the dogs are. These will be her last words.

On the floor above, Lauren's door is also open. Johnson dashes in, filled with a sudden apprehension: some disaster may have occurred in his absence. . . . It is only in the middle of the room that he sees the police lieutenant in khaki shorts and white knee socks. He turns around suddenly and sees that the door has closed behind him and that a soldier holding a machine gun is standing in front of it, barring his way. More slowly, his glance sweeps the entire room. The second soldier, in front of the drawn curtains of the bay window, also closely watches him, holding his machine gun trained on him with both hands. The lieutenant does not budge either, and keeps his eyes fixed on him. Lauren is lying on the fur spread, between the four columns supporting the canopy which forms a kind of dais above her. She is wearing golden silk pajamas that cling to her body, with a short, standing collar and long sleeves, in the Chinese fashion. Lying on her side, one knee bent, the other leg stretched out, head propped on one arm resting on its elbow, she watches him without making a single gesture, without moving a single feature of her smooth face. And there is nothing in her eyes.